ANNIE'S

NO RETURN

ARTORIUS REX

Artorius Rex

JOHN GLOAG

ST. MARTIN'S PRESS · NEW YORK

Copyright © 1977 by John Gloag

All rights reserved. For information, write:
St. Martin's Press, Inc. 175 Fifth Ave., New York, N.Y. 10010

Printed in Great Britain

Library of Congress Catalog Card Number: 76-62767

First published in the United States of America in 1977

Library of Congress Cataloging in Publication Data
Gloag, John, 1896–
  Artorius Rex.

  Final vol. in the author's trilogy, the 1st of which is Caesar of the narrow
seas; the 2nd, The eagles depart.
  1. Arthur, King—Fiction. I. Title.
PZ3.G517Ar3 [PR6013.L5]   823'.9'12   76-62767
ISBN 0-312-05548-X

CONTENTS

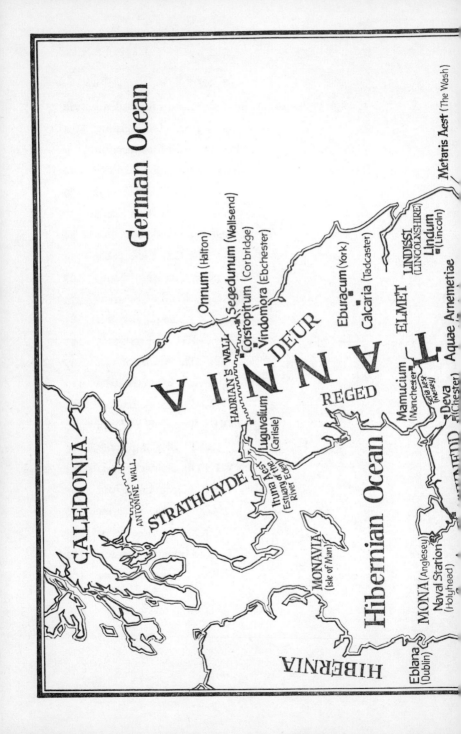

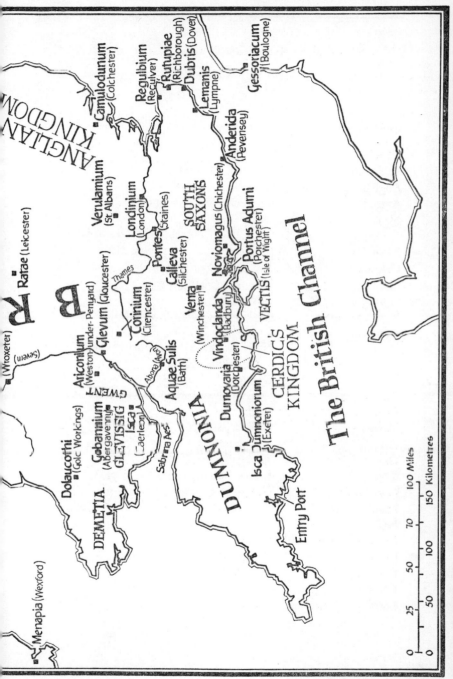

The British Channel

ANGLIAN KINGDOM

Menapia (Wexford)

Dolaucothi (Golc Workings)

DEMETIA

Gobannium (Abergavenny)
GLEVISSIG

Isca (Caerleon)

GWENT

Ariconium (Weston-under-Penyard)

Sabrina Aes

DUMNONIA

Aquae Sulis (Bath)

Abona (Avon)

Corinium (Cirencester)

Glevum (Gloucester)

(Wroxeter)

(Severn)

Ratae (Leicester)

Verulamium (St Albans)

Camulodunum (Colchester)

Regulbium (Reculver)

Rutupiae (Richborough)

Dubris (Dover)

Lemanis (Lympne)

Gessoriacum (Boulogne)

Anderida (Pevensey)

Londinium (London)

Pontes (Staines)

Calleva (Silchester)

Thames

Venta (Winchester)

SOUTH SAXONS

Noviomagus (Chichester)

Portus Adurni (Porchester)

VECTIS (Isle of Wight)

Vindoclanda (Badbury)

Durnovaria (Dorchester)

CERDIC'S KINGDOM

Isca Dumnoniorum (Exeter)

Entry Port

0   25   50   70   100   150 Kilometres
0   50   100   150 Miles   100 Miles

© Cassell and Co Ltd 1977

Ancient place-names and their modern equivalents

ROMAN	MODERN
Anderida	Pevensey (Sussex)
Anglian kingdoms	Norfolk and Suffolk
Antonine Wall	Between the Clyde and Forth
Aquae Sulis	Bath
Ariconium	Weston-under-Penyard (Hereford)
Armorica	Brittany
Calcaris	Tadcaster (Yorkshire)
Calleva	Silchester (Hampshire)
Corinium	Cirencester
Corstopitum	Corbridge (Northumberland)
Demetia	South-west Wales
Deur	Northern Yorkshire, Durham and Northumberland
Deva	Chester
Dumnonia	Devon, Cornwall, Dorset and Somerset
Eburacum	York
Glevissig	Glamorganshire
Glevum	Gloucester
Gobannium	Abergavenny (Gwent)
Gwent	Between the Usk and the Wye
Gwynedd	Clwyd and western Cheshire
Hadrian's Wall	Between the Eden estuary and Wallsend
Isca	Caerleon
Isca Dumnoniorum	Exeter
Ituna	Estuary of the River Eden (Cumbria)
Lindissi	Lincolnshire
Lindum	Lincoln
Londinium Augusta	London

Luguvalium	Carlisle
Mamucium	Manchester
Noviomagus	Chichester (Sussex)
Onnum	Halton (Northumberland)
Orcades	Orkney Islands
Pontes	Staines (Middlesex)
Ratae	Leicester
Reged	Lancashire and Cumbria
Sabrina	The Severn
Segedunum	Wallsend (Northumberland)
Strathclyde	Western Scotland between the Clyde and Ayrshire
Valentia	Locality uncertain, but probably included Wales, Cheshire and Lancashire
Vectis	Isle of Wight
Venta Silurum	Caerwent (Gwent)
Verulamium	St Albans
Vindocladia	Badbury (Dorset)
Vindomora	Ebchester (Durham)
Viroconium	Wroxeter (Shropshire)

NOTE:

The Peninsula claimed by the kings of Gwynedd and Reged is Wirral, between the Dee and Mersey.

DEDICATED TO

MIM

I

The Imperial Commission

AT THE AGE of ten Artorius was sent from Britain by his uncle and guardian, Ambrosius Aurelianus, to Constantinople to complete his education and to learn the military arts of the Empire. The young British nobleman was well received by the Emperor Zeno, who appointed me to act as tutor to the boy, and to prevent him from getting into mischief, something that is very easy to do in the city that the great Constantine built two hundred years ago. I was flattered by the Imperial choice, for I was then only a junior officer in the Household Guards, and although I belonged to the Geladii family that was founded when the Republic was still young, I had little influence and no money apart from my army pay and a modest allowance from my father. I should of course inherit the family estates when he died, but that event was, I hoped, far off in the future. So I, Caius Geladius, became the close companion of Artorius for forty years, and followed his fortunes after he returned to the lost province of Britain, that, even as a boy, he had hopeful dreams of reuniting to the Empire. He was a born soldier, and though few in the East have heard of his deeds, he was worthy of ranking with our greatest leaders, with Julius Caesar, Tiberius, Trajan, and Septimius Severus. He always outgeneralled the barbarians against whom he was fighting, and never lost hope that ultimately he would drive them back to the northern mountains and into the sea.

I am writing this account of the wars he waged against the Picts and Saxons, his victories, his disappointments, his loves and sorrows, triumphs and tragedies, because his Sacred and Imperial Majesty, the Emperor Justinian, has commanded me to make a report on the state of Britain and the possibility of reconquering the province, now that Africa, Italy and southern Spain have been reconquered; and though I doubt whether the Imperial government has the strength or the resources to defeat the Visigoths and recover the whole of Spain and to wrest Gaul from the Franks, the administration has made tentative plans for restoring the Western Empire to its former glory, and Britain is of course included in those plans. So this is the first draft of my report, and because it is only a draft I have not deleted any of my own reflections or conclusions derived from my experience of Britain and the unpredictable and often untrustworthy tribesmen who call themselves Romans, but have forgotten the law, order and discipline that had made Rome great. My report must be trimmed and smoothed to be fit for the eyes of his Sacred and Imperial Majesty and the even more critical eyes of her Resplendency, Theodora Augusta, the Empress.

I began writing this account in the year of Our Lord, 540, when our great general Belisarius had returned in triumph after subduing the Goths in Italy. I am now seventy-four, and was born in 466, ten years before Artorius, whose birth year was the most fateful in the history of the world, for in 476 the last Emperor in the West was deposed by Odoacer, a barbarian chief.

My first warning of the task I was to undertake came when Philonides, the Chief Assistant to the Grand Chamberlain, summoned me to his office in the administrative wing of the Imperial Palace. I was not apprehensive, as many of my contemporaries would have been; but I was puzzled, for I could not imagine why anybody so senior in the official hierarchy should wish to see a retired soldier, who had crossed the threshold of old age. For nearly fifteen years I had lived quietly and inconspicuously and alone since my wife died; my active military career was long past, and I was content to allow the memory of it to sleep peacefully; nor was I much concerned with the ambitions of my three British-born sons. They were all in the Army, and only one had any sense, and he was dull and correct and time dragged in his company. They do not come into my story at all. You cannot live other people's lives for them, and I had withdrawn from the world almost as effectively as a monk walled out from it by holy vows; my seclusion was protected by my refusal to become involved in politics, court intrigues, religious controversies, or the sporting inanities of the Hippodrome set. The Blue and the Green factions and their infatuation with chariot racing and their adulation of swaggering charioteers seemed to me as trivial and absurd as their passionate feuds, which often led to destructive riots. Charioteers are often homosexuals; a breed that I abominate. The Hippodrome is the home of the mob, and the mob is a foul beast. So I preferred the peace and quiet of my library, which occupied the largest room of my small house, with a wide window overlooking a well-stocked garden. Reading, good cooking, the company of friends who understand the art of conversation, satisfy my needs; I am content. There was no reason why I should ever emerge from a deliberately chosen obscurity. I have no personal ambitions; though I have helped some men to realize theirs, and intentionally hindered others, whose ambitions seemed dangerous.

Naturally the secret police knew all about me; nothing is hidden from them; but they must have been well satisfied that I was a spent force, incapable of harm. I was ignored after I had returned from Britain with my wife and family. My years in the far West were years of exile, though I was always free to return to the heart of the Empire had I wished to do so; but loyalty to Artorius held me, until I had outlived my usefulness. Nothing had disturbed my orderly, regular life until one of the household guards delivered the courteously worded invitation from Philonides.

I had never met him, but had heard that he was a remarkable and unusual character: quietly efficient, ruthless but not cruel, a frugal man indifferent to wealth, and—this was strange in a court official—absolutely incorruptible. Like many other high-ranking officials he was a eunuch; and I didn't know what sort of twisted and deprived creature I should see when I presented myself at his office in the Imperial Palace at the time appointed; perhaps a gross quivering mountain of flesh—for eunuchs sometimes run to excessive fat—or some soft, spiteful effeminate creature. But the man who rose from his seat behind a long table was tall, lean and muscular, in the prime of life and obviously endowed with exceptional vitality. His face recalled the serene dignity that Egyptian sculptors always gave to their royal portraits. Egyptian blood ran in his veins, for his mother had been a native dancing girl in Alexandria, and his father a famous Greek physician who practised in that beautiful, depraved, and turbulent city. He had thin, arched black eyebrows above intense, dark brown eyes; a wide, full-lipped mouth, and a determined chin. He spoke in a quiet, gentle voice; only those near him could hear his words, for his work table stood in the middle of a big room, far distant from any wall.

'General,' he said, using a title that I had almost forgotten, 'I shall not waste your time or mine with empty preliminaries. I have invited you here because you have some experience and knowledge that may be of value to his Sacred and Imperial Majesty in completing his plans for the reconquest of the West.'

He paused, and his searching look suggested that he was trying to read my thoughts; but my years in Britain and my dealings with native kings and chiefs taught me how to keep my face expressionless. He nodded, then continued:

'The *whole* West,' he said; 'all the provinces of the Empire that were ruled by Rome when the great Constantine was Emperor. Africa and Italy have been restored to us, as you know; we have a foothold in Spain, and when we have driven the barbarian Visigoths from that country, our next logical step would seem to be an attack on the Franks to reconquer Gaul and Belgica.' He smiled, then added: 'But his Sacred and Imperial Majesty is too subtle to be trapped by mere logic. He very rightly distrusts the obvious.'

That was a smoothly tactful description of the Emperor Justinian's inability to recognize facts or to face them when, belatedly, recognition was forced upon him. His infirmity of purpose was notorious, but when he made a decision (generally the wrong one) he was far too obstinate to change it, even when it led to disaster. He was surrounded by men who invariably agreed with him; he was, moreover, confident that Divine guidance inspired all his actions.

Philonides paused again, but I said nothing, for I had nothing to say, and I do not talk for the pleasure of hearing my own voice. As I remained silent, he went on.

'We know that ports on the north-west coast of Spain are still open. The Visigoths engage in coastal trading; so when we have regained the whole province we could assemble a fleet of fighting galleys and troop transports, and sail north directly to Britain.'

He unrolled a map and spread it out on the table. I knew something about maps, for I had made a good many for Artorius.

'I have little knowledge of the sea or ships,' he admitted; 'but if that fleet sailed on a northerly course, keeping to the west of the Great Bay and its storms, which I have heard about, it should reach Britain in, how many days? You shall tell me presently. The expeditionary force should land on that south-western limb of Britain which kicks out like a leg into the Atlantic, and is marked as Dumnonia. Do you know it?'

I did, also Marcus its ruler; a conceited man from a noble family who had so far forgotten his Roman heritage that he used, like his father before him, that most obnoxious of all titles: king.

'I've been there,' I told Philonides. 'Galleys would make heavy weather of the voyage. No course ever set can avoid storms, which are unpredictable, and can chew the oars out of the largest Imperial galleys ever launched. Two-masted sailing craft, with small auxiliary oar-banks, six a side, which can be shipped inboard in a heavy swell, would be best. Oars won't bite in a heavy swell. Enough water could be carried to last for the eight or ten days that, with fair winds, should be ample time for the voyage.'

'Is Dumnonia in the hands of barbarians?' he asked.

'Fifteen years have passed since I left Britain,' I told him; 'anything may have happened during that time; Artorius is dead, and he was the only man strong enough to prevent all those tribal chiefs or kings, as they like to be called, from quarrelling and fighting among themselves. There was a strong barbarian kingdom on the eastern border of Dumnonia, founded by a Saxon chief named Cerdic, and east of that were other Saxon states.'

I stopped; realizing how little I, or anybody, knew about events in Britain.

'Say what you had in mind,' Philonides invited.

'Cerdic would be a very old man now,' I continued; 'but Cynric,

his son, may have invaded Dumnonia. Cerdic, I think, was concerned more with keeping what he had than with making fresh
conquests of territory; but his son may be more ambitious. I am
quite ignorant of what is happening in Britain now.'

'We know a little,' said Philonides; 'information comes belatedly
to Administration, for there are still a few bold traders who risk a
voyage to Britain; some of them never return.'

He looked down at the map, and added: 'This record has been
changed by events; I shall ask you to correct it, up to the time you
left Britain; then it will only be fifteen years out of date instead of
fifty.'

After studying the map for some minutes, he said:

'If we landed an expeditionary force in Dumnonia we could
march against those Saxon states and occupy south-eastern Britain.
Then we should have only a narrow strip of sea to cross in order
to invade Belgica. We could presumably count on troops from
the regions that have kept their Roman civilization, so the fleet
that had brought our army to Dumnonia could ferry over a much
bigger joint force, Imperial and British, to the Belgic coast.'

I realized then that Philonides had military ambitions; but like
nearly all landsmen, he made plans without thinking of the sea and
its hazards. He knew nothing of winds and currents and tides; nor
did I until I left the eastern world and the Mediterranean; but nobody who has lived in Britain or sailed in the waters that surround
that island can ever ignore the sea. Also I was far from certain
that an imperial army landing in Dumnonia would be welcomed by
the British states. They had been independent for too long, well over
a century; their rulers had done very much what they wanted to
without hindrance from imperial officials; and if imperial troops
marched in, imperial tax-gatherers would not be far behind.

I hinted as much to Philonides, and he seemed mildly surprised.
But I knew that loss of freedom to have their own way and to
make their own laws and to govern their little kingdoms as they
saw fit, coupled with the obligation to pay money or its equivalent
to a distant treasury, would be bitterly resisted: especially the
taxation. The Saxons could have been expelled from Britain and

the whole of the south-east and eastern parts of the Island reclaimed for civilization if the great landholders and the cities that were still inhabited had been willing to bear the cost of an army: soldiers won't fight without pay or rations. Every petty king had his own bodyguard, every chief his band of armed followers, and if the Saxons or the Picts made a sudden, unexpected attack, some kind of force could be raised—far too late to be of much use. Apart from the stubbornness and stupidity of the kings and chiefs, there was a practical difficulty about payment; no money had been in circulation for three generations; no coins were minted in the west, and trade was conducted by barter. Soldiers would have to be paid in kind, with food, drink, scraps of jewellery or broken gold and silver, even with women, though the interfering bishops would have tried to stop that.

Encouraged by his questions, I described these conditions to Philonides. He pondered awhile, then asked:

'How was Artorius rewarded and his army paid?'

'Their victories were sufficient reward,' I told him, and knew from his expression that I was disbelieved, so I added: 'Artorius was an inspired leader: he hoped to free all Britain from the barbarians, and only recruited men who would share that hope. He never lost a battle. All he asked from the kings and chiefs whose work he was doing for them, was food and shelter for his men, fodder and stabling for his big horses.'

'I understand,' said Philonides. 'Such men at the right time and the right place can change history.' He glanced down at the map on the table, then continued. 'His Sacred and Imperial Majesty desires a report on the state of Britain and the conditions of life there, and I know now that you could write that report.'

A few days later I was granted an audience by the Emperor Justinian, who was affable in speech and manner, and far more dignified than the little British kings who took themselves so seriously. The Emperor was a good-looking man, with ruddy cheeks, a trim beard and dark, curling hair. He was of medium height, but he held his well-proportioned body so erect that he appeared to be taller than he really was; he clearly enjoyed excellent health and looked far younger than his fifty-eight years. He was very different from Zeno, the weary old man who entrusted Artorius to my care fifty-four years ago.

I was not allowed the privilege of an audience with the Empress, Theodora Augusta, nor, to my disappointment, was I permitted to meet Count Belisarius. Later, if an expedition to Britain was ever mounted, I should be called upon again; then I might meet the Empress and the ever-victorious general. Meanwhile I held the Imperial Commission to prepare 'An Appreciation of the Civil and Military situation in the Province of Britain', as my report was to be officially described.

II

The British connection

WHAT I SET DOWN in this preliminary draft is for my eyes only, though I shall probably show selected extracts to Philonides, as his help and guidance will be needed for preparing the final document; meanwhile this draft has revived old memories, so inevitably it has become a personal account. I am unable to avoid references to my own family, and in particular to the British branch that was founded by Lucius Geladius who was exiled from Rome when Caracalla was Emperor, three and a quarter centuries ago. He had been meddling unwisely in politics, and the penalty for that indiscretion was exile to the far western province of Britain, and the loss of his Italian estates. In those days it was possible to transfer money to the most distant provinces of the Empire, for the world was then civilized and secure under the strong rule of Rome, so the exiled patrician was able to save part of his fortune without impoverishing his younger brother, who remained in Italy and from whom my branch of the family is descended.

Lucius Geladius settled down to live quietly in comparative comfort on a large estate he bought in the sheltered, pleasant country that lies south-east of the River Sabrina, not far from the small city of Corinium and the hot springs of Aquae Sulis. Thereafter, neither he nor his immediate descendants did anything notable, but his great-grandson, Lucius Priscus Geladius, became a famous and successful soldier, Legate of the XXth Legion, the Valeria Victrix, and Governor-General of Britain during the reign of the usurper, Carausius. He served under Constantius when Britain was restored to the Empire, and was killed during a campaign in Caledonia. In the course of his military career, he became friendly with a Frankish chief, named Brennell, and saved the life of one of his sons during a bear hunt. The threads woven by the grey spinners wind strangely through time, for the gratitude of that long-dead Frank was expressed by a gift that, over two hundred years later, secured for Artorius a military ascendency over the barbarians, that made him seem invincible.

(Certainly this document must be hidden from other eyes: I have carelessly named the grey spinners, who belong to the ancient world of fates and furies, of great goddesses and valiant gods, that are anathema to the joyless theologians who rule the Christian world. Though nominally a Christian, my real beliefs and loyalties are older. Naturally I keep them to myself.)

The Franks were famous for the great horses they bred, magnificent creatures that could carry a lot of weight; and Brennell's gift to Lucius Priscus Geladius, all those generations ago, consisted of six horses from his stable, including a stallion and mares so that he could breed and maintain the stock. The big horses that enabled Artorius to use heavy cavalry against Saxon and Pictish spearmen, were descended from the original Frankish stock. The breed was carefully preserved, the mares well guarded from the wild hill ponies. Marcus Geladius, the grandson of Lucius Priscus, supplied mounts to the officers of the XXth, for the family had acquired large estates in what was formerly the tribal territory of the Ordovices, between the River Dee and the Black Mountains, so the stables were only a few miles from the city and fortress of Deva, the legionary headquarters.

Like his grandfather, Marcus Geladius was a famous soldier, joining the XXth when he was little more than a boy, soon becoming a leader of mounted auxiliaries, and eventually attaining the rank of legate, in command of the legion. Part of the estates were lost in the great war against the allied barbarians, Picts, Scots, Irish and Saxons, who devastated Britain a hundred years before I was born, and the part that escaped was given by Marcus Geladius to Cunedda, a chief of the Votadini, who had brought part of his tribe from the north-east to the Ordovician territory, expelled most of the Irish, and settled there. Cunedda and his followers had migrated at the invitation of Stilcho, the Vandal general who gave such good service to Rome in the twilight of the Western Empire's power, and as the Ordovices had been reduced to a few hundred tribesmen, the Votadini emigrants repopulated an almost empty countryside. They ultimately came to terms with the Irish, allowed them to settle, and intermarried with them. When I left Britain, the kingdoms of the west, apart from Demetia, were ruled by the descendants of Cunedda, and his great-grandson Maelgwyn, was king of Gwynedd, and for all I know may still be; though ruling a British kingdom is fraught with danger.

The British branch of my family retained their possessions despite the troubles and turmoil that have afflicted Britain; the Geladii were always renowned for their power of survival; we breed prudent men, whose foresight has preserved and often improved the family fortunes. The branch to which I belong, wisely moved from Italy to the East, when the Great Constantine built a new capital by the ancient Greek city of Byzantium, and called it New Rome; a name soon superseded by Constantinople, which honoured the Imperial founder.

I had known from childhood that cousins of mine were probably living somewhere in Britain, but knew nothing of their whereabouts or of their history until after I set foot on British soil. Then I discovered that there were two separate branches, one descended from Lucius Priscus, the general, the other from his younger brother, Marius, to whom he had resigned the family lands when he decided on a military career. No male descendants of Marius had survived in the fifth century, but the seed of Lucius Priscus flourished. The family lands were now near the northern border of Gwent, in the old tribal area of the Silures, twenty miles north of the Sabrina estuary, with rich farms and pastures for herds of sheep and cattle, where the great horses were bred that had once represented so much wealth. The chief of the family, Julius Nonna, made himself known to me at the first Council of Kings that Artorius attended after his return to Britain; but I am too far forward with my story; my memories are galloping away with me and I should describe events in an orderly sequence and begin at the time of my first meeting with Artorius when he was still a boy and had just reported at the Military Academy at Constantinople.

He was tall for his age, with broad shoulders and long arms. He had dark hair, almost black, with heavy, jutting eyebrows over pale grey eyes, set wide apart in a face tanned by his long sea voyage. His features were regular, his nose large and prominent; the lines of his jaw already firm; his expression open and frank, yet resolute, with perhaps a hint of obstinacy. Even then he gave the impression of knowing his own mind, and, more important, possessing strength of mind. His voice, still boyish, was quiet, and in all the years I knew him, he seldom raised it, and never in anger; he could make his words carry when giving orders on parade or shouting battle cries, and later, as it deepened, it became a richly persuasive voice, compelling attention.

I have long learnt to trust first impressions and I am seldom deceived by them. I felt when I first met that quiet, self-possessed boy, that despite the difference in our ages, he was destined to lead while I should follow. I then saw the pattern of my life; not vaguely but complete in shape and colour and detail. The gods sometimes draw aside the dark curtain that hides the future; and the revelation can be so vivid, almost blinding, that we become confused and understandably afraid, as I did at that moment of meeting.

My report is concerned with conditions in Britain as I found them, and as Artorius changed them, so I shall not dwell on his years of training in Constantinople; his instructors were delighted with him, for he worked hard, and was far more respectful to them than the arrogant sons of noblemen and army officers who attended the academy. He soon mastered Greek, and became fluent, for he had an ear for languages, though he brought to both Greek and his British rendering of Latin, an odd, not unpleasing, lilt; which was a characteristic of tribal speech in Britain as I discovered later. His chief interests were riding—he knew as much if not more about horses than the riding masters in the cavalry training establishment —and the use and making of weapons and the design of armour. He spent hours in the smoky forges of the armourers' shops, talking to the smiths, which puzzled and amused the other boys in the academy, who never spoke familiarly with anybody outside their own class unless they happened to be charioteers; nobody ventured to question or laugh at his interests, for he possessed a hard dignity, neither brittle nor assertive, that discouraged light-minded and aggressive types. None of the older boys ever attempted to bully him, though some disliked him.

One of the smiths, an old fellow named Dolti, came from Colchis on the eastern shores of the Euxine, the fabled land where Jason, aided by the magic of Medea, the royal witch, took the Golden Fleece from its guardian dragon. This skilled craftsman whose home was beyond the most easterly boundary of the civilized world was drawn towards the boy who came from the most westerly surviving remnant of the Empire. I think that Artorius realized for the first time how infinitely remote and little known his native land had become, when Dolti asked him, quite seriously, if Britain was the island in the far Ocean where the souls of the dead ultimately rested. The uneducated classes will believe anything, as priests of every religion under the sun have discovered through the ages; but the fact that a former province of the Empire could become a myth in less than a century shows how completely Britain was severed from civilization. Artorius was very far from home.

I had been instructed to make monthly reports on the progress of his education, and these I made verbally to Anastasius, the principal chamberlain, who was head of the secretarial staff at the Imperial Palace. He was an elderly man, modest and quiet, apparently without ambition, so when on the death of Zeno in 491 he assumed the purple, everybody was astonished, though there was no overt opposition to his elevation. He consolidated his exalted position by marrying Ariadne, the widow of Zeno, and so began a reign that lasted, not unprosperously, for twenty-seven years. I am concerned with this fragment of past history only because the new Emperor retained his interest in Artorius and when the boy reached the age of eighteen, granted him an audience and encouraged him to speak frankly.

'You should return to Britain,' the Emperor told him at the end of the audience, 'and apply the knowledge you have gained here to driving the barbarians from our province.'

Artorius had never concealed his intention of helping his uncle

Ambrosius Aurelianus, to make relentless and unremitting war on
the Saxons who had founded kingdoms in Britain; and so far
that war had gone badly for the Roman forces of law and order.
Civilization in Britain was being pushed westwards, and though
Ambrosius may have called himself *dux Britannarium*, commander-
in-chief of an army organized as the army used to be a century ago,
his authority stopped short at the parade ground: the components
of his legions and cavalry owed a prior loyalty to their own petty
kings and princelings. This I had learned from Artorius, and now
at eighteen he had completed his training and was ready to make the
long, dangerous voyage back to Britain. I was informed that it was
the Emperor's wish that I should accompany him. I was ordered to
render any service in my power to Artorius and his uncle; to remain in Britain as an observer, and to return when my usefulness
had ended.

Artorius carried with him a letter of formal greeting from the
Emperor to Ambrosius Aurelianus, also his commission of appointment as a tribune in the Imperial Army. The appointment was
qualified by a personal note dictated by the Emperor, that authorized 'promotion to any higher rank necessary for the better ordering
of the military establishment in our Province of Britannia'.

I was now twenty-eight, had recently attained the rank of
tribune, and as an officer of some seniority in the Household Guards,
seconded for the rather vague post of observer with unspecified
duties in a far-distant and long-lost province, I had no intention of
remaining a passive guardian to Artorius. I had experience of active
service, north of the great River Ister in the former province of
Dacia, where the savage Gepidae ruled in their muddled, barbaric
fashion; a short campaign had been mounted to check their raids
into Thrace, and I had learned to respect their reckless courage, fine
horsemanship, and accurate shooting from the saddle. Horses were
a part of their lives; in the saddle they were as accomplished as the
Huns, but not such repulsive animals. They washed occasionally;
the Huns never did. Artorius plied me with questions about their
methods of attack and their use of a handy but powerful short-
range bow.

When we sailed for Britain we took half-a-dozen of those bows with us, as well as a selection of finely made weapons from the Imperial armoury. Artorius tried to persuade old Dolti, the Colchian smith, to accompany us, but he had no stomach for beginning life again in a strange land, nor did either of his sons, although they were freedmen. That family was far too comfortable to be adventurous; the cities of the Empire are luxurious, even for working craftsmen; and perhaps that is why the Empire has continued to shrink in size and power.

We began our journey to Britain late in the spring of the year 494, sailing first to Alexandria, for no ships made a direct passage from Constantinople to Britain. Alexandria had long been the second city of the Empire and the greatest port in the world. The docks and quays extended for miles beyond the city, and the tall white lighthouse swung a tapering shadow over the Portus Magnus and the westerly Portus Eunosti; both great harbours sheltered by the island of Pharos were crowded with shipping; the merchandise of half the world was unloaded on the quays; the warehouses were crammed with the produce and luxuries of the East, the slave market was by far the best-stocked in the Empire; and, despite Christian ascendancy, the city was still the home of a hundred gods and creeds, with many temples of gleaming marble, as yet undespoiled, architecturally rivalled by spacious churches. Palaces and great houses rose everywhere; colonnades shaded and sheltered the sides of the long, straight streets; luxury shops, eating places that served exotic food, baths, and brothels that catered for every taste and the most intricate perversions, were artfully arrayed to make Alexandria a hedonistic paradise. The Christians called it the dark thief of virtue. But in art and science and learning, it was the throne of reason. No city on earth, since the great days of Athens, had the authority or the intellectual power of Alexandria.

Artorius hated it.

I had long discovered that he cherished the old Roman virtues, and they made me uneasily aware of my own weaknesses.

III

Britain in the shadows

BRITAIN COULD well be the home of dead souls, for beyond the borders of the western kingdoms and their cities the country has died. The great estates are deserted, their fields unploughed, undrained and covered by tall weeds and thickets of oak scrub; the fine villas slowly collapsing as, year after year, they stood empty and unrepaired. Even where Saxon barbarians settled, they carefully avoided Roman buildings, and put up their crude wooden huts and cultivated the ground by their own methods. As you travel eastwards all signs of civilized life disappear. The grass-grown roads are no longer thronged as they would be in any well-run, prosperous province, with farm carts and vehicles carrying government officials about their business; nothing goes on wheels; no officers on duty or couriers with imperial dispatches ride by on well-groomed mounts, and you must beware of mounted men, for they are often brigands on stolen horses. The only pedestrians are ragged beggars; shaggy, furtive savages who slink along, whining for food. The broken arches of bridges fill the beds of streams they formerly spanned; old fords, long abandoned, have come back into use; where some causeway across a marsh carried the road high and dry above the soggy ground, the neglect of years has allowed embankment and road surface to sink down into an impassable waste of scummy pools, tussocks and rushes, and an ill-made path of trodden earth skirts the whole area, a diversion that often adds four or five miles to the old straight route.

Perhaps the most depressing sights in the lost province are the abandoned cities, where the gates are either blocked up by crude barriers formed from broken columns and scraps of mouldings from some temple or fragments of a statue, bound together by mortar, or are just open gaps in the walls, flanked by humped shapes where the guard towers have sunk down into heaps of rubble. The streets are deserted, the houses roofless, and the air tainted with the smell of death and decay. Few of those silent cities have been burnt or wrecked by barbarians. The British climate has wrought most of the visible damage, for Britain is a damp, rainy land, where buildings unless they are kept in repair gently collapse, becoming in the course of years, dimpled mounds, soon covered by grass and bushes. The Saxon invaders left the cities to rot, once their inhabitants had fled; apart from taking the bronze cramps from the walls and the bronze window frames, they did no damage. They dislike towns, and had no desire to live in them.

I was not without experience of ruined and ravaged countries; my part in the punitive expeditions against the Gepidae had taken me far north into the old province of Dacia that the Emperor Aurelian had relinquished more than two centuries ago, and I knew the signs of neglect, ignorance and stupidity that are always present when natives have gained control of a once civilized land; but I found Britain far more shocking than Dacia as an example of naked barbarism, and I recall with horror my first visit to what had been the greatest of all cities in Britain, Londinium Augusta. There was some life in the place; its existence was tolerated by the German barbarians, the Saxons, Jutes and Angles, all those variously-named invading tribes, who found it convenient as a market; trade of a sort went on, for men must trade unless they want to live like animals. The natives call it Luddun or Londun; the German settlers know it as Lundenwic. The port and the docks and quays are still there, but the warehouses are mostly ruinous and empty. Few ships put in, apart from pirate vessels pretending to be merchantmen, and they are able to exchange their cargoes or their loot for skins and furs and slaves. Barter rules; a few scared native merchants control the exchange, and give value in kind for weapons and wine: both of the poorest quality. All the good wine imported from the East and from Frankish vineyards goes to the western kingdoms.

The city walls still stand, and are kept in repair; but within their circuit everything has broken down. The great forum is filled with rotting rubbish; sewers and drains are blocked, there is no water supply apart from the stream that divides the city and flows, turbid with filth, into the Thames to the west of what remains of the Governor's Palace. But upstream, above the city, the Thames is clean. The streets stink like a barbarian camp, and many, piled high with refuse, are impassable, so new ways have been driven through what were once the gardens of spacious houses. All told, perhaps two thousand people live there, and because they have dropped back so far in civilization are probably unaware of the appalling squalor of their lives. The great days of law, order, and prosperity have long passed out of living memory. But some tradition of independence impels the inhabitants to keep their walls strong and their gates guarded. If attacked the place could certainly be defended; but perhaps it is not worth attacking, perhaps not worth defending either.

Those were my impressions of Britain when I first journeyed with Artorius beyond the boundaries of the western kingdoms. When I parted from him and left the country fifteen years ago, little had changed, notwithstanding his victories and alliances and the accepted division of the Island into a Roman west and a barbarous north and east. For a few years the shadows seemed to withdraw; the hope that all Britain would be united had brightened many lives, and if Artorius had been as ambitious and as selfish and ruthless as the little kings who spent their time quarrelling, he might have been proclaimed Artorius Imperator Semper Augustus; like Constantine III, the last British Emperor. As such, he would certainly have been acceptable to the Emperor in the East. Britain would again have become, at least formally, a part of the Empire, and the complete reconquest of the West that his Sacred and Imperial Majesty, Justinian, is now contemplating would be partly accomplished.

Britain is a land of bewildering variety, in some parts mountainous, especially in the west and in the northern midlands; further north there are heather-covered uplands, fiercely hot in summer, buried in snowdrifts in winter; elsewhere narrow, dank valleys divide high ground, and thick forests form impassable barriers. You become used to the oddities of the climate, and in time, begin to enjoy the absence of bright light and intense shadow and to love the soft, pearl grey skies and the gentle south-west wind, which carries the tang of salt far inland from the Atlantic.

Our voyage ended at a small but busy port with a sheltered haven, in south-west Dumnonia. There was a fair amount of shipping, and a thronged market. We bought horses and mules and four sturdy slaves, paying for them with ten sealed amphorae of the precious Greek wine we had brought with us. With our baggage loaded on the mules, we travelled north-east along moorland tracks to the little city of Isca, where we joined the great northern imperial road that ran through Aquae Sulis to Corinium, beyond the borders of the kingdom of Dumnonia, where Ambrosius Aurelianus had his military headquarters.

Isca was a walled city, the most westerly in the whole province; the gates were strong and flanked by square guard towers; the masonry of walls and towers was in good repair, and as we rode up to the south-western gate, we heard the shouted order: 'Guard! Turn out!' And a squad of young soldiers clattered out, formed up, and stood to attention. They might have been well-drilled legionaires by their appearance, for they were equipped in the traditional style, with helmets, body armour and greaves of polished bronze, and they carried curved rectangular shields of the same metal. From a distance they looked very splendid and impressive, but when we came closer we could see dints in the helmets and shields, carefully hammered out, but here and there cracked open, where the bronze had worn thin. Bronze has a long life; those helmets must have been at least a century old, and in that time rust would have gnawed steel down to the strength of parchment.

Artorius had told me that abundant supplies of armour and weapons were still stored in military stations and the fortified cities of Deva and Eburacum, that were formerly legionary head-quarters, and from those dwindling stocks local forces had been equipped ever since Constantine III withdrew the last legions from Britain for his conquest of the West. But armour and weapons were wearing out, repairs were difficult, replacements impossible, for so many smiths and other skilled craftsmen had fled from the British kingdoms to Armorica across the British Channel. Nobody had tried to stop them.

'I shall get them back,' Artorius had told me, in his quiet, level voice. As he never made idle boasts, I knew that he had some plan in mind, though years passed before he carried it out.

Before we were allowed to enter Isca with our baggage and servants we were, quite rightly, interrogated by the officer in charge of the gate-guard. He was, I remember, an elderly man, with a weather-beaten face, who spoke Latin haltingly, so Artorius shifted to the native Celtic that, with local variations of dialect, is the common language of the ancient tribal regions of Britain. During our voyage Artorius had spent a lot of time teaching me that melodious tongue; I had acquired a large vocabulary and could converse at least intelligibly, though I found the pronunciation difficult, and always had to speak slowly. When the guard-commander heard that we were envoys from the Emperor, he looked puzzled, and said:

'What Emperor? We have no emperors in Britain.' And added: 'Better without them.'

He was apparently unaware that the Empire still existed, and that in the East the civilized world was guarded by an imperial army and administered by imperial officials. Artorius was beautifully patient with him; ignorant men can be obstructive and often resent attempts to enlighten them, but I realized then that young though he was Artorius could win the interest and confidence of all kinds and conditions of men, irrespective of race or rank; a rare gift which had been enjoyed by some of Rome's greatest generals. Julius Caesar had it, Aurelian too, and that tragic disappointed genius, Julian, who had tried to restore the ancient gods to their authority and died so uselessly in the futile Persian campaign. It is a dangerous gift, especially when conferred on ambitious and unscrupulous men, and it can also betray the best intentions of good men and lead them to disaster.

The gate-guard commander lost no time in reporting our arrival to a senior officer, who took the trouble to come out to the gate in person. We were both wearing the undress uniform of military tribunes of the Imperial Household Guards, which must have been strange to him, but he could see that we were senior officers, for our badges of rank were displayed, and I wore the two decorations I had collected in the Gepidae campaign. His name, he told us, was Crispinus, and he welcomed us on behalf of the Military Governor of Isca and the Chief of Western Command of Dumnonia. Those officers, he said, had accompanied His Most Excellent Majesty, Marcus, King of Dumnonia, on a tour of inspection to the eastern defences of the realm. Meanwhile he would advise the officials of the Royal Household of our arrival, and arrange for our accommodation. He detailed two of the gate-guards to guide us to a tavern with good stabling and adequate quarters for our servants. He was very correct and formal, and when he learned that we were on our way to visit Ambrosius Aurelianus, *dux Britanniarum*, he offered us an armed escort, which would, he said, solve all problems of lodging, as the officer commanding it would make all the necessary arrangements for us.

We saw our people settled in, and then went to the baths, which for a remote provincial city, were spacious and luxurious. The attendants were Saxon slave girls, yellow-haired, blue-eyed naked beauties, with large, muscular bodies. Artorius tried to converse with two of them, but they could only muster a few words of broken Latin between them, and though he tried them in the British vernacular, they were as ignorant of that tongue as we were of their gruff, guttural native German. Artorius said he had often heard as a boy that Dumnonia was a lax, unchristian place, and the lascivious paintings on the walls of the tepidarium confirmed it. I had not failed to notice how he gazed at the Saxon girls with unusual and even unchristian attention, and he said that he hoped his uncle had some Saxon slaves. 'For I shall then learn their speech,' he explained earnestly; 'I must be able to talk with their chiefs without interpreters coming between us to twist our words into wrong meaning.' His eyes were still following the movements of those blonde girls as he spoke, and it occurred to me that he would not confine his conversation to Saxon chiefs when he mastered the German language.

As we walked about the city after leaving the baths we saw that Roman standards of ease and pleasure had not been extinguished; brothels abounded, and there was plenty of other evidence that the power of the Church was feeble. The old gods were openly honoured, for stone temples, built long ago, were standing, undamaged and in good repair, with altars to Mars, Minerva, Neptune, and others, the ashes on some of them warm from recent sacrifice.

We found only one Christian church; a crude building, little better than a large wooden hut with a thatched roof, and Artorius entered, while I remained in the narrow, paved street, watching the people. Summer still lingered, for although we had made a fairly quick passage, we had been delayed for nearly two months in Alexandria before we were able to secure berths on one of the infrequent ocean-going trading ships. The southern part of Dumnonia is warmer than the rest of Britain, but even in summer the evenings are chilly, at least they seem so to anybody who has lived in the eastern provinces of the Empire, and I was glad of my military cloak. Artorius was spending an interminable time in the church; I looked inside once, and saw him kneeling before the altar. The place was gloomy and smelt of stale sweat and damp straw. When he rejoined me, he looked very solemn and told me that he had been praying for strength to resist temptation.

'Very necessary for some people,' I said; 'but what's been tempting you?' I knew perfectly well of course, but wanted to hear what he'd say.

'The flesh,' he answered frankly. 'If I am to reconquer Britain I must resist carnal indulgence: I could easily become a mere animal.'

'You could lose your human likeness in other ways, too,' I told him. 'Don't forget what happened to Aristides when people grew sick and tired of hearing him called "the Just". He was ostracized by the Athenians because he was too good to be likeable.'

'Aristides was a Greek,' he reminded me, adding, 'if the Greek citizens who banished him a thousand years ago were anything like modern Greeks, they would naturally detest virtue. I am a Roman, so are you, and Romans respect virtue.'

'Yes,' I agreed, 'and they are always ready to deplore the lack of virtue in others, especially when they are not virtuous themselves.'

He became even more solemn, and said: 'Caius, you are not at heart a Christian, are you?'

'I have certain reservations,' I replied; 'I am, perhaps, too comfortable to be a Christian.'

'You will change,' he predicted; 'Britain and our task here will change you.'

Even the passage of so many years cannot efface the memory of that confident prediction, which was to be fulfilled though not in the way Artorius imagined. Britain certainly taught me to value, perhaps excessively, all those comforts and conveniences of life that citizens of the Empire take for granted. I was slow to realize that Artorius set little store by civilized amenities; his task, as he saw it, was to reunite Britain to the Empire as a group of Christian provinces, after the Saxon barbarians had been driven out or subdued so that they would accept honourable alliance as *foederati*, and the independent British rulers persuaded to relinquish their regal titles and to become governors of provinces, under a *vicarius Britanniarum*, appointed by and directly responsible to the Emperor. I don't think that he even suspected the magnitude of such a task; at least he was encouraged by the fact that the British kings had agreed many years ago to the appointment of his uncle as *dux Britanniarum*, thus accepting, at least ostensibly, his overall authority as commander-in-chief when armed forces were put in the field.

We returned to our tavern at nightfall through streets brightened by the wavering yellow glare of flaming torches, soaked in oil and fixed in iron brackets that projected from the walls of houses. We found awaiting us a large, fat genial man in a spotless white robe who informed us that he was Libius Cassius, His Majesty's Chief Steward; in the absence of the Master of the Royal Household, who had accompanied the king to the eastern boundaries of Dumnonia, he had assumed the responsibility of overseeing our comfort.

'I particularly desired to save you from the limited attractions

A. R. – B

of the wine usually supplied in taverns,' he said; 'so I have had some sent from the royal cellars.'

We thanked him, and invited him to dinner; but he said that although he would like to sit with us, he had already dined, and hoped that we would be able to give him news of what was happening in the distant world of the Empire.

'We hear so little and so infrequently,' he explained, 'and our informants are usually mariners and travelling merchants and you know what liars they are.'

So for the rest of the evening and until long past midnight we answered his questions and asked a good many of our own. I think that he would have stayed all night, but we had to make an early start in the morning, for we were both anxious to reach Corinium and report to Ambrosius. We learned much about the political and military condition of Britain, for Libius Cassius was well-informed. Apparently King Marcus was always uneasy about his eastern frontier which was the only part of his realm likely to be attacked, so he kept a strong garrison in the little town of Vindocladia, which was the last fortified post of the kingdom. Beyond it a broad belt of desolate and almost uninhabited country ran northwards from the Sea of Vectis, to the Great Dyke, the sixty-mile-long military earthwork that formed an almost continuous northern boundary to the kingdom, and had been dug when the Saxon advance up the Thames valley threatened the south-west. That had happened a few years before the birth of Artorius. The empty wasteland east of the Dumnonian frontier, some fifty miles wide, had once been fertile farmland, with rich estates and populous settlements, but long before the Saxon barbarians became a growing menace, Irish raiders had sailed into the Sea of Vectis and penetrated far inland, killing or enslaving men, women and children, and burning every house and farmstead. That blackened tongue of land never recovered. Only wolves and packs of savage dogs lived there, preying on the deer and wild ponies. So a wilderness, which nobody wanted, separated Dumnonia from the kingdom of the South Saxons.

That barbarian kingdom had been founded by the chief, Aelle, who had brought his war band over from western Germania, burnt his ships, and marched a few miles inland to the edge of the Andredes Leag, the dense forest that covered the high ground to the north. There he stayed, slowly enlarging his band with new recruits from the Cantic and other Saxon states, living on the country, stealing crops and cattle, looting farmsteads, attracting to his service many landless adventurers and wandering brigands, so that in a few years he felt strong enough to attack the city of Noviomagus in the west of what was still the British kingdom of the Regni. He starved out that city, by encircl ng it with his greatly increased army, and sacked it after he had butchered the citizens when in despair they opened the gates and surrendered.

Three years ago Aelle had stormed and taken the stronghold of Anderida, which was the last of the forts built as part of the Saxon Shore defences in the time of the Imperial administration of Britain. So now this barbarian was king over the whole of the former tribal area of the Regni, where he wiped out every vestige of Roman civilization and, so it was said, massacred all the inhabitants, including the entire slave force. Shiploads of emigrants from Germania came regularly during the sailing season, so the kingdom was repopulated by barbarians who settled down to farm the land and raise families, for they brought their own women with them.

Ambrosius had tried to persuade the other independent British states to raise an army strong enough to attack Aelle and drive him from his kingdom, but in vain. Although in the past such armies had been raised and entrusted to his command, he was now an ageing man who lacked the energy and persistence to enforce his will upon the rulers of the two largest kingdoms, Demetia and Gwynedd. Had he succeeded, the smaller states that lay between them, west of the Sabrina, would have been compelled to join in; but only the King of Dumnonia believed that Britain was in danger of a new Saxon advance westwards. The north-western kingdom of Reged was too remote from the Saxon states on the British Channel for its ruler to feel apprehensive or even interested, moreover he was too deeply engaged in a dispute with the King of Gwynedd to have time or energy for anything else. The dispute was trivial and absurd, but although unimportant it had become traditional and had continued for three generations. It concerned the possession of the sparsely inhabited peninsula that lay between the estuaries of two western rivers that flowed into the Irish sea. One of them, the Dee, or Deva, was named after the strong fortress city which was in the territory of Gwynedd. The kings of Gwynedd, who were descended from the great Cunedda, claimed that because they held Deva they had a prior right to the peninsula. The quarrel periodically led to bloodshed, following border raids; though both parties stopped short of actual war. Minor, inconclusive conflicts and intermittent bickering satisfied them, for the native British are as fond of fighting as the Irish, and have indulged their taste for pointless violence ever since the strong hand of Rome was removed from their affairs.

Hearing all this from Libius Cassius months before I had seen the lost lands and ruins beyond the western kingdoms, I began to suspect that Britain was already darkened by the shadows of an irreversible barbarism.

IV

Ambrosius

FROM ISCA TO CORINIUM the distance is just over one hundred and thirty miles, and the road, like all roads in Dumnonia and the other western British states had been kept in good repair, cleared of undergrowth on either side for the length of a bow shot, so brigands had no cover to ambush travellers. Long stretches of it were spear-straight; streams were crossed by paved fords if they were broad and shallow, and there were innumerable stone-built bridges; every ten miles commodious rest houses were ready to receive wayfarers and, at longer intervals, there were military police posts manned by soldiers equipped with bits and pieces of bronze armour, like those of the gate-guards at Isca. Beyond Lindinis, a small walled town where four roads and an ancient trackway met, the country was open and fertile, with many prosperous farmsteads and here and there a great villa surrounded by gardens and orchards. But long before we reached that town, when we were only a few miles away from Isca, we learned more about Dumnonia than Libius Cassius had told us.

The armed escort detailed to accompany us was in charge of an elderly under-officer called Nen, a native name, and when it was light enough to see—for we had started before dawn—we were not impressed by the slovenly turn-out of that squad of six young louts. Their equipment was dirty, their helmets tarnished, and they had loaded their shields on to two of our pack mules when Isca was out of sight. They shambled along, chattering and laughing, and without any pretence of march discipline.

Presently Artorius reined up his horse, dismounted and said: 'This is where I take charge.'

He beckoned to Nen, who strolled across to us and stood looking up at Artorius, who was far taller. All Dumnonians seemed to be short and stocky. I could see that the man was stupid, not insolent. He said:

'You wanted me?'

'Listen, Nen,' said Artorius in his deceptively gentle voice, 'when you are called by an officer, you march up smartly, stand to attention, and salute.'

Nen looked surprised, but he clicked his heels together and raised his spear slowly.

'You'd forgotten your drill, hadn't you?' said Artorius.

'Well, no, sir,' Nen answered; 'but I didn't rightly know that you were an officer.'

'Well you do now, so there won't be any more mistakes. Send your men here, then they won't make any either.'

Nen saluted, turned about and was marching back to the squad when Artorius stopped him.

'Use your voice, man,' he ordered; 'call them to attention, and march them back here.'

At least Nen owned a parade-ground voice, but the response to his order was disgraceful. The men slowly rose to their feet, for they had been squatting by the roadside, when Artorius shouted:

'At the double!'

Then they ran towards us, halted, and one burly youngster, whose eyebrows formed a long black bar on his bold face, said:

'Who do you think you are, and who are you?'

I heard the hiss of his sword leaving the scabbard, and Artorius strode forward and struck the man across the face with the flat of the leaf-shaped blade.

'The next blow will draw blood,' he said; 'nor will you recover from it. Stand to attention. You are Roman soldiers, and while you are with me you'll behave as such. You are on escort duty, detailed for that duty by the officers of your king. You will observe march discipline henceforth. You will march three abreast, keeping your dressing, shields on your back between the shoulders, spears at the slope, and unless you are given the order to march at ease you will march to attention. Understand? Answer up smartly, now.'

'Yes, sir,' they said in chorus. And they looked very startled indeed.

Artorius continued. 'You're dirty and slack. If there is a barber at the next rest house you shall have your hair cut to regulation length. That's all. Dismiss!'

We had no further trouble with the escort; we rearranged the order of march, so the six men went ahead in two ranks, with Nen behind them to call the step, and after an interval of twelve paces Artorius and I rode together, one or other of us trotting back occasionally to check any straggling and to keep the party closed up. We halted at the first rest house, three hours out of Isca, and our escort was tidied up. After their hair was cut, their equipment cleaned and their helmets polished, those dark, sturdy Dumnonians began to look like Roman soldiers.

Although we maintained good march discipline, we could not average more than ten miles a day, and we were delayed at Lindinis and Aquae Sulis, for despite Nen's official billeting order for his men, the clerk who had made it out had not included our people, so we had to find taverns with stabling ourselves.

Aquae Sulis had been famous as a spa a century ago, and though the magnificent temple of Sulis Minerva and the bath buildings still stood undamaged, the plumbing of the great baths was hopelessly deranged and had, we were told, been out of order for many years. No skilled workmen remained to put it right; the natural hot springs still bubbled out, though much of the healing water was wasted, and the gardens that had surrounded the baths were overgrown and sodden; the whole area had become marshy and the streets were partly submerged beneath a shallow, gently steaming lake. No enemy had done this damage; the city had never been sacked; but no ruler of Dumnonia had cared enough to keep a great centre of civilized luxury in proper repair, and in common with the other British kings had failed to stop skilled workers from flitting across the Channel to Armorica with their goods and tools and craft secrets.

Five miles north-west of Aquae Sulis at the junction of the road to Corinium and the eastern route that runs through Calleva to

Londinium, we passed the border of Dumnonia, parted with our escort, and gave each man two gold pieces and Nen five. They recognized gold, though coined money was strange to them. But we had no other means of rewarding their services, such as they were.

We were now in the British state of Corinium, and a day later entered the city of that name, where Ambrosius Aurelianus had his headquarters as commander-in-chief of the armies of Britain.

The walls of Corinium were high, thick and in excellent repair, and as we approached the south gate we could see sunlight glinting on the helmets of sentries above the curtain wall that ran along the top of the main wall; just short of the gate, at the right of the road was a small amphitheatre, in active use as a riding school. The gate-guards turned out, formed up in two ranks, and stood at attention awaiting us.

'My uncle must have some armourers on the strength,' said Artorius, noting their impeccable equipment; very different from the makeshift stuff worn by the Dumnonian soldiers.

We were questioned by a young centurion, who, when he heard that we were imperial envoys, reporting to the *dux Britanniarum* said:

'You are entitled to a general salute,' and gave the order to present arms, which the gate-guard did as smartly as one could wish. The centurion took charge of us, sent an under-officer to the garrison barracks, to arrange for our servants, animals and baggage to be accommodated, and sent a messenger to Headquarters to announce our arrival. We washed off the dust and sweat of our journey in the bath-house behind one of the gate-towers, changed our clothes, and went with a guide to the basilica, east of the forum, which had been taken over as military and administrative headquarters.

There, in a small, bare room, we reported to Ambrosius Aurelianus.

He was an old man, though certainly not enfeebled by age; for, despite his thick white hair and the fine network of lines on his face, he gave an impression of great energy, held in reserve and strictly controlled. Looking at him, I could imagine what Artorius would be like in old age; for both had the same wide-set pale grey eyes below heavy eyebrows, the same regular features, and the prominent, aggressive nose. When he rose from his seat at his work table, I realized, with some surprise, that he was a comparatively small man; his great breadth of shoulder was deceptive, for his large body was supported by short, sturdy, slightly bowed legs. He wore the dark red chlamys of a Roman general, and an embossed cuirass of polished bronze.

Artorius knelt and kissed his hand.

'Welcome, nephew,' said Ambrosius, 'I had trained my patience too strictly to hope for your presence in Britain until another year, perhaps two years, had passed.'

His words had the agreeable lilt that makes the speech of all British-born Romans so melodious.

Artorius introduced me and then presented the Emperor's letter of greeting. Ambrosius read it through, then said: 'Few of the provincial governors, who style themselves kings, would acknowledge Imperial authority. They would say that we've had no emperor since the usurper Constantine III, and that after Rome was sacked eighty-four years ago and the Imperial Administration ordered the British provinces to manage their own affairs, that they have been well managed. Although you were only a boy when you went to Constantinople, you know all this.'

'But they recognize your authority as *dux Britanniarum* and you have commanded their troops,' Artorius objected.

'They only support my authority and recruit armies when some new barbarian advance has frightened them,' said his uncle. 'So far, I have been a successful general, but what counts more with the tribesmen who think that they are Romans, is the descent of our family from Magnus Maximus.'

'Another usurper!' Artorius sounded rather scornful.

'And for a time, Emperor of the West,' Ambrosius reminded him; 'his name is still revered throughout the length and breadth of the old fifth British province of Valentia, especially by the descendants of Cunedda, the grandson of Paternus, a chief of the Votadini whom Maximus had befriended. Like the Irish tribesmen, the British never forget their history. I could wish that Christ ruled their hearts as He now rules the hearts of the Irish, who, since they became Christians have ceased to be savages, though they seem unlikely ever to enjoy peaceful ways and still fight among themselves. But they no longer raid our shores for slaves and loot.'

He stopped abruptly. There was a long pause, then he said:

'The west is not and has never been wholly Christian. In Demetia and the Black Mountains, and all the west coast as far north as the Wall and beyond, older and darker gods are worshipped, and the little kings command the services and loyalty of priests who are called the royal devils. But you must travel in Britain and see for yourself. Things were not so bad when you were a boy: we held our own against the barbarians: the laws were respected, and in some regions justice was still administered. Not now. Each king makes his own laws, and has his own sworn band of armed bullies to enforce his will. This you will discover when you visit their so-called Courts. And this must be done soon.'

Before winter came to Britain that year, we began our travels, and what we saw then is, I suppose, very much what a traveller in the lost province would see today; so what I can recall of the people, the tribes, their power and their weaknesses, and the men who ruled them, and the barbarian Saxon states that have become secure and established, should be of value, when the final draft of my report has been passed by Philonides as fit for submission to his Sacred and Imperial Majesty, the Emperor Justinian.

In the weeks we spent in Corinium, I began to understand how Ambrosius had established and maintained his ascendancy over British rulers. As one of the last of the Aurelii, he was all they could never be. That family had held land in Britain for over four hundred years, since the days when Agricola was governor-general of the Province. The founder, Metilius Aurelianus, was one of Agricola's generals who had distinguished himself in the campaign against the Brigantes, and when that tribe was temporarily subdued, he married the daughter of a Brigantian nobleman. Their descendants left the north after the Brigantes had rebelled and destroyed the IXth Legion, and having acquired large estates west of the Sabrina, between Glevum and Ariconium, for many generations they lived a peaceful and untroubled country life, farming their land and quietly and unostentatiously increasing their wealth. In each generation the eldest son usually joined the army, sometimes more than one son, but though some rose to high rank, no member of the family was particularly distinguished until the father of Ambrosius became a commander of mounted auxiliaries in the defence forces raised after Constantine III had withdrawn all the regular troops from Britain to conquer Gaul and Spain. This Ambrosius, the first, as I shall call him, had married a grand-daughter of Magnus Maximus; by her he had two sons, Ambrosius and Uther, giving his second son a British tribal name at the insistence of his wife, who must by all accounts have been a troublesome woman. She was the daughter of Victor, the eldest son of Maximus who was slain in 388, the same year as his father.

Maximus had become a legend in Britain; before his appointment as *dux Britanniarum*, he had been governor of Valentia, and had married Helena, the daughter of a British chief of the old lost tribe of Ordovices. Helena was said to have been an ambitious woman who encouraged her husband to attempt his conquest of the Western Empire; but he was, as Artorius had said, just another usurper. Although Ambrosius the first was, in his own right, a soldier and administrator of exceptional ability, he owed some of his prestige to his connection with the seed of Maximus. He never regarded the separation from the Imperial Administration as more than temporary, and actively opposed chiefs such as Vortigern, who preferred to wield personal power in an independent Britain. He was the acknowledged leader of the Roman faction, though he never assumed the purple. Content with the rank of general and confident of the efficiency of the troops that he commanded, he opposed the panic decision of a few native chiefs who had begged a visiting Bishop from Gaul, who had abandoned a military career to join the Church, to assume command of the defence army, when a large raiding band of Picts had broken through the weak defences of the Wall and marched south. This bishop, Germanus by name, had been sent by the Pope with another missionary, to combat the

Pelagian heresy, which was popular in Britain, and he defeated the Picts by a trick, without bloodshed on either side.

That happened in 429, and the defeat of the northern barbarians became famous, at least among Churchmen and other devout and credulous people, as the 'Alleluia' victory. Professional soldiers thought little of the affair. The raiders had penetrated far into the former tribal region of the Brigantes, brushing aside the opposition of a few weak military posts, and reaching a long, snake-like pass through the mountain range that forms the backbone of the north midlands. Germanus with a mixed force of ill-trained troops, posted his men on both sides of this defile, ordering them to conceal themselves in the bracken and bushes that covered the rocky soil. As a soldier he knew that he led poor material, so in his office as a bishop he held one of those emotional religious services some hours before the battle; inspired the rabble with the belief that God fought for them; and told them that they must praise Him with their voices when the enemy was sighted. He noticed how the sound of the hymns sung during the service had echoed and re-echoed in that narrow pass, thrown back and amplified by the cliffs that rose above the rocky slopes, so he told his men to wait until they heard a shout of Alleluia. Then they should all repeat the shout, and God would put the enemy to flight. He chose the man with the loudest carrying voice to give the signal, then posted the rest and waited.

Now most barbarians believe that mountains and forests are haunted by demons, and in particular the Gwyllion, the female furies who are loyal to native tribes and help them to fight their enemies, so as the Picts came straggling along the pass, all over the place in the manner of undisciplined warriors, they halted, terrified, directly they heard the shouts of Alleluia, and when, the echoes helping, the cries seemed to come from all around them and rise and fall and fade and be renewed, they fled, and ran so fast that not one of them was slain or captured. This is still known as the 'Alleluia Victory', and God gets the credit: not the cunning of that old soldier, Germanus.

When Germanus returned to Gaul, to Autessiodurum, the seat of his bishopric, the quarrels between the two political factions in the province continued; never reaching the point of civil war, but conducted with implacable bitterness. At the time of the 'Alleluia Victory', Ambrosius was five, and his brother, Uther, a year younger. When they grew to manhood, Ambrosius chose a military career, was loyal to the Roman party, and, like his father, deplored the settlement of Saxon barbarians that had followed Vortigern's original invitation to Hengist's war-band to act as auxiliaries in the unending campaign against the Picts. Uther had died when Artorius was eight, and Ambrosius had adopted the boy, taken him into his household, and encouraged his military ambitions. That Uther had some fatal weakness seemed obvious, but I never learned what it was, for no word of criticism was spoken by Ambrosius, and Artorius never mentioned his father.

All this I learned during our stay in Corinium; and though it seemed even then to be the old, tired history of political feuds and thwarted ambitions, it revealed to me the quarrelsome disposition of the native British, and the waning influence of the Roman spirit that had formerly corrected or at least modified the instabilities of the Celtic tribal heritage. This we must take into account if ever we attempt the total reconquest of the west, for it is unlikely ever to change. We shall not be able to trust the British kingdoms, and certainly not their kings.

A small island, south-east of the Thames estuary, twelve miles long and five broad, was the price Vortigern paid in land to the Saxon war-band, and there they made their first settlement. Like the head of a poisoned arrow, that spreads venom through the whole body of a victim, the settlement became a military base for the barbarian raids into Britain. Although Ambrosius in two successive campaigns had tried to dislodge the Saxons, their kingdom was too firmly established. Without actually saying so he left us in no doubt that he had little faith in any future attempt to unite all Britain under Roman rule; indeed he seemed to think that the initiative lay with the barbarian states, which could one day apply the lesson Rome had taught the world: divide and rule. The British kingdoms were already divided: only ties of common fear compelled their rulers to unite when some obvious danger threatened, and apart

from Aelle's extension and consolidation of his South Saxon kingdom by the capture of Anderida, the Saxon states had been quiet,
their kings and chiefs apparently satisfied with their boundaries.

Ambrosius was oppressed by the gloomy memory of failure;
political not military failure; but he encouraged Artorius.

His parting words to him when we set forth on our travels were
far from despairing.

'Titles still have some power,' he said. 'You are a tribune, and
the Emperor has authorized your promotion to higher rank;
promotion that is left to my unfettered discretion. The Council
of Kings may not have much respect for an Imperial mandate, but
if it should put a young man of Roman descent in my place and if
you proved to be as good a military leader as your grandfather, then
you might succeed as *dux Britanniarum* where I have failed.'

V

The little Kings

WINTER CAME suddenly after a prolonged autumn, with continuous sunny weather, though the sun gives no warmth in Britain, and cutting winds make every day seem chilly to anyone who has lived in the East. Artorius seldom noticed the cold; Britain was after all his native land; only when frost whitened the ground and sharpened the winds did he acknowledge the change by wearing one of the grey woollen cloaks, best known of all British products. Those cloaks have been shipped to Gaul and Belgica and Spain for centuries, and the trade has continued to this day, despite wars and pirate-ridden seaways. Except in heavy rain or snow, Artorius went bare-headed, his helmet at his saddle-bow, his cap of short, dark hair neat and well-combed. He was clean-shaven, or tried to be, for he had to wet his cheeks and jaw with water and then use a razor without any soap to soften the stubble. Soap and oil, like many other things, were unknown in Britain.

During our travels in those late autumn weeks we visited the western kingdoms: Gwent, which was the smallest, Glevissig and, most westerly of all, Demetia, named after the Demetae, an ancient tribe with a reputation for sloth and shiftiness, though intermarriage with Irish raiders who settled in their tribal area has improved the stock during the last hundred years. We stayed at the courts of the kings who ruled those states, and though they called themselves Romans they were close to barbarism. They lacked nearly everything that makes civilized life agreeable. The only cities with baths that still worked, were in Gwent: one was Venta, and the other, Isca Silurum, for centuries the headquarters of the IInd, Augusta, and now known as Isca Caerleon, the city of the legion, for the Silures that it was originally named after have long lost their tribal

37

identity. Elsewhere, even in the so-called royal palaces, plumbing was unknown: everybody washed in cold water, nobody used perfumes, and to soften their hands the ladies of the court soaked them in urine; in other ways they were unsavoury creatures; their armpits sprouted a thick bush of hairs, for they considered hair sacred; the men wore beards and huge flowing whiskers, and although they shaved the front of their heads, the hair at the sides and back grew long and fell to their shoulders. Both men and women kept their long hair clean and constantly combed it, even at meals. The men were usually drunk after sunset and eager for women who were always willing. Everybody ate voraciously; food was prepared without art and consisted chiefly of huge roasted joints, greasy stews flavoured with onions, coarse heavy bread smeared with fat, and strong cheese made from goats' milk. Sheep, pigs and deer provided the meat, sometimes a kid. Odd and rather messy dishes were concocted from eggs and honey. Although no place we visited was far from a river or the sea, surprisingly little fish was eaten; and we never had any of the oysters for which Britain was famous. I discovered later that very few fishing boats existed; there was a constant demand for seamen to make up the crews of trading vessels and the war craft that were supposed to police the seas and deal with pirates, though now and then warships belonging to one or other of the independent kings, would turn pirate, help themselves to cargoes, and sail across the Channel to Gaul or Armorica and sell their spoils. There was much disorder at sea; no central Naval Command existed that could have ended it, and no ruler was willing to surrender his right to own and man warships.

Ambrosius had provided us with an escort; fifty troopers mounted on sturdy hill ponies, sure-footed and reliable beasts in mountainous country, though too small to carry much weight. Each man was lightly equipped with a spear, long sword, bronze helmet, round wooden shield covered with hide, and a tough leather cuirass that gave as much protection as metal. The officer in charge was a grey-haired veteran named Paulinus, who had served under Ambrosius in the wars against the Saxons; silent and reliable, a type that I was to meet over and over again during my years in Britain.

We left our baggage and servants at the barracks in Corinium, where Artorius had long sessions with the smiths in the armoury, talking to the ageing craftsmen and giving instructions for copying the specimens of bows and long swords we had brought from Constantinople. He was troubled, because no boys or young men were being trained as metal workers, for in every British state and city there was a shortage of skill. Nearly all the old families, versed in traditional crafts for generations, had long since crossed the Channel. Once again Artorius vowed to bring them back.

To avoid any confusion and misunderstanding I told him before we set out that he was to command our escort.

'But you are a senior tribune,' he objected.

'Not here,' I replied. 'I'm second-in-command, if you like, to the future *dux Britanniarum*. You didn't ask me for permission to take charge of those Dumnonian louts on our way here; you just did it. Quite rightly.'

'I should have asked you,' he said: 'but I lost my temper. I must learn not to.'

'You didn't show it,' I told him.

Indeed, during all our years together I never saw him show a trace of anger, though he was given abundant provocation, not only by the little kings and stupid officials he had to deal with and cajole, but by foolish women who troubled his peace of mind; one in particular, whom I ought to have killed. Had I done so the history of Britain might have been changed; but very early in life I learned to avoid those weak, regretful words: 'if only'.

We were riding north to Deva, along an old military road, when the first snowstorm came down on us, thick and blinding and driven by a bitter north-easterly wind. Fortunately we were within a few miles of the ancient city of Viroconium, where we found shelter. The place had been sacked and burnt many times during the last two hundred years, and was now rebuilt, stoutly and not unskilfully, in timber, for hardly any masons are left in the province, no stone is quarried and brick kilns have been cold and empty for half a century, but plenty of carpenters are available, and they can command the best of everything in food, drink, clothes and women, for

everybody needs their services. Although Viroconium has a market
and a few memories of old civilized comforts, such as piped water
to some of the houses, it is dismal with ruins; the columns of the
forum have fallen, capitals and broken shafts have been used to
repair the city walls; the baths are gaunt skeletons, roofless and
filled with rubbish; and the bridge across the Sabrina is unsafe.

We ran into the usual difficulties about payment in a land where
money no longer circulates, for we hesitated to billet our escort and
requisition food and fodder unless we could give something in
exchange, but we only had gold pieces, and nobody seemed to want
them. The keeper of the tavern where Artorius and I stayed said,
rather scornfully, that they were too small to melt down for orna-
ments or brooches, but he condescended to take two of them.
Viroconium is in the kingdom of Gwynedd, and on our arrival we
had told the Municipal Curia that we were an Imperial mission on
our way to visit King Catwallaun, but they were not impressed.
The chief decurion remarked ungraciously that at least we were not
a band of brigands, so he supposed we must be permitted to stay in
the city. He gave no help or advice about how we could pay for our
billets or food, so we troubled ourselves no more about the matter.
Artorius thanked him when we left after two days, and I added
that we should have much pleasure in telling his king what a warm
and memorable welcome he had given us.

'They keep the ancient titles, but they've lost their manners,' I
said to Artorius, as we rode through the north gate on our way to
Deva.

He smiled. 'That is their British independence,' he told me.

The snow had stopped, but the sky was dark and sullen with the
promise of more; a strong east wind lifted the powdery tops of the
drifts piled on either side of the road and drove them across it,
swirling white veils around our horses' hooves. Although we were
less than fifty miles from our destination, we were two days on the
road, staying for one night in a rest house near one of the road
junctions, and leaving it cold and hungry before dawn, for although
there was plenty of fodder for our mounts, we had to be satisfied
with a little salted meat and some thin red wine. The housekeeping

staff had run out of supplies, and told us in their surly way that nobody expected travellers at this time of the year, and implied that nobody should want to travel.

At last, while daylight still lingered, we saw the high walls and watch towers of Deva in the distance and, black against the dull bronze sky, the statue of Mars above the gate of the amphitheatre, pointing the stump of a spear upwards, for some Christian zealots had once tried to haul down the figure but only managed to break off part of the spear.

Deva, the ancient fortress, once called the North West Gate of Britain, was for centuries the headquarters of the famous XXth Legion, the Valeria Victrix; now it was the royal city of Catwallaun Longhand, King of Gwynedd, whose dominions extended from the Black Mountains northwards to the River Dee, with the Irish Sea as the west boundary, and an ill-defined border, fifty miles east of Viroconium, where a barbarian kingdom of Angles was established and strongly defended. North of Gwynedd the kingdom of Reged, sparsely inhabited, ran from the disputed territory of the Peninsula up to Hadrian's Wall, and beyond, to the borders of the kingdom that included and extended beyond the Clyde valley and was ruled by Coroticus. Those barbarous names are coming back to me as I write: some of the little kings still favoured Roman names, but some, like Catwallaun, felt that a native name proclaimed and sustained their proud independence. It was impossible for Catwallaun to resist boasting of his descent; the great Cunedda was his grandfather, but when he had a few cups of wine inside him he would drag his listeners back further still, until he reached Paternus, the chief of the Votadini to whom Magnus Maximus had given the rank of general, years before so many of his tribe were persuaded to march south to drive the Irish out of Valentia. Although all that is ancient history, it has a bearing on the present state of Britain; for tribal memories are strong, the bards keep old tales alive, and the deeds of old chiefs and heroes, their triumphs and defeats, seem like the happenings of yesterday to the half-drunk men who hear about them during the interminable feasts that take place in royal palaces and the grubby halls of British noblemen.

King Catwallaun was a thickset man, grey-haired, slow in speech and movement, well past the prime of life; his dark brown eyes were watchful, and I was unable to decide whether he was intelligent or merely cunning. At least he was polite, and welcomed us, though he was not impressed by the message of imperial goodwill that Artorius, mistakenly, I think, saw fit to give him. His response reminded me of the gruff words of the guard-commander at Isca when he heard who we were and where we came from.

'We have acknowledged no emperor since Constantine III,' he told us as we sat with him, drinking passable wine from finely chased gold cups. 'We've done well without them. We keep our taxes here; they aren't sunk in the bottomless pit of an Imperial treasury.'

Artorius smiled at that, and asked: 'Do you collect any?'

Catwallaun made no reply. He took a long draught of wine, and stared hard at Artorius, who knew perfectly well that taxes were neither levied nor collected in Britain. The practice of some kings was to send messengers with a squad of armed bullies to any un-protected rich man, who was tortured until he disclosed the hiding place of his hoard. It was a thieves' world, and Ambrosius had left us in no doubt about the morals and lawlessness of its rulers. I wondered who had been the original owner of the cups from which we drank our wine.

There was a long pause, then Artorius said: 'Constantine III was *not* an emperor. He was a usurper, and paid the usual price—with his head. Today, his Sacred and Imperial Majesty, Anastasius, rules the Empire in name and in fact.' He unrolled the parchment in-scribed with his commission as a tribune, and added: 'Read. I am not speaking without authority.'

The king shook his head; and I knew then how far Britain had fallen, for he said: 'I cannot read.'

And these crowned chiefs called themselves Romans!

I took the parchment from Artorius and read it aloud, translating the formal words as well as I could into the vernacular. We had been conversing in Celtic, for though the king understood Latin, he spoke it haltingly and with a strange accent. He made no comment, but reached out for the parchment, and then I saw why he had been given his side-name of Longhand; the length of his muscular fingers was out of all proportion to his arms and wrists, amounting to a deformity. He knew enough to hold the document the right way up, but I wondered what satisfaction he got from staring at it so long and earnestly.

As he returned it to me, he said: 'You are welcome, not because you come from the Emperor, who is far away and is unknown to me, but because you, Artorius, are the nephew of Ambrosius, who is a good man and a fine general.'

The king's house was stone-built and weatherproof; it must have belonged to some high-ranking officer in the past, for it adjoined the Praetorium; the roof was still tiled, though most of the houses in Deva had been burnt and were now roughly thatched with straw that was always damp, for it soaked up rain and snow and let water through in heavy storms. We were dry, warm and passably comfortable, but that was all: I had by this time become accustomed to the absence of luxuries, and Artorius never seemed to miss them; what I missed most was civilized conversation. Royal households in Britain were usually dull, and Catwallaun's was gloomy as well. We were presented to some members of it at the feast the king gave for us in the hall of the Praetorium.

The women, with their black hair and tawny skins, were not unattractive; their voices were low and soft, which was fortunate as they talked incessantly and were allowed to: another proof of how far barbarian manners were accepted. The men were clods, with two exceptions: Prince Maelgwyn, the king's eldest son, and Myrddin, his tutor, who was also the Court Bard.

Prince Maelgwyn was then about twenty; very unlike his father, for he was tall, graceful and handsome, with dark eyes, curly black hair and a thick beard. He was, as the British say, hard of smiling; his expression was habitually surly, his voice harsh, but his manners were those of a civilized gentleman. He talked well, chiefly about boar hunting, and hoped that we should be able to stay long enough for him to show us some sport.

His father explained to us, in a vast number of unnecessary words, the rights and wrongs of the rival claims of the kingdoms of

Gwynedd and Reged to the peninsula, which, he insisted, was the rightful territorial inheritance of the descendants of Cunedda, who ninety years ago had expelled the Irish settlers from it and reclaimed all the lands of the old Ordovician tribe on both sides of the River Dee. He droned on interminably, until Artorius said:

'Who owns that land now?'

Maelgwyn answered, not the king. The young man showed no deference to his father. He said:

'We do, of course. And we shall keep it.' His large teeth gleamed white amid the darkness of his beard: it was not a smile; more like a snarl. 'You shall understand why we shall keep it when the snow clears,' he went on; 'for then we shall parade two cohorts of the garrison for you to inspect.'

The king interrupted, by calling on Myrddin to entertain the company. The Court Bard had interested me, for he was quite unlike anybody I had met before in Britain; in any country or company he would have seemed exceptional. He was then, I suppose, about thirty: a man of medium height, with light brown hair, a long beard, dark eyebrows above a pair of pale grey unblinking eyes. When his glance fell on you it was difficult to look away: those pale eyes held you.

He rose to his feet, picked up a small harp and looking at Artorius sang this song:

> Give me a harp and I'll give you a song
> Of a sword and a shield and a helm and a spear
> And a horse and a maid and a man unafraid
> Who'll drive the blond savages back to the sea,
> Back to the sea,
> Back to the sea,
> Back to their ships with a cargo of fear.
>
> Hail to the Leader who drives them away!
> Crown him with oak leaves, with laurel, with bay!
> Hail to Artorius, ever victorious,
> Doer of deeds that will ever be glorious.

Men will remember his name and his fame
When Britain has sunk in the sea,
In the sea,
When Britain has sunk in the sea.

Myrddin sat down, and there was a long, cold silence. Artorius looked at Maelgwyn, and said quietly:

'Prince, I am embarrassed. Are you?'

'No,' was the reply; 'but that fool will regret his song.'

Artorius placed a hand on Maelgwyn's arm; a gentle, persuasive gesture; he smiled and said:

'He spoke with another voice, Prince. His hour is upon him, and for a time his tongue was not his own.'

'If he lives, he shall not own a tongue,' Maelgwyn returned.

'Surely bards are privileged, if not sacred,' Artorius objected.

Maelgwyn was silent, then he said: 'I am impolite. Forgive me. His song was in praise of you, our guest.'

'Let us forget such a piece of idle flattery,' said Artorius; 'I know how my countrymen exaggerate.'

They both laughed; but I knew that Myrddin's ill-timed prophecy might easily have angered our hosts. If we were to win the support of the little kings and draw on the manpower of their kingdoms, we could not afford to make enemies anywhere.

During the rest of our stay in Deva—and we were snowbound in that cold city for ten days—both the king and the prince took especial pains to impress us with their friendliness, and with the magnificence of their family history. We suspected the show of friendliness, and no member of the Aurelii or the Geladii could possibly be impressed by the pedigree of native rulers who were only a few generations distant from tribesmen who painted their skins blue, like the Picts of the present day. I should like to have talked with Myrddin, but we didn't see him again until we were three days' ride out of Deva, on our way north, and had sought shelter in the old deserted fort of Mamucium. There we found Myrddin awaiting us, well mounted, and attended by two armed servants.

VI

The self-appointed councillor

MYRDDIN'S KNOWLEDGE of the densely wooded countryside of southern Reged was extensive, and his two men, Bran and Thord, had foraged successfully, raiding royal hunting lodges, where salted meat was stored, and buying other provisions at farmsteads in the clearings where trees had been felled and the land cultivated. They bought oatmeal and honey and dried fruit from the farmers, paying them with small scraps of silver, fragments of cups and vessels and dishes looted in old wars, and worn smooth through passing from hand to hand. Deva was the first place where we came across this substitute for coinage. So when we arrived the empty fort was stocked with ample provisions; wood fires blazed and crackled on hearths in the barracks; the men of our escort quartered there had no complaints, especially as Bran and Thord had got hold of some casks of the thick, sweet drink made from honey, called metheglin, horrible sticky stuff that turned my stomach. We were lodged in the spacious, comfortable house of the former garrison commandant.

Myrddin had been installed there for some days, having prudently left Deva on the night of the feast, with his men and belongings, also three spare mounts. He knew Maelgwyn's savage temper. Although the persons of bards were traditionally inviolate, his immunity at the king's court was ended; never again could he return openly to Gwynedd. As we sat and talked over cups of rough red wine, he announced that henceforth he would accompany us where-ever we went. He took our consent for granted, rather coolly I thought, for although I was well aware that in Britain bards had many privileges, I resented the bland insolence of his assumption that we welcomed his company. Perhaps I showed my feelings.

Artorius, far more tolerant and charitable than I am, either noticed nothing or chose not to. He began to ask questions.

'I know your name, but I don't know *who* or *what* you are,' he said, smiling. 'Surely you are something other than a wandering bard. Some prophetic fire smoulders within you. That's obvious, but you allow it to flare up out of control. Why? What possessed you to sing that unwise and tactless song about me? You must have known that it would infuriate the king and the prince. Had you a reason?'

Myrddin stroked his silky, well-kept beard, an habitual gesture which always irritated me, though I knew it was not prompted by vanity, for that failing was alien to his strange character. He seemed to be withdrawn from everyday life, though exceedingly practical about everyday problems when it became necessary to trouble himself with them. He was deficient in compassion, apparently untouched by any common human weaknesses, coldly observing the world from some remote, external vantage point. Speaking slowly, he replied to Artorius.

'Directly I saw you, I knew what words I had to sing. Words come into my mind, suddenly and without warning; sometimes they concern the near future, that immediate tomorrow we all expect to see; at other times they reveal events that cannot possibly occur for many years; or again, they may disclose what could come to pass only in some unimaginably distant age and in a strange world.' He paused, then added: 'This I cannot explain, so I must ask you to accept the fact that some of us are able to see round the curves and corners of the endless road to the future.'

I dislike and distrust inexplicable mysteries, and said so rather bluntly. He ignored me, and, addressing Artorius, continued:

'Such revelations are true visions of what will affect our own lives, the lives of others, even the fortunes of nations. They are not dreams. They have more substance than dreams. A chosen few have experienced them since the beginning of time. They have guided decisions and influenced acts centuries before the days of the Delphic Oracle. Sometimes they have been too terrible to be given to the world, but the chosen few, the prophets, dare not conceal any truth

they are privileged to learn, however grim or tragic it may seem.
They may be persecuted or honoured for telling what they know;
but they must never be silent. Even Christians honour the prophets.'

That last sentence was edged with such contempt that I asked if
he was a Christian. He gave me a frigid look.

'There were many forerunners of Christianity, and some of them
survive today as rivals,' he said. 'I belong to the Order of the Golden
Sickle and the Sacred Oak.'

His answer meant nothing to me, but Artorius understood at
once and said:

'But, forgive me, you are surely far too young to be a Druid:
you can't be more than ten or at most a dozen years older than I
am.'

'My age is my secret concern,' Myrddin told him. 'I am older
than you think or might perhaps be able to believe. In my youth the
Sacred College still flourished in Ireland, where the Sacred Order
openly ruled, long before that interfering missionary Patrick taught
the Irish tribesmen that Christian fables and Christian rites and
ceremonies, borrowed from older and stronger religions, were
superior to ancient wisdom, and persuaded them to destroy the
College and disband the Order. That was one result of his teaching.
He also taught the Irish to fear death, much to their detriment as
men and warriors, and to expect eternal torment after death if in
life they behaved naturally and enjoyed themselves according to
their nature.'

He was silent. Artorius looked troubled. Then I remembered my
history lessons, and challenged Myrddin's words.

'The Druids were suppressed and outlawed by the Emperor
Tiberius over four and a half centuries ago,' I said.

'The power of a great Order could survive imperial edicts,' he
returned. 'That power has never been lost and is still wielded
secretly in Ireland, Britain and Armorica. You, Artorius, ask *who* I
am. Well, to you and Caius I have appeared as a bard named
Myrddin, and that is how I am known and accepted in the kingdoms
of Britain today. But I live another life and possess another name.
I am an adept, a seer, what ignorant and uninstructed people call a

magician, and I shall, if he is wise enough to accept me, be councillor to the leader who shall free Britain from the Saxon barbarians and remain great and glorious, so long as he resists the temptation to accept the crown of a king. I named him in my song. You, Artorius, son of Uther, are that leader.'

I remember thinking then that I was mistaken about the colour of his eyes: they were not pale grey: they had no colour that can be named or likened to anything. For a long time he gazed at Artorius without speaking, then said:

'My other life, for some years to come, is to be lived as your councillor, if you accept me as such. My other name is Merlin. Before you say whether you agree to accept my service, remember this: I know the road to the future. It is seldom straight: more often it is crooked and confusing, with many by-ways and blind lanes to tempt travellers from their right and proper direction; but all travellers are compelled eventually to return to the road and to follow a direction preordained by a power stronger than the will of any man.'

'That I know,' said Artorius, 'for I have been taught that God is omnipresent and to believe that He directs us.'

'God is but another name for Destiny,' asserted Myrddin.

This was more than I could stand: he sounded so solemn and pompous that I wanted to laugh, though I stifled the impulse, and as I did so realized that Myrddin (or Merlin, as I shall call him henceforth in preference to his barbarous native name), never laughed and seldom smiled. I had no intention of allowing him to elaborate his dogmatic assertion about Destiny. A man's will is his own affair; he is free to choose good or evil, and the belief that original sin is an inescapable heritage is a piece of Christian stupidity. What matters is the way a man lives; his personal morals and his honesty in dealing with his fellow men, determine the direction he takes through life. True, the grey spinners can weave a pattern that may influence some of his actions, though they do not control his will.

All this I said, and more, and spoke with the urgent conviction of belief. My words, I could see, troubled Artorius.

'That is heresy,' he declared; 'the Pelagian heresy which has been condemned by the Holy Church.'

Merlin condescended to notice my protest.

'Pelagius had abundant common sense,' he admitted; 'he could see the problems of life with a clarity denied to most theologians, who rejoice in subtle obscurities. Naturally his independent views were unacceptable to the Church, for they threatened the claim of the Christian priesthood to a monopoly of salvation by suggesting that each man could secure his own and enter the Kingdom of Heaven without a priest unlocking the gates. His personal conduct could give him the key. You must remember that Pelagius was born in Britain, and although he left the province and went to Italy while he was still a young man, no man of British birth ever loses the unruly spirit of independence that makes him question authority, a spirit that is now endangering the security of all British kingdoms. When faced with a threatening enemy the kings will appoint and obey a commander-in-chief, like your uncle, Artorius, and entrust him with the leadership of an army; but they surrender their personal authority with extreme reluctance, and with so many reservations that a general's task is rendered difficult and sometimes becomes almost impossible, as you will discover when you are appointed *dux Britanniarum*. But that is your Destiny, the power which Pelagius ignored: that was the flaw in his otherwise admirable teaching of self-reliance, self-discipline and moderation, and it weakened the force of his maxim: *If I ought, I can.* You cannot dismiss Destiny, which looms large in our youth, but gradually diminishes in stature as we age.'

He paused, then said: 'But we need not squander time on theological discussions.' And I began to like him better, for religious disputation breeds ill-will, and is boring and futile. He continued. 'Artorius, I have made you an offer: you may desire to reflect before you give me an answer. Think well.'

For a long time we sat in silence. Outside a rising wind shouted through the streets of the old fort. I sipped my wine and waited.

Presently Artorius said: 'I follow Christ and accept the authority of Holy Church. What do *you* believe?'

He seemed to be deeply troubled.

'Those who possess knowledge need not rely on any faith,' Merlin replied. 'Men have always made gods in the image of their hopes and fears, their virtues and joys. The old gods rejoiced in life, and men knew that; true, the Olympians were unpredictable, sometimes cheerful and benign, sometimes capricious and terrible, but men could generally understand them and were not miserably perplexed about them, as Christians are perplexed by the Trinity. Think of their interminable arguments about that triple mystery.'

Artorius crossed himself. 'The old gods were demons,' he said.

'That is the Christian view,' Merlin told him; 'but the Church has created and let loose on the world its own particular demon, the demon of intolerance.'

Artorius shook his head. 'Remember the words of Christ,' he said. ' "He that is not with me is against me." Either you believe in Him, and obey the Church, or you believe in nothing. The gods are dead.'

'The gods have never died,' Merlin answered. 'Here, in Britain, they live on: many of their temples have been destroyed or desecrated or become ruinous, but the gods are still with us and in many places, as you must have seen, they are openly worshipped.'

And I thought of the warm ashes on the altars outside the temples of Isca in Dumnonia; of the marble statues of Venus and Diana, lovely and serene, standing on their pedestals by the great bath at Aquae Sulis, works of art that must have been carved in Italy or Greece, for no native sculptor could have commanded such skill; of the figure of Mars triumphant towering above the amphitheatre gate at Deva; of the wayside altars and small, undamaged stone temples we had come upon so often during our travels along the old roads, far outnumbering the crude Christian shrines and ill-constructed churches. Merlin was right. The Olympians were still alive—and laughing. The ancient native gods of Britain were also alive, for men had never ceased to believe in them. Simple-minded rustics could respect and fear a god like Nodens, who became visible now and then as he charged up the Sabrina in a chariot of foam, past his great temple with the hostels for pilgrims and houses for priests, a stately group of buildings overlooking the river where it begins to narrow, erected when Julian ruled both West and East, that great and noble Roman whom Christians denounce as the Apostate emperor. The fine stone buildings, roofless now and deserted but enduringly impressive, stand in the King of Gwent's territory, neglected by royal decree and providing a quarry for builders and road menders, for the king is a Christian, though few if any of his subjects share his faith.

From Dumnonia in the south and throughout western Britain up to the Wall and beyond, scores of local deities flourish, as varied in character as their worshippers. As I told Philonides when I showed him selected extracts from this first draft of my report, the map of Britain is unlikely to have changed much since I left, and then it resembled a many-coloured cloak such as Nubian slave girls make from scraps of finery, cut into irregular shapes and sewn together, a dazzling patchwork of religions and tribal customs, edged by a long dark strip of Saxon barbarism.

Artorius at last made up his mind about Merlin's offer.

'I shall need a councillor,' he said; 'and one moreover who knows Britain and its kings and customs and people. Whatever you may believe or disbelieve, whatever you are or have been, I think that God has brought us together for His purpose. I am His sword.' He smiled; it was a boyish smile. 'Perhaps your Destiny is to be the grindstone that helps me to keep that sword sharp.'

'Your battle for Britain must be fought with words and guile as well as swords,' said Merlin. 'Properly used, they are deadly weapons. Always avoid fighting if you think you can gain your ends by other means. You should not allow Christian beliefs to restrain you from making expedient alliances. No Christian would approve of any alliance with the Saxon states, but when British and Saxons have a common enemy, they should combine their forces and march together against that enemy. The Saxons who have settled in Deur, between Eburacum and the Wall, are troubled by the Picts, and would gladly join with the British of Reged in attacking them. Have you heard this?'

Artorius shook his head. 'I can well believe it,' he said.

'Unfortunately Reged is ruled by Maël, an obstructive Christian and a remarkably stupid man who would rather allow his kingdom to be overrun by painted savages than defeat them with the help of a pagan. There are many fools like him, and as *dux Britanniarum* you will find them bitterly opposed to you, not to you as a man, but to what you personify. Although they fear Saxons and Picts, they are troubled by a deeper dread; they dread the return of Imperial authority.'

'You seem to be certain that I shall be appointed *dux Britanniarum*,' said Artorius, 'I am only eighteen, but if my uncle should die soon— and I hope that he has many years of life left to him—would the Council of Kings choose one so young?'

'Certainly,' Merlin replied. 'Your youth would commend you. The British kings are far too jealous and suspicious of each other to appoint one of their number to that high military office. Although Ambrosius rules in Corinium, he has avoided the title of ruler, and is careful to speak of that city, and to see that others speak of it, as the General Headquarters of the Army. So nobody thinks of it as a city state. When your uncle dies, you should summon the Council yourself, which would be accepted as the right and proper course for you, as his nephew. Family influence, and your ancestry, are far more important than any Imperial commission you may hold. The Council when it meets would certainly choose you for office, as collectively and individually they would feel confident of their ability to dominate one so young. That is why your youth would be an asset.'

Artorius sighed. 'I shall be happier fighting with weapons than with words,' he confessed.

Then we fell silent, until the stillness of the night was broken by a sound that reminded me of the Gepidae campaign and the forests and mountains of Dacia. Somewhere, out in the snow beyond the walls of the fort, a wolf howled.

VII

The last of idle peace

Our journey ended at Luguvalium, where the military road passes through a gate in Hadrian's Wall and continues northwards beyond Reged until it reaches Strathclyde, the kingdom of Coroticus. King Maël held his court at Luguvalium, which he called a city, though it was only a large fort, with wooden huts, a few patched-up stone houses, baths for the former garrison, granaries and stores, and a small church. The plumbing of the baths had long been out of order, but there was no shortage of water, for a swift-flowing river and smaller streams supplied all needs. The King's Hall was the newest and largest building, strongly constructed of wood and covered by a thatched roof with a few holes to let out smoke from the open fires, which also let in snow, rain and down-blasts of wind: a bleak place, that stank of dogs, urine and unwashed bodies. The rammed earth floor, covered with grubby straw, was thickly populated with fleas. Northwards the Wall rose above the roofs; the weather-worn masonry still intact; a barrier that ran mile after mile from sea to sea, a mighty monument to the power and skill of the lost Empire. Luguvalium stood a few miles from the western end where the Wall ran down to the shore.

We spent Christmas at the King's Hall; Maël was a kindly host, though he expected us to attend far too many services in the damp little church: Artorius appeared to enjoy them, and good manners compelled my attendance, though I found them even more of an ordeal than the gross feasts we sat through, night after night.

The climate of north Britain is horrible; snow storms sweep over the hills, piling up huge banks against the northward face of the Wall, level in some places with the battlements, so from the sentinels' walk behind them nothing was visible save a boundless, undulating white expanse, sparkling in the watery sunlight and slashed with pale purple shadows where the snow had wrinkled into ridges over uneven ground. Only the shrill voices of gulls, driven inland by rough seas, broke the profound silence, for thick snow muffles every sound, and in the king's city people kept indoors.

Merlin's men, Bran and Thord, were put at our disposal, and were of great service, for they taught us two useful languages. Bran was the son of a Pictish chief who had rebelled against the Royal house, and had fled with his family to the south by ship, but the vessel was driven ashore by a gale, and wrecked on the sandbanks at the mouth of the Dee. Bran, then a boy of fifteen, was the only survivor, and managed to reach an island off the tip of the peninsula where he took shelter in a cave until at low tide he was able to walk across the sand to the mainland. Like all his tribe, he was a resourceful and experienced hunter and a ruthless robber: he had one weapon; a long knife in a sheath securely strapped to his belt. For a year he lived the hard, solitary life of a brigand on the peninsula, until, as he said, he felt the world closing in on him like a prison, so he made his way to Deva, where he found employment as a stableboy in the barracks. He was a small, dark-haired youth, with little black slits of eyes, and a puckered brown face, who spoke the harsh variation of Celtic that his tribe used. When Merlin, wandering from kingdom to kingdom in the west, came to Catwallaun's court and was appointed king's bard and, after a while, tutor to the prince, he was allowed two servants: he discovered Bran and employed him. The boy had a quick mind and an eye and memory for country. Merlin taught him to read Latin and to draw maps. His second servant, Thord, was a Saxon who, like Bran, had been shipwrecked. Thord, with other survivors from a Saxon longship that foundered in the Dee estuary, had been sold in the slave market at Deva, and Merlin had bought him. He was a huge man, yellow-haired, blue-eyed, immensely strong and rather stupid. He spoke Latin badly with a thick guttural accent. He was incapable of learning how to read. Both men revered Merlin, for he knew and respected their gods, and was considerate, always giving orders in their native language which he had taken the trouble to learn. One of his first acts

A. R. – C.

after buying Thord was to have a manumission document prepared
and legally attested by an official of the King's Court at Deva as there
were no magistrates in that realm; but although free to rejoin his own
people, Thord refused to leave his master. I was surprised that
anybody so obviously devoid of human foibles and weaknesses
could command such loyalty and devotion. Perhaps fear had something to do with it, for both men thought Merlin was a magician.

Artorius was soon fluent with the Pictish dialect, which came
easily enough to anyone who had spoken Celtic since early childhood; but I never completely mastered the odd pronunciation;
and for a long time we were both baffled by the spluttering German
that Thord tried to teach us. Merlin helped us there.

'Make him sing to you,' he suggested.

Thord had a good voice, and when he sang about Saxon wars and
victories and defeats and long sea voyages and fierce storms we
found his strange words easier to follow and at last our tongues
mastered them. The tunes were invariably sad, even when the songs
were joyfully triumphant. We had to listen to them well out of
earshot of the city, for barbarian songs offended King Maël, who
abhorred anything so unchristian. I much preferred those Saxon
melodies to the monotonous repetition of a few notes favoured by
the king's harpers.

Although Maël was courteous and hospitable, I don't think he
liked us, but he concealed any hostility he may have felt. He was
a thin, sour, middle-aged man with a bristling beard, brown,
worried eyes, and a querulous voice. He had two wives, which
seemed inappropriate for such an inflexible Christian: both were
young, little more than girls, and both were pregnant. We soon
discovered that there were also royal concubines, strictly segregated,
with their own quarters apart from the king's household. Artorius
became increasingly uncomfortable, because, as he said, the Court
was a moral sty; I found that less worrying than the impossibility of
avoiding body vermin, which swarmed everywhere.

Ten days after Christmas, two messengers from Strathclyde
arrived at Luguvalium with greetings from King Coroticus and the
disturbing news that the Picts had crossed the far northern Wall,

built over three and a half centuries ago when Antonius Pius was Emperor. As a barrier it had long been breached and its forts dismantled, but it was still regarded as a token boundary, though the Picts crossed it whenever they felt like raiding. Those hardy savages took no account of seasons and were ready for fighting in all weathers. This time they had avoided Strathclyde territory, keeping well to the east of it, marching south and moving fast over the snow. They were said to number at least five hundred, but allowing for the usual exaggeration of spies, two or three hundred at most seemed more likely to be the size of a raiding force. So long as the Picts avoided his kingdom, Coroticus would leave them alone, nor would Maël take any action unless they invaded his domains. If they continued on their way south, they would soon reach that part of the Saxon kingdom of Deur which extended into the wild, largely deserted country beyond Hadrian's Wall.

Maël was happy to let Picts and Saxons fight each other so long as his own small army was not involved. Aloof and far too complacent, he relished the prospect of a battle between barbarians and was shocked when Artorius suggested that he should intervene and join with Alfin, the Saxon King of Deur, in attacking the Pictish raiders.

'Alfin isn't a Christian,' said Maël, as if that finally disposed of the matter.

'He's not an aggressive neighbour,' Artorius pointed out; 'he's never troubled you, he's quiet and, by all accounts, seems to be satisfied with the size of his domain and concerned only with the welfare of his people. Has he, to your knowledge, ever harboured any military ambitions?'

'He isn't a Christian,' Maël repeated, speaking with the grim self-righteousness that prevents so many religious people from admitting uncomfortable facts or seeing things as they really are. He added that demon-worshippers could never become his allies. And then Artorius revealed himself as wise beyond his years, for he smiled and said:

'But think of the glory of converting King Alfin. Surely you, of all men, could bring him to accept Christ?'

I glanced at Merlin, and there was a gleam in his odd, colourless eyes. As for Maël, he looked profoundly disturbed, and said:

'Alfin is a barbarian.'

'Many barbarians have become good Christians,' Artorius reminded him.

'No,' said Maël, 'barbarians remain barbarians; nothing, not even baptism, can change them.'

I knew then that he was a fool, and, moreover, a badly frightened fool, scared not only of a barbarian neighbour but of Artorius, who like all men with superior wits aroused the hostility of commonplace, unimaginative minds. This little king was incapable of realizing that the Saxons compared with the Pictish savages were the lesser of two evils. We found many like him in Britain, and I suspect that there are just as many today.

Artorius was persistent. 'If you stand idle and let savages pour into Britain, I cannot,' he said. 'I command fifty well-armed mounted men: I shall ride east and attack those Picts on the march before they reach the Wall. My men are Roman soldiers: no savages can defeat disciplined troops.'

'I cannot prevent you,' said Maël; 'and if you return here, seeking safety and shelter, I shall of course open my gates.'

Artorius kept his temper, but I lost mine and asked Maël if he always assumed that men *he* commanded would run from an enemy.

'You are my guests,' he replied, mildly, which made me feel rather foolish. 'I shall pray for your safety.'

'And for our success, too, I hope,' said Artorius, smiling.

We followed the military road behind the Wall, sheltered from the north wind, except where the Wall had been broken through and gaps left open. We passed out of Reged and into Deur, unchallenged by frontier guards; obviously King Alfin expected no attack from his unwarlike Christian neighbour. The country was wild, uncultivated and empty; only the tracks of wolves marked the snow.

We made for Onnum, where the old north-eastern road passes through the Wall. The ancient fort there was deserted, both arches of the gateway blocked, one with good masonry, the other with rubble and timber. We soon pushed this out of the way and rode out into the hilly country beyond. On Merlin's advice, we wore long cloaks of white linen, with hoods that were pulled up to cover our helmets. Maël had been willing enough to allow the women of his household, and all the slave girls who knew how to sew, to make these for us; and thus covered we could pass over snow-bound country with less chance of being seen by an enemy. Our horses were of course visible, but from a distance they might be taken for wild, straggling beasts, for we avoided riding in close formation.

We wanted to take the Picts by surprise, and we did, near the mouth of a river. They were on foot, and we rode them down and killed them like animals.

My report is concerned less with the battles Artorius won than with the conditions under which they were fought. This was the first of many victories, and altogether we killed just over two hundred of those tough painted savages. They were dark, ugly men; their smooth, hairless bodies covered with patterns in dull colours, pricked into the skin with dyes rubbed into the punctures. We cut off their heads, and with those trophies dangling from our saddle-bows made our way south sheltering for the night at Onnum. The next day, the third after we had left Maël's country, we took the military road, passing through the ruins of Corstopitum, Merlin and Artorius riding ahead with Thord to act as interpreter, for though Merlin could speak Saxon well enough, Artorius was still learning I commanded the rearguard. And so we progressed, through the white emptiness of a land that had lost its civilization, till we came to the first large settlement, adjoining the abandoned fort of Vindomora.

There we found King Alfin.

When we were in sight of the settlement we had halted; Artorius, Merlin and I rode towards the two sentinels who lounged on either side of the open gateway. Artorius and I drew our swords, and threw them down on the snow. Merlin was not armed. This sign that we came in peace was understood at once, and Thord, who had accompanied us, delivered our carefully prepared greetings. One of the sentinels nodded (for Saxons don't waste words: they prefer to nod or grunt) and went through the gate. While we waited we sent word back to Paulinus whom we had left in charge, to have the severed heads of the Picts arranged in neat piles in sight of the gate. Half an hour passed before we were allowed inside and taken to the King's Hall, which, like the rest of the buildings in the settlement, was a hut made of roughly-trimmed logs.

The Saxons, like most Germanic tribesmen, are tall and brawny; but I was not expecting to meet a giant. Alfin was over seven feet high, with a chest like a cask and a long golden beard rippling down over it, reaching almost to his waist. He was cheerfully and genially drunk, and greeted us without any suspicion of hostility. He sent for bread and salt; a slave handed us big curved drinking horns brimming with metheglin, and when we had eaten a morsel of bread sprinkled with coarse grey salt and swallowed some of that sickly drink, Alfin said:

'Now you are my guests and as such are sacred and protected: your enemies are mine.' Then he went on, speaking slowly with the excessive care of a drunken man, slurring some words and repeating others. Through Thord, we told him how and where we had dealt with the Picts, and this surprised him, for he had heard no rumours of the raid. We realized he might feel less surprise when he was sober, for he knew perfectly well that in the sparsely populated northern part of his kingdom nobody travelled in winter: wolves were too bold and hungry, and those who lived in isolated farms and coastal fishing villages, kept inside their homes.

We accepted Alfin's hospitality for two weeks, and Artorius and I both improved our command of the German tongue. His settlement was not large; Saxons had no love for town life, and seldom attempted to enjoy the comfort of well-planned, properly drained cities, though many such remained in their kingdoms. They had built wooden huts where they lived a communal life, within sight of Vindomora; the houses of the Roman fort still stood, roofless and blackened, for the place had been sacked and burnt long ago, but the Saxon settlers left it alone, fearing the presence of ghosts and revengeful spirits.

As we sat in Alfin's hall, at the high table, with members of his household seated at boards on trestles running down each side of the room, their fair hair and fresh complexions lit by the blazing logs in the fire trench in the centre, the lines of Merlin's song ran through my mind. These, then, were the 'blond savages' that Artorius was to drive back to the sea. They seemed to me to be better men and women than the dark, grubby subjects of Maël and Catwallaun. This shall certainly not appear in my report, but I felt then, and I believe now in my old age, that the Roman cause was lost before Artorius was born, and that the future of Britain lay with those tall, handsome Saxons and their fair-haired women folk.

Those women enjoyed a lot of liberty, far too much in my view, and were allowed to go about unguarded and unaccompanied, and to talk to anybody they liked, and—this struck me as particularly uncivilized—argue with and often contradict their husbands, brothers and other men who were not their kinsfolk. Alfin told us that they were far too honourable to abuse their freedom; more-over their easy manners and cheerfully argumentative conversation were accepted as part of social life in a free country. He used the word free in a restricted sense, for all the hard work in his country was done by bondsmen and slaves; but members of his warrior band and their women were free to say what they liked, and to make rough jokes about each other, which never seemed to lead to quarrels. They laughed easily, their habits were dirty and primitive, their manners especially when eating, were appalling; but they seemed to be a happy people.

Artorius was surprised by what he called their high moral standards: I think that he expected the women to be promiscuous, but as Merlin explained to him, no Saxon nobleman would dream of debauching a Saxon lady; nor was there any need, as there were plenty of willing and passably attractive slave girls available for recreation.

In the Southern part of Deur, the Saxons had been established for nearly thirty years, and during that time had come to terms with the remnants of the Brigantian tribe. Marriages between British-born Saxons and the dark-haired Brigantian women were fruitful; a generation of mixed blood was already in being, sombre youths and sullen-looking girls: we saw many of them, neither Saxon nor British, before we left the kingdom.

'This is no temporary settlement,' said Merlin; 'these people are making a new and perhaps a better Britain.'

'And are they to be driven back to the sea with the rest of the blond savages?' I asked.

'If they accept Imperial rule, they would serve as *foederati*, as other barbarians have served in the past,' he replied.

We had decided not to return to Reged, or to travel north to Strathclyde: instead we made our way south to Eburacum, which was still a living city, with a few inhabitants and a garrison. But before we left Alfin's realm, Destiny or Fate, call it what you will, caused Artorius to fall deeply and helplessly in love with Gwinfreda, Alfin's fifteen-year-old daughter, a cunning, greedy, beautiful girl, lithe and lovely, like a golden snake. Innocence wears no armour, and Artorius who, aided by prayer and fasting, could resist what he called carnal temptations, created his special image of Gwinfreda, endowing her with a superhuman purity (for which she had no inclination), and a character that even a saint would have found irksome to sustain. He had not been in love before, had certainly never slept with a woman, and was completely bewildered by this unsettling infatuation. I suppose that to some extent I was responsible for his excessive innocence, for I had guarded his growing years, though not too strictly, and never interfered with his interests. But I had interpreted my duties as his tutor in accordance with the tenets of Christian morality and had kept him away from the brothels and pleasure houses of Constantinople: consequently he knew nothing about women, and although as a military cadet he met the often lascivious wives of officers in the Household Guards, their languishing glances and sighs conveyed no message to the good-looking boy. As such meetings were always on social occasions, invitation went no further than glances and sighs.

Gwinfreda was years older in worldly wisdom, and I am sure that she knew far more about the relations of men and women than Artorius even suspected. Perhaps from practical experiments. I had realized ever since his unconcealed interest in the slave girls at Isca, that women strongly attracted him; but as he labelled such agitating inclinations as sinful, he had remained deeply ignorant.

His infatuation for Gwinfreda was no transitory emotion, no passing glow of calf-love; it was profound, and never diminished in passionate strength, bringing alternate periods of happy exaltation and black misery to his later life. But during our weeks with Alfin another, and in my view, far more important experience changed all the prospects of his military career, for the Saxon king told us about the great horses that somewhere in western Britain had been carefully bred for some two hundred years. We had heard nothing of them in our travels in the western kingdoms: and we discovered later that the breeding of these magnificent creatures was a well-kept secret and, as I have already mentioned, ownership of the breeding stock was part of the great wealth of the British branch of the Geladii family. Alfin possessed one, a black stallion, which he showed us with great pride; but even that huge beast could not bear his enormous weight; he had been unable to ride since he was a boy of twelve, he told us, for apart from his weight, his legs grew far too long and touched the ground when he bestrode a horse. Although he had hoped to improve his own stable, by cross-breeding after acquiring the stallion, the smaller stock obstinately persisted.

'It's always the same,' he grumbled; 'small breeds go on and on like the Picts and the Brigantes.'

We had seen no horses of the size and strength of that stallion since we had left Constantinople. Alfin could not tell us where it came from; he had bought it three years ago from a travelling horse dealer, who had probably stolen it, though he swore that he'd found it wandering wild on the moors. The hill ponies of our escort were serviceable beasts, good enough for riding down savages on foot, like the Picts, but incomparably inferior to the mounts of the Emperor's troops, or those used by the Huns or Gepidae. With horses that could carry weight, we would be more than a match for any barbarians in Britain, especially as the very idea of mounted men being able to fight seemed strange to them. Alfin had been astonished when he heard that we had attacked the Pictish raiders without dismounting. Fighting on foot was what the Saxons understood, and they were clumsy riders, even when they weren't huge and heavy like Alfin.

So we came to Eburacum, enriched and a little bewildered by new experiences, and once through the city gates we re-entered the old, established civilized world.

VIII

The Council of Kings

FOR NEARLY TWO DAYS we were soothed and deceived by appearances; then we realized that what seemed outwardly impressive was as empty of strength and purpose as a resplendent suit of armour with a corpse inside. The walls, angle towers and gate houses of Eburacum were intact; the administrative and public buildings and the Praetorium were as staunch and dignified as they had been when the great Legionary fortress was the military treasury of the Imperial forces in Britain and Gaul and the headquarters of the old North-Eastern Command; the garrison and gate-guards, armed in the traditional style, knew their drill, and might have been taken for legionaries of the long-disbanded VIth, the Victrix; but when we met and talked with Rufinus, the military commandant, who was also the Governor of the city, we discovered the weakness behind the intimidating façade. That man of clay lived in an illusory world. Eburacum, he assured us, was a powerful city state, well prepared to repel barbarian incursions, and though proudly and securely independent, still a part of the great Imperial world of Rome.

'We have preserved and honoured our military traditions,' said Rufinus. He drew our attention to a slab of polished grey marble that filled one wall of the atrium of his house; it was engraved with the names of the legates who had commanded the VIth from the time the Legion was first stationed at Eburacum when the fort was still comparatively new and the most northerly of all military strongholds in Britain, a record extending for nearly three hundred years until all but one cohort had been withdrawn by Stilicho, the Vandal general, early in the century for his campaign against the Goths. They never returned to Britain. The garrison of Eburacum and the small field army that Rufinus commanded were, he told us, recruited from descendants of that last surviving cohort of the VIth.

'We pride ourselves on our direct continuity with the Victrix,' he told us, not once but many times, for he was a boastful bore of the kind all armies breed. As junior officers they are not encouraged to talk overmuch; as they acquire higher rank and their seniority dissolves their caution and restraint, they talk to excess. Rufinus was a bald, bloated man of sixty; nobody had contradicted him or questioned his judgement for years, and as he was outstandingly stupid I wondered how he'd managed to keep his city state secure and independent.

'Somebody has been thinking for him,' said Merlin, 'he's supported by another mind.'

On the evening of our second day in Eburacum we met the man who really shaped and controlled policy in that city state. His name was Lunaris, a client king as Rufinus explained with an air of bland patronage, ruler of Elmet, the land that lay south of Eburacum and extended westwards to the borders of Reged, a country of varied character, consisting partly of dense forest and naked moors, divided by winding valleys, well-watered and fertile. It was peopled by survivors of the Brigantes, the redoubtable tribe that had given Rome more trouble than any other in Britain and had never lost tribal identity or pride. Even when the generous wisdom of Cara-calla allowed so many natives in the provinces of the Empire to become Roman citizens, and the Brigantians were entitled to claim the privileges of citizenship, they remained first and foremost Brigantians, and still were. In their view Rome has now sunk to a name, but they are unconcerned; their tribe, so they believe, is eternal. There was something both splendid and pathetic about the fierce confidence of that remnant of a fighting British race, but whether their independence and character can survive intermarriage with the Saxons is as yet unknown, and should his Sacred and Imperial Majesty, the Emperor Justinian, decide to reconquer Britain, he may find either hard enemies or welcome allies in the kingdom of Elmet.

Artorius and I both liked Lunaris, who was easygoing, portly and jovial, but all the same a man to be reckoned with who commanded great reserves of strength and resolution. Although he called himself a king I don't think he took his regal status very seriously; but we soon found that what he did take with great seriousness was his descent from a line of Brigantian chiefs that began three centuries before Julius Caesar and his Legions had set foot in Britain. We discovered, when we became his guests, that he lived an urbane, civilized life; perhaps the example of a well-governed, well-run Roman city as a close neighbour prevented him from relapsing into the sordid squalor tolerated by Maël; perhaps only primitive Christians become inured to dirt and vermin. Lunaris could be described as an 'occasional' Christian, for he and his people honoured many of the old gods, Olympians and native British, as well as Christ. The only missing god in all Britain was Mithras, of whom the Christians were bitterly jealous; perhaps because they had borrowed so much from the older religion. Mithras had been very much a soldiers' god, and when the regular Legions had left Britain, few if any of his worshippers remained, and the bishops and priests of the British Church destroyed every trace of the ancient and honourable cult: no temple of the secret god was left standing anywhere, though as I have said, many other temples to the old gods were still undamaged and properly served.

Lunaris was on the best of terms with Rufinus, treating him with a careless deference that the Governor of Eburacum was either too obtuse to notice, or if he did dismissed it as barbaric lack of manners, for he had hinted to us that the King of Elmet was really a barbarian.

'Amusing enough, as such,' he remarked; 'but don't take him seriously. He's a tribesman at heart, nothing more.'

'And is there anything disgraceful or inferior about tribesmen as valiant as the Brigantians?' Artorius asked.

Rufinus looked startled. 'Eh? What's that?' he said, and like many men who feel embarrassed asked for the words to be repeated. Artorius obliged him, and added: 'Every Roman in Britain has some native ancestors: my own family, the Aurelii, who were patricians before Augustus created the Empire, were granted lands by Agricola and took wives from the noble British families, who were their neighbours.'

His gentle, tolerant smile took the edge off his words; but we had had enough of Rufinus, and readily accepted an invitation from King Lunaris: after an evening of his company we wanted more of it, for although Artorius was British-born, he had only childhood memories of the still sophisticated south-western lands and cities of Britain, and knew nothing about the northern and north-western kingdoms apart from what Ambrosius had told us and what we had seen ourselves in our travels.

Lunaris was a well-informed realist with massive common sense. He didn't call his household a 'court', nor was there anything regal or formal about that cheerfully sociable establishment. His family with a few close friends, and the servants and slaves, occupied a comfortable house, spacious, well-furnished, properly heated, with baths in a large separate building adjoining. The house stood in the centre of Calcaris, the fortified city from which he ruled Elmet. The place had been a Brigantian stronghold centuries before it became the principal Roman fort on the military road that ran south-west from Eburacum to Mamucium.

The snow-covered country about Calcaris was desolate and forbidding, dotted with clumps of tall pine trees, blue-black against the surrounding whiteness and swept by icy winds from the north-east. Any expeditionary force sent to Britain should include hardy troops from the Thracian uplands and barbarians from the north, men accustomed to snow and biting cold; Syrians or Greek islanders would die of sheer discouragement in the conditions we endured in Elmet; but perhaps I should not say *we*, for Artorius thought nothing of that terrible weather, neither did the men of our escort, and Merlin always seemed unaware of discomfort. Lunaris with an alert eye for the welfare of his guests, presented me with a long, fur-lined cloak which I accepted with thankfulness; Artorius was satisfied with his grey woollen one. Lunaris assured me that brisk activity out of doors was the secret of comfort in winter, and during our stay he organized a boar hunt to prove it; which turned out to be an expensive entertainment, for although we got the boar, it killed two of our escort who had asked permission to join the hunt.

Artorius had not mentioned to Rufinus his intention to expel the Germanic barbarians from Britain. That old Roman donkey thought only in terms of defence. 'What we have, we hold,' he said. The idea of an aggressive war against the Saxon states would have been too unusual an idea to have been entertained by that small mind. But to Lunaris he was frank and open about his plans; not that he received much encouragement.

When he spoke of uniting the military resources of Britain not only to check further advances by the Saxon states but to win back the lands they already held, Lunaris laughed.

'Unity!' he exclaimed; 'you, a British-born Roman believe that's possible! Unless an enemy is hammering at their gates with a sword no British kings will exert themselves; let sleeping dogs lie, is what they say, and when they at last admit that the dogs of war are loose again and ready to bite, maybe they'll talk about uniting, but then it's often too late and useless anyway, for most of them think that words are the same as deeds, and that when an action has been discussed that it's already accomplished. The only man who's always ready and aware of danger is King Marcus of Dumnonia, a young pup who thinks so much of himself that he quarrels with everybody, but at least he's active; he doesn't sit on his arse praying like so many of the others, and he's nearer to an aggressive Saxon state than most. Now I'm close to Deur, but Giant Alfin's policy is live and let live, as you should know.' He grinned, then added: 'And when you've persuaded the kingdoms of Britain to unite, do you count Alfin as one of the enemies to be driven into the sea?'

I had asked Merlin the same question, and Artorius gave Lunaris the same answer; but the king laughed.

'Don't underrate that Saxon monster,' he said; 'you may have plans for his future as an ally, but he's foxy enough to have plans for yours.' He laughed again. He had a rich, deep, infectious laugh, that invited you to laugh with him. 'I'm glad enough to have such a stout defender between me and the Picts,' he continued. 'You've fought a battle for him—oh, we heard all about that—news travels despite snow and wolves, and he's your friend, and might well hope for a warmer relationship. Now don't be angry with me,' he added, for Artorius had flushed and his eyes grew hard. 'I was your age once, though I never let any wench get too deeply into my life. Fuck and forget is my rule: marry if you must, but don't let your wife be your first woman. She won't thank you if she is, and you'll probably not know enough to make sure you're her only man.'

'I am a Christian,' said Artorius.

Lunaris raised his eyebrows. 'Those pale followers of the meek god,' he said; 'they destroy manhood, and take everything from life that's worth having. Their priests are always snivelling about chastity and the holy state of virgins: Jesus Christ wasn't a eunuch. He had guts and courage and died like a man. How many so-called Christians today would face crucifixion for their beliefs?'

Merlin spoke. 'More than you could count,' he said quietly. 'Artorius here, for one. Believe me, I do not speak as a Christian myself, but as an observer of men and events, past, present——' He paused.

'And future,' I completed the sentence for him. 'You are in the presence of a seer, Lunaris. He can see round the next corner.'

Lunaris looked attentively at Merlin, then said:

'I have seen you before, but you seemed much older and bore a different name.' He paused, searching his memory. 'Ah, now I have both the name and the place,' he announced. 'You called yourself Myrddin then, and you were the bard who led the tribal chants at the last Council of Kings. How comes it that you now call yourself Merlin and have been able to shed so many years?

'I am older than you think or could easily believe,' said Merlin. 'Myrddin is my other name, used to suit the occasion and the company.'

We had heard those words once before, but they did not satisfy Lunaris, who said:

'Have you ever been or are you a priest? For you have given the half-crooked answer, that is no answer at all, that one expects from a priest.'

Merlin was silent, but with the forefinger of his right hand he drew in the air the outline of a half-circle. All cults have their mystical signs; the Christians use the cross; and I suppose that

Merlin's semi-circle was Druidical. Lunaris recognized it, and said:
'So that is the way of things; Rome may have gone——'
Artorius made a gesture of dissent. Lunaris laughed at him and
went on:
'Who can deny that Rome has gone from Britain? Oh, I know
that an emperor sits in power and splendour at Constantinople, but
where is the Emperor of the West? No matter: something ancient
and powerful has endured in Britain, eh Merlin? And was there,
undying, secretly defying imperial officials, provincial governors,
procurators, generals and legates and all the high-ranking army
officers. The rulers of British kingdoms know the Order survives
today, and that, Merlin, is why you were allowed to be present at
the last Council of Kings.'
'But the kingdoms of Britain are Christian,' Artorius protested.
'The Church may think that it has quenched old fires,' said
Lunaris; 'they hiss and splutter and seem to be extinguished; but
they smoulder on, generation after generation, and never go out.
So do ancient feuds and suspicions. If you had been at the last
Council, Artorius, you would have learned how bitterly the kings
of Britain hate and distrust each other. They were united only
because they were persuaded by your uncle, Ambrosius; and
because they were frightened. They chose him as commander-in-
chief because they feared to choose one of their own number. Fools
though most of them are, they could see that Ambrosius had no
imperial ambitions and was governed by one purpose only: his
desire to free Britain from the Saxon threat. He wanted nothing for
himself; and they knew he was a successful general. But they talked
for days and weeks before they could bring themselves to surrender
their personal authority and hand it over to a real soldier who knew
how to make war.'
'But they overcame their doubts and fears and jealousies and did
raise an army for my uncle to command,' Artorius reminded him.
'They won't do it again, that I can promise you.' Lunaris smiled
at him. 'He's an old man now, and I suppose you'll be his successor,
and though you may expect to become *dux Britanniarum* all you are
likely to get from that gathering of quarrelsome fools is the title

without the power. They may lend you a few men, those they don't want themselves, the dull, idle, useless types you'll find in any army however small: that's all you'll be allowed to have from their own bands, so my advice to you is this: raise your own band. Make them your sworn companions, so that you can rely on their loyalty. Now that may not suit your ideas: you're a trained professional soldier, a tribune in the imperial forces, like your companion Geladius; but there are plenty of young men ready for adventure and loot and a frolic with Saxon wenches; you'll have no trouble in collecting a band; you'll be able to pick and choose.'

Artorius was outraged; that I could see. With an effort he controlled his anger, and his voice was as mild as usual when he replied.

'Such men would have the minds of brigands,' he said. 'Men I lead must accept discipline, and must believe in the Christian purpose of the war I shall wage against the barbarians.'

Lunaris was silent, and a slave refilled his silver cup with the coarse red wine we had been drinking. The dinner had been served in the proper traditional style, and we reclined on couches, three to each low table. After a long pause, he said:

'I hear that you fought those Picts without dismounting: that you rode your horses into them and through them and round them and cut them down. Perhaps you could do that with savages; but would you try it with Saxon warriors who are, believe me, Artorius, very different fighters? They use long swords, and they don't panic and bolt. They would slash your horses to bits when you closed with them.'

'We should talk to them with arrows before they were near enough to use their swords,' Artorius explained. 'The men I lead into battle shall be trained to shoot from the saddle, like the Emperor's cavalry. I shall have supplies of bows for them: a few smiths are working on arms for me in Corinium now; unfortunately they are old and don't work fast. But I shall soon have as many smiths as I can employ.' He described the raid he intended to make on the British settlements in Armorica, to recapture the emigrant craftsmen and their families.

Lunaris nodded approvingly. 'You won't find any of my people there,' he said; 'only men from the west. Your plan may well succeed, but it depends on ships manned by experienced mariners and soldiers who have sea legs and sea stomachs. I can't help you myself; I know little about the sea and even less about ships. There are no sea ports in Elmet; only small river craft that never leave the estuaries; but the man who could help is King Marcus of Dumnonia, Marc as his people call him. He's full of silly pride, blown up with it like a bladder, and I distrust him; but Dumnonia has a long coast line, and like his father before him Marc defends it with a small fleet. He has a few warships, and can sink pirates before they are able to make a landing. He's the only ruler in Britain who has the means to make a raid on Armorica, and if you can persuade him to believe that he thought of the idea himself he might carry out your plan. That shouldn't be too difficult: he feeds on flattery, though he's no fool.'

'I must have the right weapons to arm any band I form,' said Artorius; 'so I can't delay that raid too long. I shall seek the friendship of Marcus.'

'You won't get it,' Lunaris told him bluntly; 'he has only one friend: himself. But try by all means.'

'I have other things to try first. I must travel north again. My voice will be stronger at any future Council of Kings if I have a reliable ally.'

'You have one here,' said Lunaris. 'I think your ideas are up in the clouds, but you may bring them down to earth and make some of them work. I'm not unhopeful about that, for though you're young, you don't believe that you know everything. So count me as a friend and a supporter if and when you make war against the Saxons in the south and south-east.'

Artorius thanked him. 'But I want to be sure that the north is secure,' he continued; 'and that means containing the Picts. Maël is too weak and pacific, and from what I've heard of Coroticus of Strathclyde, he won't exert himself unless his kingdom is actually invaded. He let that band of Picts through, and merely sent Maël a warning. He didn't loose an arrow or draw a blade to stop them. Nor did Maël. We did their work for them.'

Lunaris suddenly roared with laughter. 'I told you that jovial Saxon giant might have plans for you,' he shouted. 'He's used good bait for his trap, and I'll wager you're going north to get your balls caught in it.' He went on laughing, but stopped and became serious when Artorius said, very gently:

'King Alfin could become a Christian. I shall do my best to persuade him, and if he and his people accept Christ, they become our brothers and allies.'

'*Sancta simplicitas*,' said Lunaris; but there was no scorn in his voice.

IX

The Holy Band of Brothers

MERLIN ACCOMPANIED ARTORIUS on his mission to Alfin, while I divided my time between the military record office at Eburacum and the hospitable household of Lunaris. In that office I found detailed and accurate maps of all Britain, south of the Antonine Wall, with forts and towns and roads and rest houses marked, and the names of units detached for service in all fortified posts, a complete picture of the imperial military organization of the Province as it existed a hundred years ago. I am not a skilled cartographer, but any educated man can copy maps, and I spent much time during the remaining winter months making copies, for a general with a map is always more than a match for a barbarian chief who relies on what he can remember of a country; although he may possess a good sense of direction, he can't piece his visual memories together to make a coherent picture of any large area. From what I had seen on our travels, I was able to correct those maps, marking abandoned stations and towns and roads that had become impassable. Now, forty-five years later, I am doing the same work all over again in the scriptorium of the Imperial Palace on maps from the military record office of Constantinople, assisted by two staff draughtsmen. I think that this may well be the most useful part of my report.

Winter gave place to spring; not that there is much difference between those seasons in North Britain. We had rain instead of snow, an occasional gleam of faint sunlight, while sharp winds still swept across the countryside and whined through the streets of Eburacum and Calcaris. Artorius returned alone; no longer the rather too solemn, precocious boy, but a man, strong in self-confidence, though not assertive or arrogant. He had left Merlin behind at Alfin's Court to act as tutor to Gwinfreda.

'She has promised to become a Christian,' he told me; 'but I don't want her to think about Christian rites and practices as barbarians think about magic: she must understand what she is doing, and nobody should accept Christ in a state of ignorance. Merlin is teaching her to read and write.'

He could talk of nothing but that Saxon girl and Alfin's great black stallion, which he had been allowed to exercise. Lunaris, who was a patient and tolerant soul, at last got so bored by this unceasing and intemperate adulation, that he said: 'And which would you rather ride? The girl or the horse?'

I thought the remark was in rather bad taste myself; but the Christian side of Artorius was always uppermost. He smiled and answered:

'I haven't sinned by anticipating marriage, Lunaris.'

I wondered how often Gwinfreda had, but the society of army women in Constantinople had depraved my outlook. Until he actually found a trusted member of his band in bed with her, Artorius never suspected Gwinfreda of anything save playful and mischievous indiscretions. But that happened many years later.

'I must have some of those big horses to mount my band,' he told us. 'We must discover where they are bred. With fast mounts that can bear weight and the arms I shall have made, we can change the whole character of war in Britain, and teach the Saxons in the south and east a hard and final lesson.' He checked himself.

'First find your horses,' said Lunaris drily.

We were fortunate, and found them sooner than we expected, and without searching. Spring was far advanced before we left Elmet. Lunaris pressed us to stay on, and we had gladly prolonged our visit. His youngest son, Agrippa, was the first of all the recklessly brave, faithful and pious men who became sworn followers of Artorius, the Holy Band of Brothers, as they were called.

'I don't pretend to understand Agrippa,' his father told us: and we could easily believe that, for the boy (he was a year younger than Artorius) was a dedicated Christian, who abstained from every normal pleasure and positively rejoiced in discomfort. Indifference to comfort is no bad thing in a soldier, but Agrippa carried it too far.

To sleep on the ground when beds were available was a form of stupidity.

'He'll live and die a dried-up virgin,' Lunaris growled; 'Like an ugly girl who has to be one as nobody wants her. But he doesn't know what fear is, and he isn't a reckless fool either. I wish you joy of him, Artorius: he may grow up later. He's the best-looking of all my gets, in or out of the marriage bed.'

A few months earlier Artorius might have been shocked and offended; but he was learning fast; also he had grown very fond of Lunaris.

'He's your son, and that's more than good enough for me,' he said.

Agrippa was certainly good-looking, with a head that might have been fashioned by Praxiteles; a flawless profile, large, expressive grey eyes and curly brown hair. Some thread of blood, winding down the centuries from Greece through Rome to Britain, had given him those features, also the supple body of an athlete. Although, as his father said, he wasn't an impulsive fool, there was not much inside that handsome head except credulity. Agrippa was prepared to believe almost anything. And yet, few people took advantage of his innocent good nature, and—this I found difficult to understand— no woman ever attempted to seduce him.

Merlin returned after seven weeks at Alfin's court, bringing with him as a gift for Artorius, the black stallion which was probably the king's most treasured possession. At that time I knew little about Saxon customs, so I wondered if Alfin's generosity signified a betrothal; but I was wrong. His gesture was one of pure friendship; the exchange of betrothal gifts is a formal occasion, with both parties present. The ceremony varies with different Germanic tribes; some regard it as binding as marriage, others more lightly, though if the pledge is broken the injured honour of a family might lead to bloodshed and a feud lasting for two or three generations.

Artorius now had a serious problem to solve: what sort of gift should he make to Alfin that would show his gratitude and suggest the character of their future relations. I told him that he should anticipate his coming authority as *dux Britanniarum* and act with the authority he already possessed as an Imperial envoy, and send to Alfin the insignia of a Roman general's rank: the deep red chlamys. This would be a strong hint that if and when Imperial authority returned to Britain, the King of Deur would be regarded as an honoured ally of the Empire.

He accepted my suggestion with cheerful alacrity and welcomed the excuse for yet another visit to Alfin. It should, he said, be a formal presentation, not merely the occasion for a reciprocal gift.

'And another opportunity for toying with the Princess Gwinfreda, no doubt,' said Lunaris. 'Better let me get that chlamys for you,' he added; 'Rufinus would ask too many silly questions if you approached him; but I'm entitled to draw anything I like from the military stores at Eburacum, as I hold the rank of general: all the kings who took part in the last war were made generals by Ambrosius. I'll requisition enough cloth for two, and have it made-up here, so we shall have a chlamys large enough for Alfin.'

Artorius thanked him, and a week later we rode north to the little wooden city by Vindomora. We were accompanied by Agrippa and two elderly priests, appointed by Eutropius, the bishop of Eburacum, as missionaries to Alfin's kingdom, and, more specifically, to prepare Gwinfreda for Baptism. The bishop had strongly objected to the whole idea of converting barbarians to Christianity.

'If they become Christians they are no longer barbarian enemies,' said Eutropius; who was almost as obtusely bigoted as Maël.

'Of course not,' said Artorius; 'they become Christian Saxons, and the glory is all yours for having thought of converting them.'

The bishop remained doubtful. 'I don't like it,' he said, shaking his grey head. But eventually, after prolonged discussions, he was convinced, as Artorius had intended he should be, that the idea of extending the work and influence of the British Church was his own. Nobody, as Artorius pointed out, could deprive him of the credit for such noble work. He spoke as if the conversion of the whole Kingdom of Deur was already accomplished.

Other difficulties arose, as it was no longer possible for Rufinus to remain unaware of the alliance that Artorius hoped to bring about. But Rufinus, who revered tradition, could be awed by precedent; and Artorius cited an imposing number of examples when official recognition of friendly barbarians had led to their enlistment as *foederati*, and thus enlarged the effective military strength of the Empire. Without any boastful display of erudition, he disclosed the depth and breadth of his studies in Constantinople: he certainly knew far more about military history than I did, and tactfully assumed that Rufinus was just as well-informed. That old fool was ultimately persuaded that imperial policy would be best served by allowing Alfin's Saxon warriors to protect north-eastern Britain from Pictish incursions. I realized that very soon he would accept sole responsibility for the whole conception of an alliance with the Kingdom of Deur. When Artorius deployed his powers of persuasion, you forgot his extreme youth and the fact that he spoke without any recognized authority; you were conscious only of the profound sincerity of his words, uttered in that gentle voice: of his excellent manners and pellucid innocence. It was impossible to suspect him of guile, and yet he was always able to delude men with stupid or commonplace minds, so that they honestly believed themselves to be the originators of ideas and plans and actions that he had suggested. His gift for imposing his will or characters as different as Alfin, Rufinus and, when at last we met him, Marc of Dumnonia, was exerted so naturally and easily that men were aware only of his irresistible personal charm: the fact that most women were also acutely aware of it only troubled him later in life. He was now relieved from all the old sinful temptations, thanks to his infatuation for Gwinfreda; this he confessed to me, rejoicing in his happy, and almost holy, immunity.

So we came once again to Alfin's city, where Artorius invested that convivial giant with the visible emblems of his rank as a general of the Imperial forces. Before we left there was another ceremony: Artorius having sought and gained Alfin's sanction, tendered the oath of betrothal to him so that Gwinfreda was pledged securely and honourably, and their marriage became inevitable. She had assumed for the occasion a demure and innocent air, but I noticed that her large blue eyes strayed rather too often to the handsome figure of young Agrippa. I think I was the only man there who intercepted those ardent glances, but they evoked no response from Agrippa, and I began to suspect that he might be a well-controlled homosexual. Like Artorius, he was an earnest, dedicated Christian; apparently he never indulged any unnatural inclinations; or, if he did, was too discreet or too lucky for them to be discovered.

We stayed for three days after the betrothal feast, one of them devoted to a wolf-hunt. For once the weather was fine, no rain fell, and a breeze came softly from the south-west. Our horses were brought round by grooms, and Artorius asked for a mounting block. Gwinfreda giggled, a silly habit that irritated me, though it seemed to amuse Artorius, and said:

'Oh, bring him an *estrifa*, somebody.'

'What's that?" he asked, puzzled as indeed I was by the barbarous German word.

'Something you wouldn't need if your legs were as long and strong as father's,' she told him. 'I know they're not as long, but I hope they're strong.' Saxon girls may be honourable, but they are coarse creatures. 'Here it is,' she added, as a stable boy ran up with a long leather strap, looped at each end. He threw it across the saddle of the big black stallion, held one end, and to Artorius, said:

'Put your foot in the loop your side, and heave yourself up. That's it: makes mounting easy.'

'Don't take it away,' said Artorius when he was up. He sat in the saddle, easing both feet into the loops that hung down on either side. Then he rose from the saddle, and the strong looped strap allowed him to stand upright. He laughed, and addressed Merlin.

'What was it that old Greek shouted when he'd discovered something?'

'Eureka!' Merlin answered.

'Eureka!' shouted Artorius. He settled himself back in the saddle, urged the black stallion forward, and without warning it reared up, striking out with its hooves, scattering the grooms. The looped strap slid to the ground. Artorius kept his seat, and soon regained control.

'If those straps are fixed to the saddle you can ride with your feet in them,' said Gwinfreda.

'I'd thought of that,' he told her; 'and it means a lot more than keeping a firm seat in the saddle.' He turned to Alfin who had been looking on, envying the ability of other men to ride. 'Give me the loan of a saddler for three hours, Alfin,' he said, 'and then I'll be able to show even the Imperial Cavalry something new.'

The first rough model of the new saddle was made then and there, and when we returned to Eburacum we had it copied and much improved by skilled leather-workers, so that we left the north equipped with the new pattern and becoming accustomed to keeping our feet in the loops of those supporting straps.

'When I get some smiths to work, we'll make those loops of iron,' said Artorius; 'we shall soon wear through leather. We *must* have smiths.'

We kept well to the west of the regions held by the Angles, another of those land-starved German tribes, who came to Britain originally as raiders, and, liking what they saw of the flat, well-drained fertile country behind the uninviting North Sea coast, came again, year after year, thousands of them, not only fighting men, but whole tribal units, farmers and their families, who settled, as Alfin had settled, determined to make the old Roman province their future home. They didn't sack the towns in the conquered territory; they left them unmolested, to decay through poverty and starvation, for all trade ceased and the townsmen who had hitherto lived on the produce of the countryside could no longer grow enough food in the remnant of land they still possessed.

Artorius wanted to see Londinium; but I opposed his wish. I thought that we had seen all we could usefully see, and had been away from Ambrosius and his army headquarters too long; but Merlin said that as peace of a sort still prevailed between barbarian settlements and British kingdoms, we should visit the once-great city while the country was quiet. We should travel as a small party, and send our escort back to Corinium, which we did in charge of

Paulinus. Our party included Merlin's servants, Bran and Thord, and the first member of the band, Agrippa: six in all. We passed through an empty and lifeless land; I have described that scene of desolation; and although we visited two cities that still had walls and garrisons and some semblance of civic order and government, they were evidently fighting a rearguard action against chaos and barbarism. Our last halt on the road to Londinium was Verulamium where we found that the citizens had accepted barbarian settlers as neighbours: a Saxon village and a group of farms flourished five miles south-west of the city, and relations were amicable. The farmers sold some of their produce in the market in exchange for metal work, for there were smiths in Verulamium, which Artorius coveted. On rising ground overlooking the city, a shrine and a small church stood, built in honour of Albanus, a member of a noble British family and a tribune in the army, when Caracalla was Emperor. He became a Christian, refused to obey orders, and was executed on the hill where the shrine now stands; other versions of the story give the theatre as the place of execution. Albanus has long been acclaimed as the first British Christian martyr. He died over three hundred years ago and is probably remembered because he was a well-born man with high military rank.

Of what we found and saw at Londinium Augusta I have already written, and we were glad to leave the depressing place and ride along the great western road through Pontes and Calleva to Corinium, where bad news awaited us.

Ambrosius was a harassed and very sick man. We found him fragile and shivering, with fur rugs piled on him as he lay on a couch in an overheated room; his cheeks were sunken, his eyes dull, and the skin of his face darkened by a feverish flush. He smiled at Artorius, and said:

'You may have to preside, if they come.'

He spoke with difficulty, his voice so weak that it was little more than a whisper.

'Messengers were sent ten days ago,' he continued. 'Only Marcus of Dumnonia has come so far, but some of the others may be on their way. Danger has been Marc's close neighbour ever since he succeeded his father as king, and the news came first from patrols policing his eastern boundary.'

From his disjointed sentences, we gathered at last that three shiploads of Saxon pirates had sailed into the Sea of Vectis and landed in the wild wasteland between Dumnonia and the South Saxon kingdom. They were commanded by Cerdic, some adventurous petty chief of whom nobody had ever heard; but he must have planned something more ambitious than a piratical raid, for he drew his ships far up the beach, left them, and with his small band marched inland. Marc's spies reported that they numbered less than two hundred; all well-equipped with leather body-armour, round wooden painted shields, iron helmets and long swords. King Marc had lost no time. He personally led two fighting patrols past his boundary to the landing place, where he found two of the Saxon ships and burnt them.

'If they come here, then they can stay here to be buried,' he told us, when we saw him later.

The words were brave enough, but were not swaggeringly boastful: Marcus had an air of cold determination that made you condone his defects, of which self-satisfaction was the most obvious. He was a short man, and far too fat for one so young—he was a year older than Artorius—but men of the western British tribes run to fat. The Dumnonians are much the same stock as the Silures who formerly lived on the lands north of the Sabrina estuary, until they were displaced by Irish settlers; many families of that lost tribe fled across the water and made new homes in Dumnonia, where there was plenty of room for them, and the king welcomed reinforcements for his army.

Marcus, or King Marc as I shall continue to call him, had black hair, a swarthy complexion, intensely dark brown eyes, and a black beard, clipped so close that he looked less like a bearded man than one who had neglected to shave for three or four days. He seldom looked you in the face, and habitually stared over your shoulder as if he saw something standing behind you that needed watching; his voice was harsh and penetrating, and, like Merlin, he never laughed, and rationed his smiles; perhaps he thought that smiling relaxed his dignity. I was inclined to distrust him, largely because of a trick he had of revolving his tongue in his mouth, moving the tip of it against the inside of his cheeks, as if trying out the flavour of a lie before uttering it, like a Syrian trader selling worthless rubbish to innocent strangers in the bazaars of Antioch or Alexandria. His conceit was so blatant that it was often embarrassing to be in his company, and his sense of proportion was defective in every way. He had a bodyguard of two gigantic Nubian slaves: he may have thought that they added to his dignity, but they certainly diminished his height. He had inherited them from his father who had bought them long ago when they were boys, from an adventurous merchant who had risked the long hazardous voyage to south-west Britain to bring a cargo of exotic wares from the Alexandrian slave markets. They were named Samson and Goliath: faithful, fearless and always cheerful, they were devoted to their master. In addition to those black-skinned giants, one or other of whom was always on duty, for the king was never left alone by day or night, he had what he called his household guards; twenty well-armed mounted men, all young, and they rode with him everywhere.

While we awaited the arrival of the other British kings we got to know King Marc as well as anybody could know a man so self-absorbed and confident of his personal rectitude. Later we uncovered some of his hidden virtues. He seldom promised to do anything, but when he did give his word he kept it, so that Artorius could rely on him when, after hours and sometimes days of argument, he would agree to a course of action. Artorius said nothing to him in those early days about his plan for raiding Armorica.

'I shall wait until we are friends,' he told me; but we soon found that Lunaris was right; Marc's only friend was himself. Ultimately he became a rather grudging ally, but never one of the Holy Band of Brothers that Artorius formed and led to so many victories.

X

The royal voices

DIRECTLY AMBROSIUS HEARD of the new Saxon landing, he exercised his authority as *dux Britanniarum* and summoned a Council of Kings; after five weeks they had finally assembled, even Maël of Reged and Coroticus of Strathclyde, though Catwallaun Longhand of Gwynedd, who was suffering from some mysterious illness, had sent his son Maelgwyn to represent him. I anticipated trouble when I saw that tall, black-bearded, good-looking prince ride up to the west gate of Corinum at the head of a bodyguard of a hundred armed men. I told Merlin to keep out of his way; but my advice was coldly received.

'I mastered the art of survival many years before you were born, General,' he said.

'I am a senior tribune, not a general,' I reminded him.

'I was not describing you as you are now,' he told me, 'but as you are to be; sooner than you would perhaps believe. But have no fears for my safety: Maelgwyn will not recognize me as his father's bard and his own former tutor.'

And what followed I cannot explain; indeed there seems to be no credible explanation; for as he spoke I realized that I was no longer talking with a man of thirty or so, with light brown hair and a beard of the same colour, but with a white-haired man, whose face and hands were engraved with the lines of old age. Of course it was some clever trick that would be accepted by the ignorant as magic; but I was annoyed. I dislike the inexplicable, which is perhaps why I can never be a sincere Christian. But that transformation showed that Merlin knew how to take care of himself.

He saw that I was both puzzled and annoyed, and he almost smiled.

'I have resumed an old and more accustomed shape,' he said gravely; 'and when the kings have met in Council, I shall be accepted without question, as I was at their last Council.'

He was right: his presence was taken for granted when at last the kings assembled in the great hall of the basilica, but Lunaris of Elmet recognized him at once. 'So you've put on your former face, eh?' he said, grinning. 'You're Myrddin again. Well, ancient man, we shall need the protection of your magic, for our dark friend from Gwynedd has brought the king's devils with him though he's left the king behind.'

'Lunaris, what do you believe?' I asked.

'Nothing,' he replied; 'just like you. If there are gods, then they made the world for a joke and have been laughing at it ever since, although it's a bad joke. If you think it isn't then look around you at the might and majesty of the noble rulers of our kingdoms.'

For an hour or more, before Ambrosius was carried in and helped from his litter, those self-made kings had been quarrelling in pairs and groups. Not all. Marc of Dumnonia, silent and aloof, stood near the platform of the apse, regarding the assembly with critical disapproval. His vigilance was responsible for their presence, for he alone had taken action against the new barbarian invaders, and was daily informed of their movements. Cerdic and his couple of hundred Saxon sea thieves had reached the high ground thirty miles north from the coast, and settled into a disused military camp. This became their base for raiding isolated farmsteads in north-east Dumnonia. Marc had since learned that they had landed from three ships, but one had been sent back, presumably for reinforcements; the other two, as I have said, he found and burnt.

Artorius moved from group to group, listening intently and asking a question now and then, when some point of military interest emerged from that swirling torrent of boastful talk. He wore the undress uniform of a senior officer in the Emperor's Household Guards; so did I, and the only men who looked like Romans at all were Lunaris, who wore the red chlamys to which he was entitled, and King Marc, who had, rather unwisely, squeezed himself into an old but still serviceable bronze lorica. With the exception of Prince Maelgwyn, tall, elegant and soberly clad in black, the kings and noblemen gathered there were unkempt barbarians, with big bushy beards and manes of long hair, save those from the far western kingdoms between the Sabrina and the Black Mountains who shaved the front of their heads, exaggerating the length of their faces which appeared to be topped by enormous foreheads. Most of them wore woollen cloaks, dyed in garish colours, long grey woollen breeks, leather jerkins pricked and stamped with barbaric patterns, and high boots of soft leather, brown or dark red, reaching to just below the knee; all were armed and, with a few exceptions, they favoured that most serviceable of all weapons, the short, leaf-shaped sword, that had for centuries been the legionary's best friend. They used the sing-song lilting vernacular speech; they disputed without dignity; there was much shouting, and I recalled the scornful laughter of Lunaris when Artorius had mentioned his hopes of uniting Britain.

In appearance and behaviour these representative rulers of British kingdoms were incredibly remote from their civilized great-grandparents who could say with pride, *Civis Romanus sum.* The Roman citizens from whom they were descended might never, have existed; they might soon revert to the squalid savagery of their tribal ancestors, twelve or more generations ago, the half-naked animals that Julius Caesar saw and described who painted themselves blue and wore skins. If civilization in Britain sank still lower, the grandchildren of these men would be like that. And then I remembered that Ambrosius had on former occasions dominated this rabble, soothed their antagonisms, so that the Council of Kings was transformed, at least temporarily, into the likeness of a civilized assembly, deliberating with the gravity of the ancient Senate. But now Ambrosius was too old and feeble, and Artorius too young and without authority: so I thought, but I was wrong about Artorius.

Little slave girls moved silently about the hall, bearing flasks of wine, and making sure that no man's silver cup remained empty for long. I thought that this hospitable gesture by Ambrosius was a mistake: wine so easily melts the control of quarrelsome men, and more than one of the company seemed intent on making trouble. The outstanding trouble-maker was Maelgwyn, who went out of his way to insult Maël of Reged by informing him that the forces of Gwynedd had now occupied the whole of the disputed peninsula and the frontier of the kingdom would soon be moved further north; but Maël refused to be drawn into a quarrel, though he was angry, and showed it when a tactful centurion on the staff of Ambrosius tried to change the subject by asking him if he intended to visit Aquae Sulis, where the hot, healing springs were still in use though the luxurious pleasure city was greatly decayed.

'I've heard of Aquae Sulis,' said Maël sourly; 'I've also heard of Sodom and Gomorrah.' And he turned his back on Maelgwyn and the centurion and moved to another part of the hall. Maelgwyn laughed, looked about him, and slowly made his way towards the solitary figure of Marc. I followed him, and presently Artorius joined us.

Maelgwyn began by asking Marc about the numbers and arms of the Saxon raiders, and expressed mild surprise that the mighty army of Dumnonia had not swept them back into the sea.

'Have you ever fought a Saxon force?" Marc enquired coldly; 'but I suppose you've been far too busy making useless war against friendly kingdoms, like Reged.'

With an insolent smile on his face, Maelgwyn looked down at the squat, tubby little King of Dumnonia, and said:

'If any horse in my stables had a shape like yours, I'd slaughter it at once and feed it to my boar-hounds.'

His fingers rested lightly on the hilt of his dagger.

Marc said nothing: his sword was half drawn when Artorius stepped in front of him. 'We have only one enemy,' he said; 'the Saxons are nearer to Marc than to you, Maelgwyn.'

'Near enough to be vigorously attacked, I should have thought,' the prince returned. Then, with one of those swift changes of mood that make the British-born Romans so unpredictable, he became conciliatory and almost reasonable. 'I have a century of experienced fighters with me,' he continued: 'shall we join forces when the Council has finished talking, and hunt down these Saxon barbarians?'

Marc surprised me by accepting the offer. 'That would allow us to meet Cerdic and his band on equal terms,' he said: 'I can muster a hundred well-drilled men, but I can't spare more without leaving my kingdom unprotected. We have a long coastline, and every bay and inlet and beach has to be guarded; we never know when an enemy like Cerdic may land, and although I have some warships, and have fought off raiders at sea, only a strong fleet could keep the Channel free.'

From what I had seen of Dumnonian troops, I doubted whether they were as well-drilled as Marc claimed.

I shall not record the discussion that followed, though I shall describe it to Philonides, so he may understand how preoccupied with trivialities and personal dignity British rulers were when I knew them. I doubt whether they have changed much. Marc and Maelgwyn are still living; now they are middle-aged men, both experienced in war, and Marc was defeated in battle by Cerdic and his Saxons some years before I left Britain. In their own individual way they were identical in character with the old tribal British, half-savage and half-child; half-drunk when sober, and mad, impossible and dangerous when intoxicated. Always quick to anger, they were boastful, valiant and infinitely cunning, especially those from the far west, the old and now forgotten province of Valentia.

Few promises made by these little kings were ever kept; Maelgwyn never marched with Marc against that Saxon stronghold, though I think that he might have done so had he not returned to Gwynedd when news came to him of his father's death. He left the Council while it was still in session, to claim his rights, before his younger brother or his uncle could attempt to supplant him. We heard later that he had secured his kingdom by murdering most of his relatives, and there were many imperial precedents for such ruthlessness; the brothers and sisters of a king can be as embarrassing as those of an Emperor.

Old men's memories become misted over, and when I try to describe that Council, I find that I have lost so much of what was said; but what I do remember is the dignity and wisdom of Ambrosius Aurelianus, and the silent and respectful attention his words commanded. He spoke in Latin; his British accent hardly noticeable; and he spoke as a trained orator should, clearly and to the point, and —this I found astonishing at the time—he seemed to transfer some of his personal serenity to that unruly mob of barbarians; for that is how I had begun to think of the British, and I still do. But if they spoke Latin, as they did occasionally, they changed perceptibly, because then their thoughts marched at the steady pace and with the precision of an imperial legion instead of rushing about in wild confusion; the discipline of that well-ordered language steadied those emotional, impulsive minds. I could see that as they listened to Ambrosius, his reasonable good sense helped them to recapture—or so I thought—something of that understanding of universal citizenship, which had been Rome's greatest gift to mankind. He was urging them to sink their differences and unite. Britain united could again be the powerful province it had been when Magnus Maximus ruled in the West. That was his message to the Council of Kings. Old and ill though he was, his final words, stirring as a trumpet call, were:

'Unite! Unite! Unite!'

Momentarily we heard the challenging voice of a young and virile man.

For some minutes the assembly was silent; then one of those infernal harpers struck up and started bellowing out a song in praise of battles long over and victories long forgotten. Those kings and noblemen who had for a brief space remembered that it was still possible to justify their claim—which they all made—to be called Roman citizens, relapsed into incoherent squabbling, and loudest of all the angry voices was that of Honorius, king of the tiny state of Gwent.

'Unite indeed!' he bellowed. 'How well we all love each other and help each other. Why, only a month ago when that Irish pirate raided as far as the walls of Venta and captured half a hundred girls for the slave market, did the rulers of Glevissing or Demetia or Dumnonia send a ship to pursue them? No! They prate enough of brotherly love and fight with their mouths, but when it comes to sending men or ships, oh no! We're told then that God helps those who help themselves, so go and pray, brother.'

Somebody told him to shut up. He had a grievance, certainly. The Irish after they became Christians ceased troubling the western British kingdoms, but latterly they had acquired an appetite for sacred relics, and these were shipped to them by enterprising Alexandrian and Syrian traders, who wanted to be paid with slave boys and girls for the eastern markets. The relics were supposed to come from holy places in Judea, and already in Ireland there must have been enough fragments of the true cross to build a sizeable ship. Slave-snatching by pirates has been going on for more than a century; ever since Magnus Maximus threw open the western gate of Britain by withdrawing the Valeria Victrix in 383. Patrick himself, who converted Ireland to Christianity, was abducted by Irish raiders when he was a youth; two shiploads of those pirates had rowed by night up the Sabrina, landing and dragging away boys and girls, slaves and citizens alike, from the villas and villages that fringed the river.

Patrick, the son of a rich landowner, endured some years of slavery in Ireland, but he possessed courage, also immense patience, and, inspired by the spiritual power of a born teacher, converted his savage masters, who presently released him. After a few years of freedom and training he returned to Ireland to teach and tame the tribesmen; and, as Ambrosius told us, they abandoned their raiding and left the coast of western Britain in peace; but had recently resumed their old ways, not because they had forgotten Patrick's teaching, but because of its effect on their superstitious minds. They enjoy fighting and raiding, and now their religious faith condoned their natural taste for violence and robbery, ever since those enterprising businessmen of the eastern Mediterranean began to export holy relics. And as Irish pirates increased and multiplied their slave raids seemed to the rulers of the western kingdoms to be a greater menace than the Saxon states and settlements, while Cerdic's recent landing on the south coast appeared to be relatively unimportant, though nobody ventured to say so. Why should they heed a call for unity and action? The matter was not even debated; indeed no rational discussion of any problem took place, and that noisy session of the Council ended when Ambrosius, too exhausted to exercise control over that wrangling mob of barbarians, rose from his chair of carved ivory and called for silence. Surprisingly enough he got it, at once. He still had some power, and they listened respectfully when he announced that they must meet again the next day, when some decisions must be taken.

After Ambrosius left the basilica, the kings and their councillors and ministers resumed their noisy discussions; even when they were agreeing with each other, they made as much noise as they did when quarrelling. No dignity. No trace of the ancient Roman *gravitas*. Just a crowd of bawling natives—yes, natives is the word that comes as naturally to me now as it did to the officers and officials who first brought Roman civilization to this wild island when Claudius ruled the Empire. That desolate spectacle of human indiscipline depressed me, but Artorius thought nothing of it. He was cheerful and confident when we were alone together, and talked over the day's events.

'They're frightened of the Irish,' he said; 'and that's something new we have to take into account. My uncle said nothing about such raids; but of course they hadn't started when we saw him a few months ago. I think that something may be done with these people. But not yet. What I must do as soon as I can is to recruit my own band.'

His resolve was favoured by events, for when the Council met the next day, Ambrosius announced that his office as *dux Britanniarum* should henceforth be held by a younger man. He said:

'Before this Council disperses, you, the assembled rulers of Britain, must confirm the choice of my successor.' He spoke slowly and clearly, but with obvious effort. 'I name as my successor my nephew Artorius Aurelianus,' he continued.

One or two protesting voices were raised; but nobody questioned his right to do so; there were so many imperial precedents, and as Commander-in-Chief of the British Army, when there happened to be one in existence, his authority was unassailable.

'A young man is needed,' he went on; 'I am an old and a dying man.'

At that some fool wept aloud, but nobody took any notice. Then King Maël of Reged said:

'He's too young. What wisdom and experience can he bring to this great office?'

Lunaris, who detested Maël, snapped out: 'Young enough to win battles. He went after those raiding Picts and killed them off as raiding savages should be killed off, while you sat on your arse and prayed; neither you nor Coroticus did anything to stop them; so long as Strathclyde and Reged are not invaded, you're both content to leave the hard work of fighting to other and better men.'

Maelgwyn, glad of the chance to mock Maël, said:

'The great and noble king of Reged fights when he must, but has the unfortunate habit of losing battles. Perhaps he's unlucky as well as incompetent.' He laughed unpleasantly, then surprised me by adding: 'I can speak for my father, King Catwallaun, who gave me authority to do so; and in his name I would pledge the support of the kingdom of Gwynedd to Artorius as *dux Britanniarum*.'

Then that self-important fool, Honorius, of little Gwent, had to bray out a promise of support in far too many words. His armed forces, he announced grandly, were at the disposal of Artorius.

'Two men and a boy, I suppose,' Maelgwyn sneered. A new quarrel was checked by Lunaris who said, with great sense:

'We cannot shape or settle the future by shouting at each other. Ambrosius Aurelianus, you command here as chief of the army: I support the choice of Artorius as your successor, but here and now you must order the rulers who are present to signify whether they accept or reject your nephew.'

Ambrosius rose slowly—and I saw how difficult it was for him to stand unsupported. He swayed slightly, then with an effort stood firmly upright. His voice was strong and steady when he spoke.

'Whoever commands the armies of Britain is the servant of the rulers assembled here,' he said. 'He can serve Britain well only if those rulers accept his authority. Does any British ruler here contest my choice of a successor?'

There was absolute silence. Then Ambrosius said:

'You have confirmed my choice, and without words.' He sat

down, settled back in his chair, and said: "That concludes the business of this Council.'

His body went slack; his head fell forward; and we knew he had died.

XI

The successor

WHEN THE BRITISH are frightened they forget their quarrels and mutual jealousies; memories of old tribal hates and feuds and suspicions melt away; at such times they could become a united people if only the mood lasted, but it doesn't; what could be the dawn of national amity is a false dawn which soon fades. The death of Ambrosius caused those quarrelsome kinglets to reconcile their differences, for they were afraid, though most of them hid their fear. They did not immediately apprehend the magnitude of their loss. They had trusted and obeyed Ambrosius; their trust was unequivocal, their obedience reluctant and qualified though ultimately effective; but now they realized despairingly that there was nobody else like the victorious general who, as a living embodiment of the Roman virtues, was all they could never be.

Within a few hours of his death, when his body lay in state in the small Christian church that a hundred years earlier had been a Mithraeum, I learned something of the depth and breadth of the respect those kings and their followers had for the great Aurelii family and especially for their blood link with that ambitious adventurer, Magnus Maximus, whose name, like that of Cunedda, was honoured by all descendants of the old far western tribes. Because of that family connection, Artorius, the untried youth, was acceptable.

Very wisely, when he delivered the funeral oration, Artorius spoke not in formal Latin but in the vernacular. I thought that Merlin had advised him to do so; but I was soon to learn that he seldom sought advice, or paid much attention to it when proffered. 'Sometimes it may be expedient to fight with words,' he told me; 'then Merlin may have his uses; but I prefer to say what I have to say to Britain's enemies with swords and arrows.'

The day after the burial, when all the religious ceremonies were concluded, the Council reassembled, and Artorius addressed them. His opening words were well-chosen, for they acknowledged the regal status of his hearers but also recalled their imperial heritage and all it implied.

'Romans and rulers of Britain,' he began, 'I am here to give to the land of your fathers the service that my uncle Ambrosius gave; and though I lack his years and experience, I am not without military knowledge and have already won my first battle on British soil against the painted savages of the north.'

This time he spoke in Latin; again wisely, for he dwelt deliberately on the relationship Britain could still claim with the Empire and the support her rulers might receive from some future emperor. All unknowingly, he anticipated the plans that his Sacred and Imperial Majesty, the Emperor Justinian, has already made for the recovery of the lost provinces of the West. But he was careful to avoid any suggestion that imperial authority might be resumed as the price of military aid. He spoke without passion, without rhetorical flourishes; calmly, reasonably and with deep conviction. Had he used the vernacular he might have roused that audience to bawling enthusiasm; but his sedate, restrained description of the power conferred by efficient military organization, steadied those emotionally untidy minds.

'I do not ask you to fight for me,' he said; 'but I do ask you to pray for me. God is on our side, for the barbarians are the enemies of God, but we must serve Him with our swords. Prayers are not enough.'

A few people were fidgeting uneasily, but were reassured when he explained that they were not expected to supplement their prayers with much practical help. The small force of trained troops which his uncle had established as a permanent garrison at Corinium, would, he assured them, remain as his only standing army. They were disciplined, competent soldiers, and he had good proofs of their worth as fighting men, for fifty of them had attacked and ridden down a strong band of over two hundred Picts. He asked for no more than a score of young men from each ruler's own band. He qualified his request by saying:

'But I want willing men, not men who have been ordered to join our British force, and they must be men who can ride and use a long sword and send an arrow home to its target.' He paused and after regarding his audience for a space, added: 'The day of the legion is over for ever. Marching men with big, heavy shields and old-fashioned spears belong to the past. This is the day of the arrow and the long sword and the horse, especially the horse, for men who can shoot from the saddle will always be masters of men on their feet. Now in addition to the men you send me,' he went on, 'I am raising my own band of trained warriors; I am already re-cruiting them.' (He forbore to mention that so far Agrippa was his only recruit.) 'I shall accept only those who are prepared to fight until all Britain is once more a peaceful, Christian land; strong, secure and prosperous. This should be our aim; this we can achieve; but purely defensive war is not enough. We must attack, conquer, and expel.'

I could never be quite sure when Artorius was deceiving himself; I knew that he was too honest, too innocent, to try to deceive others; but his British blood, that strange, unstable, heady blood he had inherited from generations of native ancestors, enabled him to believe sincerely and passionately in what he said, when he was actually saying it. And presently, quite unknowingly I think, he changed from Latin to the vernacular; and then I knew that while he continued to speak the truth, it was not the whole truth. To restore Britain to Christianity implied the expulsion of all the Germanic tribes and the conquest of the kingdoms they had founded; but he said nothing about the possibility of converting such kingdoms and persuading them peacefully to abandon their heathen beliefs, or accepting their rulers as *foederati*, so that their states and subjects became part of the imperial establishment. Although everybody present must have known of his visits to King Alfin, no awkward questions were asked, nor was the name of Gwinfreda mentioned.

That night there was a feast, and good wine imported from

Aquitania mellowed and cheered even such austere chiefs as Maël
and diminished the sour dignity of Marc: I call them chiefs, for king
is a barbarian title that for over a thousand years has offended the
ears of every true Roman. My tongue rebels against it. Prince
Maelgwyn sat on the right of Artorius, for these latter-day British
chiefs and nobles preferred to sit at high tables on stools or benches
instead of reclining on couches, three to a table in the traditional
style, and Artorius to avoid offending anybody about precedence had
arranged many tables in a circle, with a few gaps between them for
slaves to pass through and serve from the inner sides: so everybody
faced each other across a big circular space, as if they were sitting
at one great round table.

An hour before midnight, we heard the sentries outside the hall
challenging somebody who had ridden up; then the guard was
turned out, and presently a weary messenger entered, demanding
speech with Prince Maelgwyn.

'Grieve for the news I bring,' he began in a lugubrious voice.

'Say what you have to say and get out,' growled Maelgwyn.

'Your majesty, it is with sorrow that I report the death of your
royal father, Catwallaun, King of Gwynedd.' The man paused, then
shouted: 'Long live King Maelgwyn.'

Artorius rose to his feet.

'My lords,' he said, we cannot continue feasting after such
tidings. I shall go to the church and pray for the soul of a wise
the noble king; I have no doubt that you may all wish to join me
and add your prayers to mine.'

Maelgwyn shook his head. 'I have no time to spare,' he said; 'I
must ride north at once to claim my kingdom and my rights.'

'Of course,' said Artorius; and he embraced the young king.
Then he left the hall, followed by all the kings except Honorius of
Gwent, who, helplessly drunk, had fallen asleep. I was leaving too,
when Maelgwyn touched my arm, and said:

'Ride with me a little way, Caius Geladius.'

We left by the West Gate, and took the road to Glevum, accompanied by a score of men from Maelgwyn's bodyguard. The rest
would follow with the baggage as soon as they were assembled and

everything packed. The night was moonless, but the road was wide
and well made and two armed men rode ahead of us.

For many miles my companion was silent, then he said:

'Caius,' (and like most British-born Romans he shortened my
forename to Cay), 'I wanted to talk to you about Artorius. You are,
in some sort, what churchmen might call his guardian angel, though
angel is not the right word: not for *you*. But I recognize your
responsibility, though you wear it lightly.'

I decided to be frank with this perceptive barbarian, so I told
him what my orders were about Artorius and what I was supposed
to do in Britain.

He made no comment, and for a mile or so we trotted on together
in silence, then he said:

'You serve Artorius——'

But I interrupted. 'I serve his Sacred and Imperial Majesty, the
Emperor,' I told him, 'I am second-in-command to Artorius and as
such serve him, but only because I am thus obeying imperial orders.'

'The Emperor is far, far distant,' he said.

I replied with an old proverb: 'Rome's arm is long.'

He laughed harshly. 'That arm withered years ago,' he returned.
'Come, Cay. Let me make you an offer. I have an army, well-drilled,
well-equipped. You have seen detachments on parade when you
were my father's guest. So you know that I'm not boasting.
Commanded by a professional and experienced soldier like you, it
would enable me to conquer Reged and Strathclyde and unite the
whole of the north-west.'

I stopped him. We both halted, and faced each other.

We had been riding for nearly three hours, and the early summer
night would soon end. Already the stars had lost their brightness.

'My lord Maelgwyn,' I said (for I could not bring myself to call
him king), 'if I disobeyed the orders of the Emperor, would you
ever trust me to obey yours if I entered your service?'

'No,' he answered at once, 'but I don't trust anybody. No king
can afford the risk, and that is one of the reasons why I am hastening
to make sure that my orders have been carried out.'

I think that he expected me to ask what those orders were; but after a long pause, while our mounts fidgeted and the eastern sky began to pale, he said:

'I knew my father was a dying man when I left Deva; and three men of my personal guards knew what to do directly he died. I cannot allow my uncle or my two brothers to live. That's all, Cay.'

'I thought you trusted nobody,' I said: 'can you trust those three guards of yours?'

He laughed. 'Some men love their wives and children a little too much for their comfort,' he told me; 'all three are devoted family men, and I have taken hostages to make sure of their obedience.'

'So if I entered your service I should know what to expect,' I said, and laughed. To my surprise he laughed too.

'Farewell, Cay,' he said; 'go back to your *dux Britanniarum*. When I have conquered the north-west and dealt with those imitation men, Maël and Coroticus, I shall have done much to unite Britain: more perhaps than he will ever achieve. I'm Roman enough to believe in unity through conquest.'

So I rode back to Corinium that summer morning, with the words of a mournful song running through my head. One of the bards had sung it at the feast, before the messenger had brought the news of King Catwallaun's death.

> When all the last battles were lost,
> And the might of the victors unshaken,
> When the vanquished had counted the cost,
> And the last of their tribute was taken,
> And the lords who had ruled were enslaved
> And the king they had followed had perished
> And nothing they fought for was saved,
> No customs or laws that they cherished,
> Then the name and the fame of the land of
>   their fathers
> Were lost in the darkness of shame.

The singer's voice had been deep and mournful, and he had sung the last line over and over again, a little lower at each repetition, until at last the minatory words had been scarcely more than a whisper.

His song was listened to in silence, and some time passed before conversation had come alive again.

Did these latter-day Roman-Britons ever see themselves as they really were? I wondered then, and I am still wondering. They have delusions of grandeur and military prowess. Their leaders have never realized that a Roman helmet does not make a Roman general. At heart I think they know what failures they are, and perhaps that is why they hymn their defeats and disasters. Some of those defeats have been heroic and magnificent occasions of courage and fortitude, darkened by depressing incompetence. The time may come, perhaps it has come already, when they have tasted defeat too often, quarrelled among themselves too long and too bitterly, and so weakened their powers of resolution and lowered their courage that apathy may seem a better choice than action. If they have sunk so far, their condition might, as I suggested to Philonides, make the task of any future imperial expeditionary force easier, for though it might not be welcomed it could not be resisted.

'If they are still like that, they would be useless as allies,' he said.

'Not altogether,' I disagreed. 'They may be weak and divided and dishonest, but I believe that they might respond to leadership, as a chosen band of them responded to the leadership of Artorius.'

I knew that no British-born Roman could take up the task Artorius had begun and left unfinished. British chiefs and nobles thrived in an atmosphere of tawdry ambitions, treachery and secret murder. Civilization would depart from that unhappy island, and law and order become memories, recalled only by the very old. But a leader there must be, inspired and fortified by belief in ultimate victory, as Artorius had been—at first. He existed.

Britain and the politics of its small, squabbling states seemed so far away in space and time, as I sat in the office of the Chief Assistant to the Grand Chamberlain of the Imperial Court, going over the first rough draft of my report. Philonides was impassive as usual: his steady brown eyes and calm Egyptian face concealed his thoughts, though he was able to read mine, for presently he broke into them.

'Count Belisarius is unlikely to be entrusted with the command of the force that must reconquer the West,' he said.

Belisarius was the leader I had in mind; the greatest general since Julian.

'Let me explain,' he went on. 'Continued success may be as injurious for a general as failure or defeat. Too many victories often arouse the envy of those who cannot claim personal credit for them; while defeat may be condoned and pitied.'

I was horrified when he amplified that explanation, and in my innocence of the devious ways and intrigues of the Imperial Court, I found it difficult to believe that his Sacred and Imperial Majesty could be jealous of the reputation of his ever-victorious general. Lesser men might feel belittled by a great soldier whose military skill had won back some of the Empire's former power and splendour, but surely the Emperor was immune from and far above such frailty. Philonides hinted—it was no more than a casual remark—that the favour and friendship of the Empress Theodora Augusta, which Belisarius enjoyed, were also serious liabilities. Apart from formal meetings at Court functions they carefully avoided each other; that friendship, long established and well-known, was not nearly so damaging as the general's enormous popularity and the adulation, unsought by him, of the great mass of the people.

Having lived for years in seclusion, I was happily ignorant of the corruption and pettiness and political plots of the Imperial Court. The lies, follies, vices and concentrated selfishness of politicians and prelates and officials were so detestable that almost I wished myself back in Britain, taking part in events that were now an old man's memories.

Again Philonides picked up the thread of my thoughts.

'You are not so old as you think you are,' he said. 'You have the vigour and the mind of a far younger man: you are an experienced general. You know Britain and, what seems to you very important—and you have half persuaded me that you are right about this—you have experience of seafaring and sea warfare.' Then he used the identical words Maelgwyn had used when a newly-made king. 'Let me make you an offer.' He paused, then added: 'His Sacred and Imperial Majesty would certainly consider favourably a suggestion that you should command an expedition to Britain, if one is mounted.'

I was silent, and he smiled and said:

'Think well, General. Nothing is settled: but when you have completed your report and it has been considered not only by the Emperor but by his military staff, I shall expect an answer from you.'

I wondered whether Philonides would have second thoughts about his offer when he had read my final report. He might learn the truth about my abilities and limitations, might understand as well as I did, that I could never be more than a trustworthy follower, never a leader.

Back in my quiet, comfortable house, I reread my draft, picking up old memories. That warm, moist summer morning when I returned to Corinium after my ride with King Maelgwyn became vivid and real again. What happened then was as fresh in my mind as if it had happened yesterday.

The road ran on high ground, straight, well-kept and clear of undergrowth on either side as a military road should be; as the early morning mists thinned I could see the way ahead for some miles, as I was riding south-east not straight into the dazzling sunrise. Presently, in the distance, I saw a body of mounted men approaching. They rode slowly, and were escorting a train of baggage mules; but what controlled their pace was an advance guard, on foot, not marching in formation at the old regulation pace of troops, but strolling— there is no other word. Now and then they broke into a run, howling like wolves. Between those bursts of animal noises they chanted in unison, over and over again, words charged with menace.

'Mark the passing, mark the passing, we must slay to mark the passing. Slay! Slay! Slay! Slay!' On the fourth repetition of 'Slay!' their voices rose to a shriek.

I reined up my horse and counted them. There were twelve, and as they drew near, I saw that they were young men, far taller than stocky British tribesmen, clad in some material that looked like polished black leather, for it glinted in the sunlight. Their headgear, also black, rose to a point and flopped out behind. They carried long

A. R – E.

whips, which they flourished and cracked. Now and again, after running far ahead of the riders and baggage mules, they would halt, form a circle and dance, leaping high, and howling.

I knew that the mounted men were Maelgwyn's warriors; I had expected to meet them; but had not expected a body of raving savages. Then I remembered what Lunaris had said to Merlin about needing magic protection against the king's devils that Maelgwyn had brought with him. He had kept them well hidden during his stay in Corinium; this was my first sight of the creatures. When they were almost level with me I drew my sword; but they never even glanced my way, and passed on, still leaping and shouting and cracking their whips.

The officer commanding the troopers rode up to me, saluted and said:

'There's nothing to be afraid of, sir. They have no authority to take action until they reach His Majesty's territory.'

His insolence was unintentional; like so many tribesmen he was ignorant. I resisted my impulse to tell him that I was seldom scared by barbarians. I knew he expected me to ask him about that queer advance guard, but I contented myself by saying:

'I wish they'd make less noise.'

'They aren't under my command, sir,' he replied, then saluted and rode back to his place at the head of the column.

When I returned to Corinium I went to Merlin's quarters and found him studying an old map, showing the bays and capes and peninsulas of Armorica.

'I've seen the king's devils,' I told him; 'why didn't you tell me about them?'

'You never asked,' he replied. "When Lunaris told you that Maelgwyn had brought them, you changed the subject, and asked him what he believed. I hope his answer pleased you, though you must have guessed that he had no religion. Now about the king's devils. Old traditions live long, especially when they are evil; this one has survived for over a thousand years; even barbarous British chiefs have heard of King Romulus who founded Rome, and have heard too of his celeres, the band of three hundred noble youths who formed his bodyguard, gave him unquestioned obedience, and were professional murderers who removed anyone the king found troublesome. Many of these little kings have their dedicated band of killers, Maël and Marc and even that pitiful fool, Honorius of Gwent. They don't of course call them celeres; *devils* has a more terrifying and dangerous sound to so-called Christians; and the bands are small but well-trained, and ruthless. King Catwallaun used them to collect his taxes; so will Maelgwyn, and he will turn them loose on anyone who might question his authority.'

'What did they mean about slaying to mark the passing?' I asked.

'You must remember that these people are savages,' said Merlin. 'They have long neglected the laws and rejected the guidance of the Druids who regulated their life before the Romans came. At first Rome ruled them with the sword, then by corrupting them with wealth and luxurious living. Christianity was never taken seriously. These latter-day tribesmen are slowly sinking down to the old, dark primitive life; and unless Artorius unites them, they'll be swept away by the Saxons, who are savages too, but superior savages. Maelgwyn's subjects accept the ancient custom of sacrificing twelve men and twelve women when a king dies. That's what the royal devils meant: they slay to mark the passing of the king.'

Merlin told me that Artorius had called another meeting of the Council for noon, and had invited some of the great landlords of the West to attend, with their eldest sons.

'They will certainly come,' he said; 'for they are determined to resist exactions to support an army; but Artorius has no intention of asking for taxes: he wants to recruit his band. They will be so agreeably surprised when no demands are made, that many of the younger men may decide to become his sworn followers.'

Two of the kings were preparing to leave that morning: Maël, who feared that Reged might be attacked by the belligerent Maelgwyn, and Coroticus, who, quite groundlessly, feared that Maël might attack Strathclyde, unless he returned. He overestimated the ability of that pious monarch, whose only ambition was to be left alone in peace to enjoy his prayers, his wives and his concubines.

I had been up all night, but I could do without sleep for long periods easily in those far-off days; so I spent an hour in the baths, then went to the great hall of the basilica, where members of the Council and the noblemen Artorius had invited were chatting while slaves served them with wine. For once there was no quarrelling, no loud boasting: for a British assembly this was remarkable, and I attributed the prevailing good manners to the presence of so many civilized landowners who, unlike the little kings behaved as one expected Roman gentlemen to behave.

One of them introduced himself to me. He was tall, slender, on the young side of middle age; dark-haired, clean-shaven and with large grey eyes.

'My name is Julius Nonna Geladius,' he said, 'so we are in some sort, kinsmen. It is good to know that a member of our family is second-in-command to the *dux Britanniarum*. The Geladii have a long tradition of military service in Britain. Welcome.'

XII

The sinews of war

MERLIN WAS RIGHT about the eagerness of young British noblemen to join a sworn band. When Artorius asked for recruits he got
them, though he was bluntly discouraging about prospective re-
wards. The concluding business of the Council had made it clear
that troubled kingdoms must see to their own defence, without expecting help from their neighbours; King Marc was disappointed
when he was told that he must cope with Cerdic's band of Saxons
himself.

'You are vigilant and have an army, ships too,' said Artorius, 'and
unless I am wholly mistaken, you have the will and the skill to use
both. Britain is ably protected in the south-west while you reign in
Dumnonia.'

Cold comfort, perhaps, but common sense. Marc took it quietly;
but Honorius of Gwent, given the same advice about tip-and-run
Irish raiders, protested vociferously. Somebody shouted: 'Quiet, Big
Mouth!' and a quarrel might have flared up, but Artorius stopped it
before preliminary insults could be exchanged.

'I have nothing more to say to the present rulers of Britain,' he
announced; 'but I have something to say to the young men who
have come here by invitation.'

He knew as well as I did that nothing could be expected from the
kings except words, though Marc and Lunaris were exceptions.
They stayed to hear him, while the others took the hint and left the
hall. Out of the corner of my eye I saw one of the bards pick up his
harp, and I strode over and stopped the fool before he could open
his mouth. He started to say something about it being customary,
and I told him that obedience to an officer's orders was customary
too and advisable unless he wanted a sword in his guts. The shuffling

and noise of people leaving died away, and Artorius began to recruit his band.

He was honest with his hearers.

'So far my band consists of one, Prince Agrippa, son of King Lunaris of Elmet,' he said. Then he told them what he expected of a sworn band, and what the members of it could expect from their service, and after explaining briefly how he intended to wage war and the weapons he would use, ended by saying:

'I can offer nothing but hardship; hard living, hard fighting, hard riding. Henceforth for those who follow me there are three chief things in life: the sword, the bow and the horse. Dismiss all thoughts of ease or pleasure. You are never off duty. It would be wise to forget your homes. I promise nothing: war is uncertain: indeed one thing only is certain, and that is the rightness of our cause. Some men say that God is on the side of big armies, but God is on the side of any army that fights for a great and good cause.'

Unlike so many British noblemen, Artorius knew how much to say, how to say it, and when to stop. He inspired those boys, and as Marius, the eldest son of my newly-found kinsman, Julius Nonna, said to me later: 'He seems to be in God's confidence.' Marius was one of the eighty-five young men of good family who had taken an oath of loyalty and service to Artorius. His words conveyed an undertone of doubt: his grey eyes twinkled, and a smile transformed his small, tanned face into something monkeyish and full of mischief.

'I should advise you, cousin, to take the *dux Britanniarum* seriously,' I said.

'Oh, I do,' he replied; 'very seriously indeed; that's why I'm going to leave home and follow him. My brothers can manage the estate when my father dies: that's about all they're fit for. I want more than that out of life.'

Artorius, who was strolling about the hall talking to his recruits, overheard that. 'Don't try to get more out of life than there is in it,' he said, smiling at the boy. There could only have been a couple of years between them in age, but Artorius seemed very much older.

Marius, quite unabashed by this advice, became serious and said:

'My lord, may I ask a personal question?'

'Ask anything you like.'

'I saw you riding a black stallion. Where did it come from?'

'I wish I knew.' Artorius looked at him keenly, and added: 'Why do you ask?'

'It's from our stables,' Marius told him. 'It strayed some years ago, and father has been worried ever since. We are very careful of our breeding stock.'

Artorius crossed himself. 'I see God's hand in this,' he said. Turning to me he added: 'Cay, this is a matter that I must leave to you.' He had dropped into the habit of using the shortened British form of my forename.

So early the next day I rode westwards with Marius and his father, leaving the military district of Corinium and passing through Glevum into the kingdom of Gwent, turning north to Ariconium, deserted and dismal with ruins of the iron foundries that once made armour and weapons for the legions of Britain, then west again along rough roads that twisted through narrow valleys, crossing and recrossing small rushing streams by paved fords, while the encircling hills rose higher and higher, until we were within sight of a mountain with a flat top that towered above the surrounding highlands.

'We live in the shadow of the Black Seat,' said Julius Nonna, pointing to the mountain; 'it's called that because the guardian spirits of the Black Mountains sit there, watching the south and west for enemies. But they've been asleep for half a century or more. Irish raiders seldom came so far north. There's an old fort on the slopes and a military settlement named Gobannium. We've taken that over, and the foothills and the valley south of them are all part of our estate, which begins at the river, and the western road runs through it.'

'Good fishing in that stream,' Marius remarked.

We had ridden all of seventy miles since we left Corinium at dawn, and the long summer day had nearly ended when we turned off the made road to follow a dusty track through fields covered by a purple mist of thistles. The warm evening was heavy with the scents of a rich countryside; we passed through orchards, and beyond

to a spacious garden set out in terraces, while our shadows length-
ened, until the last of the slanting sunlight was shut out by the great
flat-topped hill. The loose gravel of the track was replaced by a
broad paved roadway that curved up through the gardens to the
portico of a long white house. Servants ran out and held our horses
as we dismounted; in the portico three young men and two girls
awaited us, and Julius introduced his family.

During that long day's ride Julius related the history of the British
branch of the Geladii, and I have already said all that needs to be said
about their fortunes earlier in my report. They had kept up the
breed of great horses, and that was my chief concern, though I was
naturally interested to meet and hear more about my remote and
unknown cousins. Apart from Julius Nonna and Marius, only one
of them comes into my story, for something quite unexpected and
disturbing occurred a few minutes after I met Lavinia, the eldest
daughter of the house, a quiet, solemn girl of nineteen. I fell in love
with her, and that had never happened to me before.

Julius had been a widower for several years, and Lavinia ran his
household, managing the domestic affairs of the estate, the slaves and
servants and housekeeping, with great competence. Her father had
never remarried, contenting himself with pretty slave girls that he
had the good taste to keep out of sight. The family lived a secure
life of quiet luxury, their needs supplied by their own crops and
herds of sheep and cattle. They had plenty of slaves, and were well
protected, for Julius had a trained band of bowmen, and all his sons
could ride and knew how to use weapons.

'The laws here, are made by the strongest,' Julius told me.

Nobody ventured to interfere with him; brigands avoided his
well-guarded valleys; King Honorius made no demands or requisi-
tions.

After a couple of restful hours in the steam of the baths, we dined,
sitting on chairs at a long table. So many of the refinements of
Roman civilizations had survived in that household that I half
expected to find couches and low tables in the dining-room; but
although the decoration was lavish, with gay patterns painted on the
walls and floors glowing with mosaics depicting the exploits of the

old gods, the furniture was simple and crude, made from oak by the estate carpenters. The daughters of the house dined with us, and although this was customary in Britain, I resented it on this occasion, for I found the presence of Lavinia distracting, and wanted to be alone with Julius and his sons. Love is an untidy emotion: fatal to a professional soldier if taken seriously. My business with these British relations was to secure mounts that would make Artorius and his band invincible. What puzzled me was the family policy of restricting the breeding, for those big horses could be a source of wealth as they had been a hundred years ago. Of course I understood that when the military establishment of Britain shrank, and no more troops came from the Empire to reinforce the garrison and to man the forts and stations and the Wall, the market for that special breed had vanished. The chiefs and kings preferred the sturdy little native ponies that cost nothing, for herds roamed the hills of the West and the deserted parts of central Britain, but the secrecy of the proprietors about their magnificent stock seemed odd, and when I said so a chilly silence followed. Julius glanced at his sons, Marius looked at his plate; they all avoided looking at me, except Lavinia, who smiled gently and said:

'Why not tell him about the prophecy, father?'

Julius shook his head. He seemed troubled, and muttered something about old wives' tales and unchristian superstitions. Marius laughed.

'Don't let that worry you, father,' he advised. 'The *dux Britanniarum* believes that the hand of God is opening our stable door. If you won't tell our cousin Cay, then I shall.'

I said hastily that I had no desire to probe family secrets; but Marius dismissed that objection. 'You *are* family,' he said.

Julius sighed and admitted that I had a right to know. Then he told me that over two centuries ago a wise woman, a Sibyl named Brid Rhua, lived in a cave on an island at the mouth of the River Dee, off the north-west point of the peninsula, that disputed tongue of land which had caused unending strife between Gwynedd and Reged. It was still known as the Sacred Island, though the Sibyl was slain long ago when the Christians gained power and began to hunt down and persecute all who had served the old gods. Brid Rhua was always attended by an acolyte, who after five years was sent out into the world to spread wisdom. One of those acolytes had come south to the Black Mountains, where she lived to a great age, well over a hundred years. She had named the Geladii as the sacred guardians, chosen by Epona, of a breed of great horses that would bring victories to the last of the Romans. Such was her prediction. Epona was the goddess and protector of horses, and the family, although Christian, had taken it seriously. Even today Epona was acknowledged; Merlin had told us, and we had seen for ourselves, that the gods lived on in Britain, and in the secluded far western hills and valleys they were not condemned to the furtive, apologetic half-life forced on them in regions where the Church was powerful. Unlike pronouncement by the Delphic Oracle, there was no ambiguity about the wise woman's prediction. Marius, who had been watching me to see how I took it, said:

'The *dux Britanniarum* needn't hear anything about this: serious Christians are so easily upset.'

The young man's casual irreverence amused me, for what he said was also in my mind; but he would have to learn discretion. I told him so.

'Oh, certainly,' he assured me, lightly; 'I can be discreet, and silent in the right places too; but surely I needn't be with you? As I said just now, you're family; and I think we share the same beliefs and disbeliefs.'

Lavinia smiled. 'Marius often talks for the sake of talking,' she warned me; 'but he thinks too. Of course talking gives him time to think.'

'Pay no attention to those sisterly remarks,' said Marius; 'we are a united family, though we seldom agree with each other and often take opposite sides in an argument for the fun of it: quarrelling is the spice of life. Lavinia and I quarrel all the time, possibly because we are so alike. She'll miss me.'

In appearance they were certainly alike: Lavinia had the same wide-set grey eyes and small round face as her brother: both had dark brown hair with a slight reddish tinge. Lavinia was grave,

Marius was gay: they both had hard, resolute minds. I discovered that after I'd served two campaigns with Marius: Lavinia's strong will stayed in hiding until after our marriage. But I spent little time then on personal matters. My immediate task was to get as many big horses as Julius Nonna could let me have now, and to persuade him to breed and increase the stock, so that in the near future Artorius could confront Britain's enemies with heavy cavalry, trained and armed like the Imperial Household Guards. Meanwhile his Band would have to be mounted and trained on tough native ponies, reserving the big horses for his officers.

Julius Nonna employed many free craftsmen, carpenters, plumbers and smiths; only his field hands, gardeners and household servants were slaves; iron for his forges came from two mines that were still worked, one near the deserted temple of Nodens. He paid dues in kind to King Honorius for the use of it, and found the labour, for the king's officials were too lazy and incompetent to organize or supervise such work; mines had been imperial domains in the old province, but nearly all were now neglected or abandoned, though tin was still mined in Dumnonia, and King Marc paid for his wines by exporting it to Gaul. No craftsmen had ever left the Geladii estates for Armorica.

When Marius and I returned to Corinium, two of the smiths came with us, lent by Julius so that they could copy the weapons our few ancient craftsmen were making. We could not long delay the raid on Armorica to impress the invaluable ironworkers who had so foolishly been allowed to settle there.

I had been away for twelve days, and during that time Artorius had been drilling his Band, and had increased their numbers by inviting our original escort of troopers to join. They did not hesitate: they believed that Artorius was lucky in war, and he had proved it by winning his first battle. Forty-eight out of the original fifty—we had lost two in that boar hunt—gave our small army a fine stiffening of veterans, and moreover we had that tough under-officer, Paulinus, who knew his drill so thoroughly.

This addition to our force revealed some odd weaknesses among the young noblemen. Some of them objected to being on terms of perfect equality with the troopers. One fastidious youth, with a womanish face and hair as dark and sleek as a starling's plumage, was fool enough to explain why in a rather shrill voice.

'They are common men, *humilores*,' he protested.

'They have legs, arms, heads and hearts like you,' Artorius told him; 'they have experience of war and of the comradeship that war brings. You haven't. There's nothing wrong with them, but I'm not sure that there isn't something wrong with you. What is it? Vanity or just bad manners?'

Far from silencing him those words caused the critic to stand on his dignity. 'Had I not sworn a solemn oath—' he began; but Artorius stopped him.

'Say no more,' he advised; 'otherwise you may say too much. I can forget stupid words, but I don't forget obstinacy or forgive it either. That's enough.'

Members of the Band who felt superior to their new comrades were exceptional. A few may have regretted their own impulsive enthusiasm that had prompted them to join; but nobody wanted to leave, and before summer ended they became happily united, for the first of the northern wars began. Messengers from Coroticus and Maël had hurried south, with panic-stricken requests for immediate help, as the Picts had invaded Strathclyde. Couriers left our head-quarters an hour after Artorius received the news, bearing his written promise of armed support. He also dispatched messages to Lunaris and Maelgwyn, informing them of his intention to ride north and inviting them to send contingents to join him, and to Alfin of Deur he sent Merlin to explain verbally his plan of campaign to the Saxon king.

'If the father of my future wife desires to march with me, he will be very welcome,' he said; 'I think he will, so he'd better know exactly what I'm proposing to do.'

He assumed that the joint armies of Strathclyde and Reged would be able to hold the invaders for several days, though that depended on the size of the savage horde. The message from the kings had said that the Picts were massing in their thousands, whatever that might mean. Frightened men always exaggerate. Artorius could muster just under one hundred and fifty mounted men, including the forty-eight seasoned troopers of his original escort, the first volunteers for his band, and some young nobles who had joined since it was formed. All were equipped with bows and knew how to use them; there was a shortage of armour but every man had a long sword, and hanging from the sides of each saddle were riding irons, as we now called them, for Artorius had improved on the original looped straps by substituting iron foot-rests. With his weight thus supported, a rider cound stand upright and wield his long sword with deadly effect. We still relied on the preliminary showers of arrows, loosed off as we rode round the advancing troops. No savage or barbarian enemy in Britain ever thought of using horses to fight back. They always fought on foot, never in formation like drilled troops, but charging in disorderly mobs, 'every man his own general', as Marius said, after his first encounter with the Picts.

Compared with the rumoured thousands of the enemy—if there were thousands—our force would have seemed hopelessly outnumbered to any professional soldier who judged by numbers only; but we had better arms, better training, good discipline, mobility; and the secret weapon of surprise. Our plan was to ride north-east through Elmet to Deur, adding reinforcements if Lunaris and Alfin gave us any, then north again, passing Hadrian's Wall at Onnum as we had on the way to our first battle, and further north still, into Caledonia and beyond the Antonine Wall, then we should turn west into the Picts' homeland and attack the left flank and rear of their army. The ravaging of their villages could be left to Alfin's Saxon warriors, who were welcome to anything they could find in such poverty-stricken places and to any women and children fit for a slave market.

In Elmet fresh mounts awaited us, for Lunaris had requisitioned them after receiving our message; he also increased our numbers by a score of men from his own small army and had used his authority as a general to draw helmets and spare weapons from the stores at Eburacum. The issue of helmets reconciled the young members of our band, to the military hair-cut that Artorius insisted on: they had resentfully parted with their long, flowing locks.

'War demands its sacrifices,' Artorius told them crisply; 'you don't want your heads to become cities for lice, do you?'

When we left Elmet and rode into Alfin's settlement, we looked more like imperial cavalry; those old bronze helmets with their tufts of horsehair dyed red were impressive; the mounted youngsters now seemed far taller than they really were.

Alfin also reinforced our little army, and thirty of his large, muscular Saxons rode with us; Alfin, unable to ride himself, watched us depart; Gwinfreda and Merlin accompanied us for the first fifteen miles, turning back when we reached Onnum. Once past the Wall we sent scouts ahead and westwards, and a messenger to Maël at Luguvalium. We had left Alfin's settlement at dawn, and by dusk that day were deep in the heather-covered hills of northern Deur.

When making war against savages and barbarians no preconceived plan can be rigidly followed; their movements are unpredictable, for they are not led by professional soldiers who usually think in a professional way and are conventional and cautious. We could only hope that we had guessed right about the Pictish advance. Unfortunately we underrated their imagination, for one large party of them had seized some trading ships in the Clyde estuary, sailed south to the western end of the Wall, and landed below Luguvalium. When our messenger reached the place all he found were smoking ruins and the mutilated corpses of men, women and children. He told us that the Wall north of the city was intact, and though the gates were open, they had not been battered down, so presumably the place had not been taken by assault. Maël had lost his city, his hall, and probably his household: he may even have lost his life, but that seemed unlikely, for even so pacific a king would feel obliged to lead his forces to war in person, without waiting at home to be attacked.

Our messenger brought us the news as darkness fell. We had camped in an old fort, and sat up half the night discussing the changed situation. Finally we decided to modify our original plan. We invited Harad, the leader of Alfin's Saxon contingent, to join our Council of War; Artorius now spoke his tongue fluently, but although I understood it, the pronunciation often defeated me; so I kept quiet and listened when Harad spoke.

The Saxon was an elderly man, tall and powerfully built like most of his people; his long yellow hair dangled in two plaits to his belt; a thick beard hid his chest. Before we heard of the Pictish sea-raid, Harad had mentioned it as a possibility; seafaring Saxons understood the mobility of ships, which was more than I did at that time, for imperial military training ignored sea-power and in common with most soldiers I thought of ships either as floating fortresses or troop transports. Artorius, who had far more imagination than I could ever claim, grasped the point at once. If some Picts had come by sea, they could easily have taken Maël's city without having to break through the Wall. After sacking the place they may have gone south into Reged to ravage the country; so we divided our forces, and the next day Artorius led his band and the Saxons north, while I turned back accompanied by a score of veterans. We reached the ruins of Luguvalium in the afternoon.

On our way we discovered some fugitives from the city, hiding in one of the Wall forts, and from them we heard that what our Saxon ally had conjectured, had actually happened. Among the survivors were three seamen from the captured ships, who had managed to escape, and they told us where the vessels were lying; from some house slaves who had fled to safety we heard that Maël had divided his army, and sent part of it to protect his southern border, for he feared that Maelgwyn would seize the chance of invading Reged. So much for British unity and trust between Christian kings. The rest of his men he led north to join forces with the army of Strathclyde, leaving his city unprotected.

Details of the campaign and my part in it are of little value in this report. Artorius fought and won two battles, one far beyond the Antonine Wall on the foothills of the Caledonian mountains, the other further south, near the west coast. He lost fifteen of his band who threw their lives away in reckless exhibitions of what they called valour and Artorius called stupidity. All I did was to hunt down the Picts who had come by sea, recapture the trading ships, and rejoin Artorius when the country was clear.

We knew now that our horses, our weapons and the way we used both could bring victories, and we had also learned that the sea which surrounds Britain must never be forgotten.

XIII

The years of preparation

DURING THE FIVE YEARS that followed the early battles of the long Pict War, the map of Britain changed, for Maël lost southern Reged which was taken by Maelgwyn. That ruthless and ambitious young king now ruled a fertile province, which extended eighty miles north of Deva, bordered on the west by the Irish Sea and on the east by the kingdom of Elmet. His plan for uniting north-west Britain by conquest was now partly accomplished, for Maël, pious, peaceful and hopelessly ineffective, was incapable of expelling the invader: he had no army, no capital city, no home, hardly any wealth and lacked the ability to recruit and lead fresh forces. His long and earnest prayers were unanswered; so, like many disappointed Christians, he concluded that God was punishing him for his sins. In desperation, he swallowed his pride and pious prejudices and rode to Alfin's city in Deur, where Artorius was making a prolonged stay.

The Picts had been driven back into their mountains; their settlements in the lands beyond the Antonine Wall had been destroyed, and they were now a scattered nation of fugitives. They would recover in time, but our successful campaign had won some years of peace. Artorius felt entitled to what he stupidly called selfish indulgence, so preparations were made for his marriage to Gwinfreda, that was to take place just before the midwinter pagan feast of Yule, celebrated by the Saxons and other German tribes, to mark the turn of the year, and by Christians as the anniversary of Christ's birth. As Yule and Christmas coincided, Alfin's followers and the handful of Christians in Deur, including the prelates who were to officiate at the marriage ceremony, could meet without rancour, unless some bigoted fool destroyed the harmony of the occasion.

When King Maël arrived to beg for help in reconquering his lost territory, Artorius told him firmly that his sworn band would take no part in wars between British kingdoms. Maël then offered payment for help, though without specifying how such payment would be made; but that proposal was rejected even more firmly.

'We are not mercenaries,' said Artorius. 'We have vowed to free Britain from savages and barbarians. We fight for no other cause.'

With more spirit than we expected from him, Maël asked:

'Then why are you here in a barbarian's stronghold?'

'King Alfin of Deur is a loyal ally, and his warriors helped to defeat the Picts,' Artorius replied. He added that Maël must make his own peace with Maelgwyn; he offered no help or comfort to that weak king, who returned to what was left of Reged, disappointed and apprehensive.

'Woe to the weaker,' was Alfin's comment, when Artorius told him what had happened. He reflected, then said: 'Maelgwyn is now my neighbour. We must keep our swords very sharp.'

We spent the rest of the winter in the bleak and bitter north-east, though not in idleness, for Artorius drilled and exercised his band. Meanwhile Britain was quiet, and remained so for some time. We made good use of those peaceful years. For Artorius they were happy years, for he was blindly in love with Gwinfreda, blissfully unaware of her appetite for illicit adventures, and always eager to satisfy her whims. She was too wily to allow him to suspect the variety of her roving interests, but although much could be hidden from a husband, many members of his band became uneasily aware of what was happening; three of them deserted, which wounded Artorius, but his first and most trusted follower chose a tragic way of escape after we had left Deur and returned to our military headquarters at Corinium.

One spring morning, Agrippa, that good-looking, austere son of Lunaris, was found in his quarters with his throat cut, and a blood-stained knife beside him.

My cousin Marius had been in his confidence, for although

utterly different in temperament, they had become close friends, and he told me what had happened. Gwinfreda had pursued Agrippa relentlessly, and at last she tried the oldest trick in the world. Unless he yielded, she had threatened to tell Artorius that he had attempted to rape her: she gave him a week to think it over. Agrippa was in despair: he asked Marius for advice. Now my young relative was a realist, unfortunately in this case. 'You have three choices,' he told Agrippa. 'Sleep with the bitch, which would be *my* choice; run away and leave the band; or, if you can overcome your Christian scruples, end your life by your own hand.'

Marius was horrified when Agrippa had chosen the third way out of the trouble. 'I never thought he would,' he said, 'for suicide is a deadly sin, and he's lost his hope of Heaven, for he really believed in Heaven. If he'd only done what she wanted, she'd have soon grown tired of him as she did of me.'

He stopped abruptly. 'I didn't mean to tell you that,' he went on.

'I shall forget it,' I assured him, 'and I hope that you will too.'

Several peaceful years passed, while our strength as a warrior band increased in skill and size.

In the south-west, King Marc had waited too long to make an attack on Cerdic and his Saxons; year after year those barbarians had been reinforced by fresh shiploads of settlers, who gradually reclaimed the wilderness east of Dumnonia; so now Cerdic ruled a populous state, with prosperous farms and industrious farmers. Caution can be overdone, and Marc had been over-cautious. Swords need more than sharpening; they must drink blood. But Marc was a good friend to our plans; he had his price, of course, and it was a reasonable and sensible price.

We wanted ships and crews for our expedition to Armorica: Marc wanted big horses for his cavalry. Those splendid creatures eventually enabled us to mount the whole of our band, which now numbered over four hundred trained men. All our losses in the first and subsequent battles of the Pict War had been made good. We needed more armourers, for some of the smiths at Corinium had died of old age, others were becoming too feeble to work, and those em-

ployed on the Geladii estates could hardly keep pace with our needs.
We needed helmets, as those we had were old and wearing out, also
mail shirts to cover body and arms, close-fitting mail for the legs,
and longer and heavier swords. Native ponies would have foundered
under such a load of equipment, but our great horses could carry
any amount of weight. Thus armed and mounted our band was
invincible; nothing on foot could withstand our charging lines; no
enemy in all the battles we fought ever attempted to meet us on
horseback. Also we had weapons no armourer had made, something unknown to savages and barbarians, namely detailed maps
of Britain, covering the whole land south of Hadrian's Wall, also
sketch maps of the land far north, beyond the Antonine Wall, to
the distant northern coast of Caledonia; maps originally made by
surveyors and cartographers on the staff of Septimus Severus when
he marched his field army to the uttermost limits of the island, and
corrected and brought up to date a century later when Constantius
I and his son, the Great Constantine, followed the same route in
their Caledonian campaign.

(And here, in my report, I may venture to suggest that if and when
Britain is reunited to the Empire, the whole island should be held
and garrisoned, all Caledonia cleared of the Pictish savages, and the
Orcades, those islands of the northern seas, should be held too, so
that no sea raiders can land. Where Septimus Severus and Constantius failed, His Sacred and Imperial Majesty, Justinian, may well
succeed, for the campaigns of Artorius have prepared the way, and
the Picts are still cowed by the memory of his victories.)

We perfected our plans for a descent on Armorica, timing the
expedition for the late spring of the year 500, which Artorius considered a propitious year, as it marked the half millennium since the
birth of Christ. Merlin, for totally different reasons of some dim,
magical kind, also believed that it was a fortunate year. In my own
view, one year was as good as another; but the state of our armour
and weapons was such that further delay in replenishing them would
endanger the effectiveness of our band. We were well-informed
about our objectives, for Merlin had travelled in Armorica, which
the British settlers had already renamed Britannia; he knew where

their foundries and workshops were located, and could guide us to a sheltered inlet on the south coast, facing the Great Bay, two hours' march from the main settlement of craftsmen. I was in charge, and chose Marius as my second-in-command, for he was resourceful and reliable. With fifty veterans, half of them from the original force who had fought in our first battle, I led a manageable body, all men who had an eye for country, and could move silently. We proposed to land and march by night, and surprise the settlement just before dawn. A good many people would probably be hurt, and some killed; but I felt no tenderness for men who had bolted to safety and deserted their country when it needed them.

King Marc lent us a large, two-masted ship, the biggest in his small fleet, fast sailing, easily manageable, with that invaluable small sail, an *artemon*, set forward in the bows, so we could keep on course against the wind. Aft an auxiliary oar bank, four-a-side, was used for manœuvring the vessel in and out of harbours; in open water the oars were shipped inboard. There were big holds for cargo, which gave us ample room to accommodate our unwilling passengers.

We left at the beginning of the sailing season, embarking at the port where Artorius and I had landed six years earlier. Our course was almost due south, for Armorica juts out into the Atlantic, a big peninsula corresponding to Dumnonia. Our ship-master was Corimac, a tall, sinewy man of sixty, with a white beard and a dark tanned skin, who had followed the sea since he was a boy of nine. Although I commanded the expedition, I had no authority over the ship's company: I could give my orders to my own men but to nobody else. Corimac could read maps; those we brought with us were copied from an old imperial survey of southern Armorica, and Merlin had shown him where we wanted to land.

I shall not forget that voyage. On the passage from Alexandria to Britain I had mastered sea-sickness and acquired the art of walking on a heaving deck without falling over, but I soon discovered that the British Channel was alarmingly different from other seas; cross currents and odd gusts of wind that seem to blow from every quarter, and banks and patches of fog constantly challenge the skill of mariners. After three hours I had lost my sea-legs, as well as everything I had eaten that day. The trouble passed, and for a few hours we hoped to make good time, but a south-west gale caught us when we were within sight of the Armorican coast, sweeping us far up the Channel, almost to the Straits. We ran before it, and took four days to beat back to our destination.

We met no opposition on land or sea. Apart from fishing vessels and a few small trading ships, the British settlers have nothing afloat, certainly no warships capable of intercepting an invading force. The coasts of Armorica, Belgica and Aquitania lie open to attack from a British base; though any large expeditionary force ferried over from Britain would have to be protected by a fleet, not as large as the old imperial *classis Britannica* that formerly patrolled the narrow seas, but powerful enough to deal with any Frankish or Saxon warships. Pirates used to infest those seas, but for seventy years traffic between Britain and the old trading ports of Belgica has shrunk, and further west where the waves of the Channel and the Atlantic mingle, cargo vessels plying between Dumnonia and Aquitania sail in waters regularly patrolled by King Marc's cruisers. Pirates do occasionally raid the coasts of Armorica, but they never go far inland, unless they can steal some horses.

When subjects from British kingdoms emigrated to Armorica, often under the leadership of some local nobleman, their native habits were unchanged; congenital inability to work together for a common cause left their new homes defenceless: no army was ever raised, no protective warships ever built. They were armed, but used their weapons for fighting among themselves as senselessly and happily as they did in Britain. From what I heard such inter-tribal warfare (for that is what it really was) still continued, on and off, when I returned to the East, twenty-five years later. Philonides at our first meeting had suggested invading Belgica from Britain by crossing the Straits; like so many landsmen he was misled by the map. True the distance was shorter, but the Franks now held Belgica and they were warriors to be reckoned with, on land and sea; so I recommended Armorica; there were good landing grounds, and only a disorganized and divided enemy whose opposition imperial troops could easily brush aside.

When I described our successful raid, Philonides agreed that Armorica was a sensible choice. Merlin had been an excellent guide, and had taken us to a thick belt of woodland, half a mile from the settlement where the majority of the skilled workmen lived, and there we waited until the eastern sky paled.

At least a thousand people, men, women and children, must have inhabited that settlement; we wanted the men, not their families. There was no resistance; men sluggish with sleep were easily over-powered; they obeyed our orders, collected their tools and other belongings, and, roped together, two by two, we marched them down in columns to the sea and the waiting boats. The women were troublesome, screaming and clinging to their men; we tried not to be too rough with them, for I was anxious to avoid bloodshed, but one woman snatched a hammer from her man's tool-bag and attacked a trooper who had foolishly taken off his helmet to wipe his fore-head. It was a short-handled, heavy hammer and she smashed his skull with it, so we had to kill her. The captive men were a craven lot, and made no attempt to resist or escape.

We had found some ponies stabled in the settlement, so were able to mount some of our men. Both Marius and I had become so accustomed to the use of riding irons, that we felt strange without them. We also took a score of pack-mules, and loaded them with spare tools and equipment from the workshops. One of the troopers asked if we should set fire to the rows of workshops, but I detested wanton destruction. There is too much of it in the world today.

On our way back to the sea, we were accosted by a well-dressed young man, riding a splendid black horse and accompanied by an armed servant, also well-mounted. A long sword in a gilt leather scabbard hung by his side, and a black leather helmet cross-banded with polished steel crowned his long, curling yellow hair. A fair complexion and bright blue eyes proclaimed his Saxon origin, but he spoke the native Celtic tongue of Britain. He rode up to me, and with the confident authority of a nobleman said:

'And who in the name of God and His saints are you and *what* do you think you are doing here?'

I told him briefly the purpose of our mission and who had sent us.

'I have heard of this Artorius,' he said; 'a leader of mercenary troops, I believe.'

'Nothing of the kind,' I told him. 'Artorius is a senior tribune in the Household Guards of his Imperial Majesty, the Emperor, and is *dux Britanniarum*, commander-in-chief of the armed forces of Britain.'

'Yes,' he said, 'yes, no doubt. But who the devil *is* his Imperial Majesty and what is he emperor of?'

He was a well-spoken youngster, probably educated after a fashion, but I could never get used to western ignorance of the world. I tried to enlighten him, though he was far more interested in Artorius than in the Roman Empire of the East.

'If Artorius isn't a leader of mercenaries, then *what* is he? What is this band you speak of?'

His questions were insistent, but I don't think he understood all my answers. He rode down to the shore with us, where the ship's boats awaited our return. King Marc's warship was anchored half a mile offshore; a light breeze ruffled the surface of the sea; the boats with their passengers and guards rose and fell as they were rowed from shore to ship and back again. We had captured nearly four hundred men, and the embarkation took all the morning. There were only three boats.

The yellow-haired youth stayed to watch. Presently he said:

'You should know my name. I am Wencla and my family was founded by Swarf, the Saxon sea-king who ruled the narrow seas before he was defeated by Carausius over two hundred years ago. Men of his blood seized land here, and the family has held it ever since. I am the last of my line, the only child of my father, who died two years ago. God never intended me for a farmer: any clod can manage an estate and live in ease. My lands are some miles from here half-way to the northern coast.'

Having said so much, he fell silent, nor did he speak again until the last boat was ready to leave. We had turned our horses loose and they had wandered inland: some were caught and led away by a few women from the settlement who had trailed after us, and stood a little way off, watching us and shouting imprecations. I was about to bid farewell to Wencla, when he turned abruptly to his servant.

'Take my horse home,' he ordered.

'Yes, my lord,' said the man; 'and what shall I tell the manager?'

'Anything you like,' Wencla snapped; to me he said: 'I am coming with you.' And with that he stepped into the waiting boat and sat down by the man at the tiller. I hesitated a moment before giving the order to shove off, but I decided to say nothing. Wencla smiled at me; a friendly smile that did something to diminish the arrogance of his next words. 'I have a mind to join that band you speak of,' he said; 'I have no doubt that Artorius will recognize me as an asset. I can use weapons.'

'Can you swim?' I asked.

'Swim?' he repeated; 'why of course.'

'Just as well,' I said; 'you may have to if you should change your mind.'

Our passage back to Britain was favoured by a steady south-easterly breeze, so we made good time, until we rounded the westerly capes of Armorica, when the long Atlantic swell treated us roughly. Most of our prisoners and some of the troopers were sick, but I survived the crossing without trouble; so did Wencla. That young man was intensely curious about everything connected with the working of the ship; he spent much time with Corimac, plying the master with questions, and listening to his yarns. All seamen tell interminable stories about their voyages and adventures, willingly enough if you encourage them and like listening to expert lying. Wencla could read and he understood Latin though he seldom spoke it; he had never seen any maps and soon grasped their meaning. He was very quick-minded.

'This is what we see in bits but made flat,' he said, when I had unrolled maps of western Armorica that Merlin had prepared. He improved his knowledge after we landed and rode to Corinium, for I gave him maps of our route, and he followed them carefully, checking the course of the road, the streams we crossed, and the position of rest houses and military stations. He stored this information in his head, and gave it all back to me, mile by mile, without any omissions, when we reached Corinium. Barbarians have astonishing memories; unable to read or write they rely on their innate gift for recalling everything they hear, unaided by notes and records. In this, Wencla was like a barbarian, but in no other way. He was not an easy man to understand; his independence, his almost fierce self-sufficiency, would have seemed intolerably arrogant had it not been accompanied by an eagerness to learn and a readiness to listen. He was argumentative, he asked challenging questions, and if the answers didn't satisfy him he said so with such innocent frankness that nobody could feel offended by his doubts and reservations.

Artorius welcomed him, and was surprised and rather puzzled by some of the objections he made to taking an oath of loyalty and service to the band and its leader.

'I am prepared to learn your ways, and to accept your discipline,' said Wencla; 'you have your own methods of warfare, so I shall learn them, drill with your band and follow you in war and obey your orders; but I do not nor shall I ever surrender the right to private judgement. I am not without experience: I have killed men and fathered men. Is that enough for you?'

'No it's not,' Artorius replied. 'Are you a Christian? You don't sound like one.'

'I have been told that my parents had me baptized,' said Wencla; 'so I suppose I am a Christian because of that, but for no other reason. I detest priests; they talk too much and teach hard-working slaves to be idle and to justify idleness.'

They continued arguing, and after a time I stopped listening. It ended when Artorius said at last:

'I believe that you are at heart a Christian, though you don't seem to know it. So I shall accept you for my band.'

'You won't regret that decision,' Wencla said; then checked himself and added: 'I hope my deeds will prove my words.'

He had no false modesty, though his good opinion of himself never tempted him to boast; he was a cheerful companion, and time passed briskly in his company. He soon became popular with the band, and very friendly with my cousin Marius. But I was worried about him, for when he was presented to Gwinfreda, her considering look of appraisal reminded me of the way she had looked at the wretched Agrippa the first time she met him.

The summer passed, we put our captured smiths to work, and that autumn were able to re-arm the band. As I have said before, this is not a personal account; but before winter came I had married into the British branch of the Geladii family. Lavinia became my wife, well aware of all the disadvantages of marrying a serving soldier, for I had concealed nothing from her or from my father-in-law, Julius Nonna. She knew that for weeks and months at a time I should be away on campaigns; a year or more might pass without her knowing where I was or how I fared, for in the lawless land we lived in, solitary couriers with letters did not always survive the hazards of travel: brigands had increased their numbers even in the few years I had been in Britain, and no king used his army for policing the surviving roads. Only parties of six or more armed men could be certain of reaching their destination.

Julius Nonna gave us a suite of rooms in his spacious house, so Lavinia was spared the cramped married quarters which were all I could have offered her if we lived together at military headquarters in Corinium; she knew that at some time in the future I should have to return to Constantinople, and that we'd end our lives far away from Britain, unless I happened to be killed in battle. All this she accepted cheerfully and without complaint, and although I saw more of her than I'd expected to during the first years of our marriage, there were long periods of separation later, when I was with Artorius and his band in Caledonia, and beyond in the Orcades, those storm-swept, treeless islands where barbarians from the white lands of the north had tried to settle. So Lavinia remained in the home of her childhood, and there our three sons were born and grew to manhood. I had little to do with their upbringing; as boys they were almost strangers to me, and when they grew up, strangers they remained. As I said earlier in this account, they are outside my story, and I am conscious of my shortcomings as a father for we have few interests in common and nothing to say to each other when we meet.

Artorius and I made plans together for the invasion and reconquest of the old kingdom of the Regni, where the Saxon king Aelle now ruled. For this we should need more than our band, and as we'd both wearied of the obstructive and unhelpful kings of Britain when they met in Council, we decided to make sure of some reliable allies before we began a campaign. The most promising was King Marc; but he refused to join us unless we first helped him expel Cerdic from his settlement. This seemed sensible. Our plan was to invade the south Saxon kingdom of Aelle from the north; if we first disposed of Cerdic, we marched in from the east instead.

'Why march?' asked Marc. 'I shall attack Cerdic from the sea, where he least expects attack; then your band can come in from the north. Later, when you invade Aelle's kingdom, my ships can land an army anywhere along the coast.'

Once again we had forgotten the sea. And as we made our plans and studied our maps we also forgot how tempting Britain must seem even in its present state, to the sea-rovers from the bitter lands of the far north. Those plans for attacking Cerdic and the South Saxons were indefinitely delayed.

XIV

The Easterlings

MERLIN as a recognized bard enjoyed freedom of movement throughout Britain, and except in Maelgwyn's realm was sure of a welcome everywhere, even among the Angles in the kingdom they had founded in the flat, fertile lands facing the North Sea. He could sing the traditional songs those former Germanic tribesmen understood and liked to hear; the verses he composed also won their applause; the themes were as familiar as the poems of the skalds which Merlin knew well; long depressing poems that preserve gloomy legends and tales of terror and towering courage, of doomed heroes, of battles lost and joyless victories; tragic tales of endless strife beneath an ever-darkening sky of hopelessness, with warriors awaiting Ragnarök, the final battle that destroys the world. Those German and northern barbarians are not cheerful peoples; perhaps that is why they habitually drink themselves into oblivion, to shut out the vision of a frightful future. Merlin was familiar with their ferocious, hard-drinking gods, and the servants of those gods, like the Wish-Maidens, the Valkyries, who rule and decide the fate of warriors; he knew the characteristics of that savage crew of deities as well as he knew the civilized pantheon of Rome and the complexities of the Holy Trinity. His training as a Druid had given him immunity from the variously ridiculous beliefs that sustain so many men and comfort (or delude) nearly all women. Perhaps that cold immunity, and his complete detachment from ordinary life and human foibles, enabled him to see things as they are; hard and sharply defined in what he claimed to be the clear light of ancient wisdom.

I was frankly bored by his pontifical pronouncements, but I respected his common sense and I realized that his powers of observation and persuasion (when he chose to be persuasive), were of immense use to us in our dealings with British kings and barbarian chieftains. Young members of the band, like Marius and Wencla, were unimpressed: they scoffed at his pretensions. Wencla as an Armorican nobleman knew something of the influence Druids had formerly exercised in his country, and which they still wielded in remote parts of it. What Merlin called ancient wisdom, they called magic, and although they laughed at his solemnity and Wencla mimicked him, I could see that neither of those youngsters, so different in upbringing and yet so strangely alike in many ways, wholly disbelieved in Merlin's powers. But Merlin's status as a bard served us well, for during the winter months he travelled widely, accompanied by Bran and Thord, spending weeks at a time as the welcome guest of kings and nobles, in different parts of Britain, returning to our headquarters when the dark months had passed, bringing news of happenings in far-off places, and rumours he had picked up which gave us early warning of trouble brewing in lands beyond the seas that girdled the island.

Early in the spring of the year 501, he came back to Corinium after a long visit to the Angles, where he had spent Yule and the rest of the winter with their king Ringvald, who ruled over a mixed population of German settlers and native British, the latter descended from the ancient Iceni tribe whose queen, Boadicea, had nearly succeeded in regaining British independence. They still sang songs about her, and thought of themselves as the Iceni; their German conquerers called them the Ickenny folk. Much of their land was below sea level, and as the sea-wall, built by Roman engineers generations ago, had been damaged and never properly repaired, good corn land was gradually being swallowed up as the marshes advanced and the draining ditches became blocked and useless. It was the old story of ignorant barbarians without technical skills losing every benefit that civilization confers. King Ringvald was greatly troubled, not by the inroads of the sea and the loss of fertile fields, but by the increasing number of raids by Easterlings, as the Saxons and Angles call the sea-rovers who come from the bitter northern and eastern lands, men of a kindred race who live by ravaging other countries, and are as much in love with fighting as the Irish, and even better at it.

Artorius held a Council of War to consider Merlin's report; senior members of the band attended, and some junior officers too, among them Marius and Wencla, for the latter had soon proved to be a born leader, and a popular one, who wore his authority easily. Gwinfreda always attended our Councils, for Artorius honoured the Saxon custom of allowing women liberties that no Roman lady of noble birth ever enjoyed or even expected. Although she took part in our deliberations, attempting to sustain an unnatural solemnity though unable to control her impulse to giggle, she was a light creature; all she ever contributed was the barbarian point of view, which was occasionally valuable, as barbarians, especially those of German origin, think quite differently from Romans and Greeks; in fact they seldom think at all; they are moved by impulse and would be completely governed by their appetites which are restrained only by their sense of honour and respect for truth. Crude savages they may be, but they always tell the truth and keep their promises.

I resented Gwinfreda's presence at those council meetings; she was a disturbing influence, perhaps for the reason Wencla gave when he said: 'She's all body and no mind.' At heart she was concerned only with her father's kingdom of Deur; for her the conception of a united Britain was incomprehensible, perhaps understandably, because it implied the ultimate dominance of the Roman-British over the Saxons and Angles and other Germanic settlers; her interests and loyalties were made sun-clear when we discussed the growing threat of the Easterlings and King Ringvald's fear of them.

'The best defence is often attack,' said Artorius thoughtfully; 'with a few ships we could land armed parties to destroy one or more of their ports.'

He was beginning to think constructively about sea-power; but our strength lay in our use of heavy, armoured cavalry. True, we could find men for such raids if we could persuade King Marc to find the ships to carry them; but to make the best use of our forces we should meet the Easterlings on land and ride them down; that meant waiting until they invaded some part of Britain. I said so.

'That is the course of prudence,' Merlin observed, smoothing his beard. He added that although Ringvald's kingdom had been attacked, no landings had been made elsewhere; hitherto the raids were on a small scale, intended perhaps to probe Ringvald's defences in preparation for a full-scale invasion, something sustained and aiming at permanent settlement.

'We could easily reinforce Ringvald,' said Artorius; 'would he welcome our help in preventing the Easterlings from getting a footing in Britain?'

'No!' Merlin was emphatic. 'He thinks of the British as Romans. Ringvald hates everything Roman,' he went on; 'he has rooted out all traces of Roman power; he's destroyed forts, signal stations and marching camps, even rest houses on the main roads; but he has left the native population unharmed, because they hated everything Roman too, and kept their tribal pride and identity as the Iceni. They preferred a barbarian ruler to a horde of imperial officials. The Ickenny folk are Ringvald's loyal subjects: they would be against you too.'

Gwinfreda made a grimace when he said 'barbarian'. I saw Wencla grinning at her, so she laughed and put in her word.

'Is Ringvald important?' she asked. 'Surely we should be thinking of helping my father if the Easterlings attack Deur.'

'I don't think that the Easterlings are likely to,' said Artorius; 'King Alfin as our ally would of course have our immediate help; but we cannot predict where they'll make their next attack. I'm afraid that King Marc is going to be disappointed; we can't begin a war against Cerdic and dissipate our strength. Cerdic will have to wait.'

The expulsion of Cerdic and his Saxon settlers came up year after year for discussion at our war councils, but Artorius and his band had far too many urgent calls on their strength to spare time for a campaign in the south-west; meanwhile Cerdic's power increased; the population of his small, compact state expanded steadily as shiploads of his land-seeking countrymen arrived regularly in the sailing season. Some years after the victory of Badon, King Marc resolved to attack Cerdic alone, and did so, with disastrous results. His army was broken and scattered at a river crossing on his eastern border. That battle of Cerdicsford, as it was named, was never forgotten: it ended Dumnonian military power. But that happened many years later than the raids of the Easterlings. Two months after Merlin had told us about them they landed in the thinly populated marshlands of Lindissi, the country that lies east of Elmet and takes its name from the walled city of Lindum, which, like Londinium, had been slowly dying for over half a century.

We heard that a fleet of two hundred long, black-painted undecked ships had brought them from their northern homelands; so at least ten thousand warriors were loose in Britain, huge fearless men, accustomed to victory who welcomed death in battle. Any other form of death they held to be disgraceful. Against this army we brought an armoured and disciplined band, superior in weapons and mobility. Our numbers by comparison seemed absurdly small, but although we felt confidently superior, we didn't belittle the enemy: these northern giants were very different from wiry, half-naked Pictish hordes. The Easterlings were above all other things, cunning.

They were quick to learn. Our first encounters taught them that a shield wall could not stop a charge from mail-clad men superbly mounted. After heavy losses they gave up trying to stand against us: instead they threw themselves flat on the ground with their shields held over their heads, and let us ride over them; after our line passed they sprang up and slashed at the horses' hocks. A hamstrung horse is useless. Dismounted, we were hampered by the weight of our armour, and no match for a leather-clad Easterling wielding a double-edged sword or a long-handled double-axe. So we changed our tactics and relied far more on our initial attack with arrows shot from the saddle.

Lunaris sent his small army to join us; they marched in from Elmet, and few survived. Our losses in men were not heavy, but the maiming of so many horses by depriving us of mobility and superior weight in battle, prolonged the war, and six weeks passed before we could bring remounts from Gwent.

AR –F

While we were fighting the Easterlings in Lindissi, Maelgwyn seized the opportunity to complete his conquest of the north-west. He invaded what remained of Reged, and marched north into Strathclyde where he defeated the army of King Coroticus. King Maël, dispossessed and a fugitive, found refuge in Deur, where Alfin with characteristic generosity treated him as an honoured guest.

'My father has always been kind to fools,' was Gwinfreda's comment.

Maelgwyn soon discovered that a military victory, however glorious and heartening it seems to be at the time, does not guarantee docile acceptance of alien rule by the vanquished. The field army of Strathclyde was dispersed; men who prefer flight to death in battle can in time recover their courage and be willing to fight again; so Maelgwyn had the task of controlling a large kingdom, with only one city, scattered villages that were little more than groups of miserable huts, no towns, two old military roads in bad repair, and a half-savage population, as hostile as an angry sea. Warfare continued. Coroticus, unable to muster an army strong enough to meet the invader in battle, used small groups of archers to harass his enemies by day and night, but more especially at night. If Maelgwyn's men camped anywhere on the heather-covered hills and shallow valleys, they were smoked out; dry heather burns fast, and although the natives were destroying their bee pasture they did so willingly at the bidding of their king. As the summer months passed, the campaign must have become a nightmare for Maelgwyn; he was tormented by the tactics of his enemies, but even more by his own fears. Unable to trust anybody, he was suspicious of the motives of Artorius, and bewildered by his silence, for no word of protest or warning was sent from our headquarters; we were far too busy dealing with the Easterlings, and when at last we cleared Lindissi of their roving bands, we had another little war on our hands, for Ringvald marched his army west and invaded the Midlands.

He had to be stopped. Fortunately replacements for our maimed horses arrived from Julius Nonna's stud before he had reached

Ratae, that almost empty little city. Instead of pursuing him, we rode south-east skirting the Metaris, the shallow bay that separates Lindissi from the old Iceni territory, for we intended to invade his kingdom. We forded the rivers that flow into the bay, crossing expanses of marshy land on causeways still intact, until we reached Ringvald's chief settlement. We were angry with that barbarian, for by fighting and defeating the Easterlings we had dealt with his enemies as well as our own, and his unprovoked aggression confirmed all Merlin had said about his hatred of everything Roman. In Ringvald's view the kingdoms of Britain were merely components of an imperial province, while our band represented resurgent Roman power.

Bad news has wings, so Ringvald soon heard that we were loose in his lands, burning settlements and farmsteads and collecting saleable stock for the slave markets of Corinium, Gwent and Demetia. He halted his invading force within sight of Ratae, turned back and rode eastwards as fast as stolen ponies and farm horses could carry his men; and when he met our band, he also met death and defeat, for his warriors were not quick learners like the Easterlings. They dismounted to fight on foot, and were demoralized by the shower of arrows we loosed as we circled about them; their small round shields of painted wood gave little protection from steel-tipped shafts, winged with goose feathers. Our first charge scattered them, and as they ran we cut them down without mercy. We took no prisoners.

Compared with the Easterlings they were a poor lot; two generations removed from the tough sea-rovers who had originally conquered the land and softened by years of security and fat living. Now we were faced with the task of occupying and trying to govern that land, a task which will also face the commander of any successful expeditionary force His Sacred and Imperial Majesty, the Emperor Justinian, may at some future time order to Britain. Our numbers were far too small for effective military occupation, and no civilian help was anywhere available; no trained administrative staff existed outside a few shrinking cities, and their members were always fully employed, responsible to a Municipal Curia, and tied to their day-to-day work. Provisionally we had to leave the government of that sparsely populated region to the chiefs who owned the largest estates and had some local authority. Germanic tribal customs had long replaced Roman law and order; crude codes that at least prevented the illiterate farmers and their slaves and bondsmen from robbing and murdering each other; allowing them to pass their dull brutish lives in lonely villages and farmsteads, in peace if not in amity.

We were as unwelcome to Ringvald's Angles as we were to those descendants of the original British stock, the so-called Ickenny folk, proud and obstinate people who rejected any form of orderly government that suggested bygone imperial rule. Temperamentally quarrelsome, unstable and shiftless, chained to tribal memories of defeat, conquest, oppression and futile rebellion, they were unable to work together or agree among themselves. They repudiated Christianity, and condemned the Church as an instrument for extending and perpetuating Roman rule. As native British stock, they were preferable to those alien land-thieves, the Angles. Nothing more could be said in their favour.

This intractable problem troubled and divided our war council every time we discussed it. The simplest solution—brutal and final—was to massacre the entire population of Angles, but Artorius objected. Barbarians and demon-worshippers though they were, he urged that some attempt should be made to convert them. Once they had abandoned their pagan gods, they would be acceptable as an allied Christian state.

We had forgotten the promise in Merlin's provocative song that had made Maelgwyn his enemy. I couldn't resist quoting one line.

'Who'll drive the blond savages back to the sea?' I asked.

Artorius was silent; he may have been pondering an answer, but Wencla spoke first.

'I hope, my lord, that members of your band whose hair happens to be fair, like mine, will not be regarded as savages; and what about our Saxon allies in Deur?'

This barbed reference to Gwinfreda and her father irritated Artorius, but he kept his temper and replied calmly enough:

'This is no matter for jesting.'

'My lord, when I joined your band, I took no vow of solemnity,' said Wencla; 'when I feel like laughing, I shall laugh. Laughter is a Christian privilege and no sin; laughter is ennobling, a gift from God enjoyed by man alone and not shared by any other living creature, and being God-given it makes a laughing man almost god-like, especially when he laughs at himself.'

'Are you certain that you are not in spiritual peril by uttering heresies of your own contriving?' asked Artorius.

Wencla had the good sense to stop. After a long pause, the Council resumed the unprofitable discussion about governing that Anglian kingdom. No conclusions were reached then or later; events moved too fast for us.

XV

The relief of Deva

••

THE EASTERLINGS came again: tireless, warlike, adventurous and masters of sea-craft. Britain attracted them as a prize of great promise. Some hundreds had escaped from Lindissi in their long ships, and summer was over before they made their next raid. Not so many came this time. The fleet that carried them sailed down from northern waters and, keeping within sight of land, followed the west coast of Caledonia, shortly after the first of the autumn gales had blown itself out, passing the straits between north-east Ireland and Britain, down through the Hibernian Sea to the Dee mouth. They found their way through the winding channels that threaded the sandbanks of the broad estuary, rowed upstream and landed on the Peninsula where the river suddenly narrows, and besieged Deva.

This invasion brought Maelgwyn and his army hurrying back from Strathclyde by forced marches. The king, impatient and furiously angry, behaved like a rash fool. His men, exhausted and in no condition to attempt the relief of his chief city, were ordered to attack the Easterlings. They had the worst of it. Accustomed to victory and always expecting to win, wounded pride destroyed his judgement, and tempted him to further folly. After a few days' rest he made another effort to cut his way through the Easterlings who surrounded Deva. Rage and courage were of no avail against their overwhelming superiority of numbers, and when his second attack failed he was no longer in command of an army; merely a disorganized rabble of weary and frightened survivors. He retreated in shameful haste, barely escaping capture. With less than four hundred men he marched south to Viroconium, and from there dispatched couriers to Artorius, appealing for help. His ambitious dream of unifying and ruling the north-west was fading; survival was now his chief concern, and he stayed behind the walls of Viroconium, anxiously awaiting Artorius and his band. His messengers went first to our headquarters at Corinium, but we were still in Ringvald's former kingdom, so some weeks passed before we heard of his plight.

Meanwhile the Easterlings remained in their camp, hoping to take the fortress city, but like so many other barbarians, ill-equipped with knowledge or technical skill for such an enterprise. At least three thousand of them waited patiently in a great circle round the city, beyond the range of catapults and arrows, but patience is useless without siege engines. Impregnable Roman walls guarded Deva, rising in places to forty feet, with catapults mounted on the tops of alternate guard towers. Every man of the garrison was a trained archer. The city wanted for nothing, and could resist for months, relying on deep wells and great stores of provisions.

Those rust-hued sandstone walls had withstood many sieges in the past; by raiding tribesmen of the Ordovices and Deceangli; by Irish armies and other sea-borne enemies. The lives of hundreds of warriors were spent in vain attempts to scale the walls and batter down the iron-banded wooden gates. The fortress city had never yielded. Nobody ever forgot that it had been the home base of the XXth, the Valeria Victrix, most famous of the three legions which had once formed the old British Army; like Isca in Gwent, the old headquarters of the IInd, the place was also known as the City of the Legion; so it came about that nearly one hundred and twenty years after the XXth had paraded there for the last time before they marched away with Magnus Maximus to conquer the West, Roman military power was reasserted by a greater general, by Artorius, *dux Britanniarum*, whose name seems likely to be remembered in that strange and savage island, long after that of Maximus is forgotten.

Autumn had ended before we were able to complete our plans for attacking the besiegers. We had withdrawn every available trained man from Corinium to reinforce our band, and fresh recruits came in to swell our numbers, which were still greatly inferior to those of the Easterlings. We kept the recruits in reserve: eager young men, inexperienced in war and without military discipline, are often an encumbrance on a campaign, for nobody has time to teach them sense.

Our command was not divided. Artorius refused to share responsibility with Maelgwyn.

'Obey my orders, or fight on your own,' he told him; adding: 'And if you do fight on your own, don't get in my way.'

Maelgwyn who had not suspected this hard side of his character, was surprised by it, so were many of the band: but the king had to swallow his pride and agree; apart from the imperative need to relieve Deva, other troubles were darkening the future. King Coroticus had become active directly his lands were clear of Maelgwyn's occupying troops; assembling a fresh army, he invaded Reged. Before the first snows had made the country impassable, he had established winter quarters some eighty miles south of Hadrian's Wall, manning all the forts that had been left empty and neglected under Maël's pacific rule, and settling down comfortably with his staff and bodyguard in the barracks of a large military station a little way inland, between the coast and the hills. While he was enjoying his bloodless conquest of Maelgwyn's recently-acquired territory, the Picts encouraged by his absence were massing on the northern border of Strathclyde. War breeds war. Coroticus had forgotten how quickly those resilient savages could reassemble their tribal units; but many weeks passed before any warning reached him of this menace from the Caledonian highlands, and by then he was snow-bound.

Although the truth was not apparent until much later, the invasions by the Easterlings and Ringvald and the revival of the Picts marked the beginning of a war that lasted for nearly twenty years; long years they seemed, with the seat of war shifting to different parts of Britain, and beyond, to the Orcades. We fought and won many battles, and of these, two were outstanding and lit the imagination of British bards. For a change they sang the praises of victory instead of glorifying defeats and disasters. The first was the relief of the City of the Legion, and that was achieved by craft and careful planning; not by costly fighting, and victory came on Christmas Day, when the Easterlings were celebrating their Yuletide feast and drinking deeply.

Winter in Britain tests the endurance of the hardiest: men freeze to death, lose their way in the snow that hides all landmarks, and sink helplessly in deep drifts. Hardened from birth by the rigours of an even colder region, the Easterlings fared better than the British, and knew how to keep warm. They were skilled axe-men who felled trees and built strong, weather-proof huts of trimmed logs. They ringed Deva with a wooden town, protected by a palisade of stakes ten feet high. Heavy, well-guarded gates let their foraging parties and hunters pass out. Beyond their fortified camp our lines formed an outer circle of leather tents and shelters of intertwined branches, neither warm nor weather-proof. But we had plenty of food, and knew that the Easterlings were short of it, for they made many sorties in pursuit of game, and lost heavily in men until the whole countryside lay under thick snow and our great horses were useless. We sent them back to our headquarters, and so lost our military superiority; but we still had two assets denied to the Easterlings; discipline and archers. The Easterlings made little use of the bow; perhaps because they were poor marksmen; they preferred fighting at close quarters; man for man they were heavier, taller and more powerful than we were. Their fighting patrols challenged us daily, attacking in all weathers, the big men charging through blinding snowstorms, swinging their axes, clad only in their shirts, scorning body armour, but with black iron helmets protecting their heads, and small round shields of wood and leather on their left arms to ward off arrows. Before we sent our mounts away, their object was to break through our lines and maim as many horses as they could reach, for they knew how much we depended on them; but thereafter their aim was to reduce our strength, and no day passed without some loss to our band. They outnumbered us by at least five to one, though they always attacked in small groups and never sent a great mass of warriors to overwhelm us.

I have said that we were well-provisioned; we also had many casks of metheglin, kept under guard in a stone-built store down by the river, a mile behind our lines. Four days before Christmas we rolled those casks by night to our camp, and distributed them among the tents and shelters. Then we formed up, and marched south down the road to Viroconium. The first part of the battle plan was completed: we were sure that the Easterlings would willingly carry out the rest of it, nor were we mistaken. We posted a few well-hidden watchers to keep an eye on enemy movements and they sent runners back to report to us, for we had only marched some ten miles south of Deva, halting at the disused potteries between the military road and the Dee, which was narrow there and frozen from bank to bank. We sheltered from the biting wind in the ruined huts of former slave quarters, and some of us crowded into the larger tile kilns, which were at least weather-proof: the huts were roofless. The news we had hoped for came soon.

The Easterlings had found out almost at once that we had deserted our camp, and poured through their gates to overrun our lines. Satisfied that we had accepted defeat and gone for good, they settled down to feasting on the smoked deer meat and bacon we had left, and broached the casks of metheglin. Those huge men have vast appetites; eating, drinking and fighting are their chief pleasures, and their great reserves of strength enable them to continue fighting on little or no food far longer than any other barbarians and infinitely longer than soldiers of professional armies.

We allowed them three days of intensive self-indulgence, then we returned on the afternoon of Christmas Eve, marching slowly. A strong north wind stormed down the road against us as we approached our old lines in the deepening dusk. Darkness had fallen before we reoccupied them, and were joined by our watchers. The Easterlings, they told us, had shut their gates, but had posted no sentinels, so their camp was unguarded while they settled down to their Yuletide drinking. We ignored the gates; any attempt to batter them down would have wasted time and made a lot of noise, and it was easy enough to scale an undefended ten foot barrier of stakes. We climbed over the north side, which we chose so that the wind would favour our enterprise.

Although snow covered everything, none had fallen for over a week, so the wooden huts, well-warmed by fires burning night and day on stone hearths and in sunk trenches, were dry. The Easterlings had felled a thick wood of tall firs to build those huts; drops and trickles of resin oozing from the log walls diffused an aromatic fragrance. From within the larger huts, shouting and singing and gales of laughter marked the progress of riotous feasting: now and then men staggered out to spew: none returned. We saw to that. Nobody in the unguarded camp suspected our presence; the snow underfoot silenced our stealthy passage from hut to hut, as we carried armfuls of brushwood and dried twigs and bags of fir cones which we piled against the north walls. We found our way about easily; the white ground lessened the gloom of a moonless night, and no clouds hid the pale starlight.

Artorius lit the first fire, and that was the signal for kindling all the others. As hut after hut caught and began to blaze and crackle, those within seemed unaware of what was happening; many were asleep, others helplessly drunk. Only those with the strongest heads managed to stagger through the doorways, and the last sound they heard was the whistle of our arrows.

I saw Wencla waving a flaming branch and dancing.

'Smell the burning meat?' he shouted; 'we've given the wolves a hot meal.'

Long before dawn, Deva was surrounded by an irregular wall of trembling flames, which daylight changed to rosy smoke and later to black, billowing clouds, while sooty smuts rained down on the relieved city. No Easterlings escaped: our victory was complete, and Wencla, cheerfully boastful, put into words what many were thinking.

'This night's work will be well spoken of,' he remarked.

'We have been doing God's work,' Artorius reminded him gravely; but Wencla was irrepressible. 'And Maelgwyn's,' he said, grinning.

The young king ignored him: recent misfortunes had cooled his temper though he was still incapable of understanding the motives of Artorius, for he said:

'Now we must drive that insolent animal Coroticus out of Reged, back to his hovels in the heather of Strathclyde. My lord, Artorius: you and your band are fortunate in war: may we march together and win another victory?'

We stood there, in the light of a wintry sun: Artorius, his staff, and a group of junior officers, Maelgwyn and two of his captains; all of us dirty, dishevelled and clammy with dried sweat. Only men of British stock could at such a time argue about the rights and wrongs of fresh wars.

'Maelgwyn, we have been and shall, I hope, again be allies,' said Artorius, speaking slowly (and I realized that, through desperate weariness his patience was near breaking point); 'but I take no part in wars between brethren. They are unchristian, evil and senseless, as so many evil actions are. The kingdom of Reged has its own ruler: King Maël. Neither you nor Coroticus have any right there at all.'

'My right is the right of conquest,' Maelgwyn retorted; 'that imitation saint who called himself a king couldn't defend his kingdom; as for Coroticus, he wouldn't have dared to march south if I hadn't been compelled to fight the Easterlings.'

'Forget such sinful ambitions, and give thanks to God rather for your happy deliverance from peril,' said Artorius. 'Now, Maelgwyn, your chief city, the City of the Legion, is free. Go to it, so the defenders may open the gates and welcome their rightful ruler.'

'Not alone,' Maelgwyn told him; 'they owe their deliverance to you, so we go together.' His generosity had, for the moment, vanquished his arrogance.

So they marched side by side away from the charred and smouldering camp of the Easterlings, past the amphitheatre gateway where the statue of Mars still brandished his broken spear, to be saluted by the garrison, drawn up on parade outside the city walls.

That night Maelgwyn gave a feast for Artorius and his staff, in the hall of the Praetorium, where his father had once entertained us and Merlin had sung his tactlessly prophetic song.

The next day we began our march back to Corinium. Maelgwyn had his city again—and something more. Ice-bound but undamaged, the Easterlings' long ships were locked in the frozen river alongside the wharves of Deva. The king had lost an army and gained a fleet.

XVI

British quarrels

WE SPENT the remaining winter months peacefully in Corinium, our days fully occupied by routine drills and training exercises, activities that disillusioned many youngsters who had recently joined the Band, filled with high hopes of exciting adventures and warlike expeditions. As time passed they discovered that the day-to-day enemy, and most persistent one in a soldier's life, is boredom. Corinium offered few diversions; although the city had formerly been a pleasant enough place, its civic and social character had changed when over forty years earlier it became British military headquarters, taken over and governed by the *dux Britanniarum*. Life in barracks can be tolerable if you are a professional soldier; there are sporting and other relaxations though some were denied to the young volunteer members of the Band, for while Artorius allowed and promoted riding contests and horse racing, he abolished the military brothels; a futile gesture as any man desiring recreation could pick up what he wanted in the luxurious City Baths that still flourished despite the efforts of successive bishops to have them closed. A few members got married. Artorius might agree with St Paul that 'It is better to marry than to burn', nevertheless he discouraged such marriages though he didn't forbid them. He believed that a soldier should remain single without domestic ties, though he couldn't say so in view of his own marriage and mine.

Young Marius attributed this semi-official discouragement of the married state to Gwinfreda's influence.

'She likes plenty of young innocents to play with,' he said; 'she relishes variety too, but knows that young wives protect their husbands even from would-be queens.'

'What folly is this about queens?' I demanded.

'Perhaps I'm looking ahead too far, cousin Cay,' he said; 'but as a junior officer I hear far more gossip than you do, and Artorius naturally hears nothing at all, for two good reasons: he's the commander-in-chief and a husband.'

The malaise that descended on the Band could have been lifted by active service, though we were denied such relief because Artorius would make war only in a just cause and against barbarian enemies. He invariably refused to become involved in British quarrels and rightly so; nor would he help those well able to help themselves as Coroticus found out when he begged for immediate aid against the Picts who were probing his defences and threatening to spill over their frontier into Strathclyde.

'If you can raise an army to invade Reged, you can use it for defence instead of aggression,' Artorius told him.

There were other requests for the services of the Band, including some from that unpractical ass Honorius of Gwent, who wanted a punitive expedition dispatched to Ireland to stop raiders. There had only been one raid by Irish pirates since he last complained. King Marc came with his bodyguard on a prolonged visit, with renewed proposals for the expulsion of Cerdic and his Saxon settlers. He seemed friendly and apparently enjoyed the company of our officers: he may have thought that he could secure support for his plans by cultivating the impulsive young hotheads among them, but soon became aware that they regarded their oath of service to the Band very seriously. He was told so firmly but quite politely. Wencla saw a lot of him; they used to go for long rides together, and I gathered that King Marc did most of the listening. He probably felt more at ease with an Armorican nobleman than he did with any of us.

No matter how friendly and familiar Marc became with members of the Band and our staff at headquarters, he was no longer on intimate terms with Artorius, who was expertly evasive, like all British noblemen when they are asked to promise anything. Greater experience of war and military success had hardened his resolution to conserve the strength of the Band and to engage his forces only against aggressive savages, like the Picts or Easterlings. If the Picts had mounted a large-scale invasion of Strathclyde, he would certainly have ridden north to support Coroticus; but he had long since modified his views about Saxons; apart from his alliance with Alfin of Deur, Gwinfreda's influence encouraged him to regard her countrymen as potential allies; he was even prepared to believe that some day Cerdic might be as amenable as Alfin and as trustworthy. Some years later that Saxon chief destroyed such innocent hopes by gathering an army while we were fighting Easterlings in the Orcades, and clearing them out, island by island, through a hard year of constant warfare. Cerdic led that army into the Thames valley, then turned westwards to the Sabrina, invading our military zone and besieging Corinium: but those events are described later in my report.

Artorius never suspected how deeply Gwinfreda's influence shaped his thinking, though it never eroded his resolve that one day Britain must be united. That was still in his mind as a sacred, duty, though he seldom talked about it. As time passed, he recognized the obstacles that barred the way to unity: they resembled the political and racial problems we encountered when we occupied Ringvald's former kingdom. Perforce, we had left those unsolved, and ultimately the Anglian kingdom was divided between Ringvald's two sons, Haldred and Cuthvald, an unambitious pair who had no other wish than to be left alone to rule in peace. While British brothers would probably have quarrelled fiercely over their patrimony, German tribesmen seem to manage family affairs amicably. Haldred took the north half of the kingdom, and Cuthvald the south, and both were troubled by the intermittent belligerence of the Ickenny folk. Unlike Alfin's subjects in Deur, who had intermarried with the surviving Brigantes, the Angles preferred their own German girls to Iceni women, so there was no hope of fusion between natives and settlers at that time or when I left Britain years later. The north folk and the south folk of the Anglian kingdoms are unlikely to have changed their preferences or habits, and the Ickenny folk haven't changed at all since the days of Bodicea.

In the north we heard of Pictish raids, accounts exaggerated by the messengers Coroticus sent from time to time. Like the Easterlings, the Picts were undeterred by winter weather, and before Coroticus had withdrawn all his troops from Reged he was involved in a defensive frontier war. When his appeals to Artorius were rejected, in desperation he sent an embassy to Maelgwyn, who had already reoccupied southern Reged. Maelgwyn was perfectly willing to join Coroticus in fighting the Picts, and named his price. It was a high price.

Maelgwyn was to have sole command of the joint forces; the frontier of northern Reged was to be advanced forty miles north of Hadrian's Wall; and as ruler of Reged he should receive an annual tribute from Strathclyde in the form of supplies for his troops. Coroticus agreed to those terms, with every intention of breaking the agreement when he felt strong enough to do so, and as Maelgwyn knew this was likely to happen, he insisted on having strong garrisons of his own men in strategic positions throughout Strathclyde, ostensibly to discourage fresh incursions by the Picts. He now referred to Coroticus as a 'client king', and already his dream of ruling the north-west, from the Dee to the Clyde, in addition to his rightful kingdom of Gwynedd, seemed to be coming true.

Some years went by before he thought of using the fleet he had acquired from the Easterlings for anything except piracy and slave-raiding. He made sudden descents on the eastern coast of Ireland, where he stirred up a hornet's nest. His raiding parties brought back cargoes of boys and girls for the slave markets, and the Irish retaliated by raiding Gwynedd and Demetia and even the north coast of Dumnonia. When at length Maelgwyn began to understand sea power, he used this new accession of strength to consolidate his rule of the north-west, then picked a needless quarrel with Alfin over the boundary line between Deur and northern Reged, and sent thirty of his ships round the north of Caledonia and down to Segedunum at the eastern end of Hadrian's Wall. Only twenty-two arrived there for his mariners were neither experienced nor well trained; six ships were wrecked in the western islands and two in the Pictland strait, between Caledonia and the Orcades.

Alfin maintained a small fleet of twelve longships to guard his coast, and these were manned by men who had made trading voyages, and knew how to handle sea-going craft. What was left of Maelgwyn's fleet fared badly in battle. Of the thirty that had rowed down the Dee, over the bar and out to sea, only six returned to the docks at Deva. Maelgwyn hanged the captains, and on second thoughts all the other officers as well.

This stupid escapade embarrassed Artorius, particularly as Maelgwyn informed him in advance that in the course of rectifying an unsatisfactory frontier position, he might be compelled to declare war on a Saxon kingdom which had, so far, enjoyed immunity because of the close personal relationship of its ruler with the *dux Britanniarum*. This message, publicly announced by Maelgwyn's envoy, infuriated Gwinfreda. She had just borne Artorius a son, and was urging him to exchange his imperial military title for something regal, 'befitting your power and dignity', she said.

'Should he ever be tempted to call himself king, he will betray Britain,' Merlin had warned, when she first spoke openly of her ambition.

'He will also lose the confidence of the Emperor and betray the trust his Imperial Majesty has reposed in him,' I told her.

'The Emperor—' she began, then stopped. Her eyes told me better than words could how greatly she distrusted me. She knew that I had no illusions about her; but she said, mildly enough:

'Cay, it is a different matter for you, as you are still an imperial officer, almost a personal servant of the Emperor who is far away and unknown: He is only a name; will he ever be anything more to us? Artorius should be the first of a royal line, a line of great kings who will rule Britain, his people and my people, in unity and amity. He now has a son who will inherit his royal authority.'

I knew enough about women to allow her the last word. Distrust me she might, but I didn't want her to hate me as well. She resented the fact that I kept my family life separate from my military life; such deliberate segregation may have seemed like criticism of her presence at military headquarters; but I could never guess what thoughts floated through her shallow mind. She had often told me that a wife's place was by her husband's side. 'I would go on every campaign with him, if he'd let me,' she said.

'He loves you too deeply to allow that,' I replied; and had just stopped myself from saying 'blindly' instead of 'deeply'.

I saw little of Lavinia during our early married life, and should have seen even less if I had not been stationed at Corinium for many months each year, and able to snatch a few days' leave and ride over to the Geladii estate. Though so much of my life was spent in Britain, I never felt at home in that island; gradually I got used to the climate, and as time passed was able to enjoy some aspects of it; but I could never get used to the erratic character of the people. Even my cousins of the British branch of the Geladii often baffled me, though I understood Lavinia well enough. In the first five years of our marriage, she bore three sons, of whom I saw little in their childhood, for after a comparatively peaceful year at headquarters I was on active service, with rare intervals of leave, until the last great battle that ended the wars in Britain.

Lavinia was a shrewd judge of character, and in after years I often recalled her assessment of Wencla after she met him for the first time. I had brought him over from Corinium as my guest, and for a few days he stayed in our quarters on the Geladii estate; I made a practice of inviting young officers from the Band from time to time, because Artorius and I both believed that military leaders who met only those of senior rank lost touch with their command. The rigid, exclusive hierarchy of professional armies was alien to the spirit that pervaded the Holy Band of Brothers, as we were still sometimes called, and off parade the social relations of senior and junior officers were happily informal, never marred by constraint or undue familiarity. Unfortunately Artorius and I were regarded by most of the youngsters if not with awe then with excessive deference and I tried to break through that barrier of respectfulness as often as possible by personal hospitality.

Lavinia seldom criticised the juniors I brought to our home; nearly all came from noble Roman-British families and were the sort of people she had met socially all her life, but Wencla was a new experience for her. Though indistinguishable in speech and manners from men of British stock, his appearance proclaimed his Saxon descent, and she soon discovered that the young Armorican nobleman was something special and in some ways rather frightening.

'He's dangerous, ambitious and could be wicked,' she told me.

'He certainly likes living dangerously,' I replied; 'he may well be ambitious, and I know that he's a good soldier, a resourceful and responsible officer who can lead men and knows a lot about them and how they are likely to behave when their courage and endurance are challenged; but he's fortunately light-hearted, too light-hearted to be wicked. Few men with a strong sense of humour are capable of evil: they are often sinful, but cheerfully sinful and their slips from virtue are just a part of their zest for life.'

'Marius tells me he's very popular with the Band,' she said. 'He's certainly attractive to women,' she went on; 'he takes trouble, listens to what you have to say, and you never know what he's going to say next or what he's thinking about. And he can make you laugh; a man who can make women laugh can do anything with them. He told me that one of his ambitions was to make Artorius laugh: it might make him more like a human-being and less like an elderly priest.'

I heard something of Wencla's ambitions on our way back to Corinium from that visit. We had stopped at a wayside rest house at midday, and were refreshing ourselves with smoked mutton, sliced onions soaked in vinegar, followed by goatsmilk cheese and coarse bread, when he became so expansively talkative that I might have thought that wine was speaking, only we had drunk nothing but milk.

'I suppose I should ask officially,' he began: 'but I want long leave of absence from the Band. I want to visit my estate in Armorica, probably marry and start a family, raise a few men and bring them back as recruits for the Band under my command, or if that doesn't please the commander-in-chief, start a band of my own. King Marcus will lend me a ship; I've arranged that with him already, and later I might be able to get a ship of my own, and train a fighting crew. We should use ships. We should have taken those the Easterlings left at Deva, instead of allowing Maelgwyn to grab them.'

He went on in this strain for some time, and I allowed him to talk unchecked. There was sense in much of what he said; the Band could always do with fresh blood, and he was right about the ships we had left ice-bound in the Dee; for, as I've related, when Maelgwyn used them eventually, he used them foolishly.

Wencla told Artorius about his intentions, when we returned to Headquarters: he didn't ask permission: he made an announcement, and a few weeks later off he went, making no promises, but saying airily that he might be back in Britain when the sailing season began early next summer.

'But I may decide to stay longer,' he had added; 'so expect me when you see me.'

This was rank insolence, and I said so; but he laughed and said: 'You'll be glad of my help when I do decide to rejoin the Band: and I shall not be alone.'

Artorius let him go without protest.

We heard that King Marcus had lent him a fast-sailing well-found ship, and that was the last we heard of him for nearly four years.

They were not quiet years: we refused to be drawn into British quarrels, but could not avoid a wearisome, inconclusive campaign in the mountains of Caledonia to prevent the Picts from over-running the south, for, predictably, Coroticus and Maelgwyn had quarrelled and were at war with each other and fighting up and down the whole kingdom of Strathclyde. We tried to stop this nonsense; Artorius tried to bring the two kings together; but they refused to meet, so we ignored their bickering and got on with our own war, the one that really mattered, to contain the painted savages. Only after we had, at least for a time, discouraged the Pictish bands and chased them back to their lairs in the highlands, could we hope for a period of peace; then Maelgwyn reasserted his claim to rule the north-west, and began his foolish adventure against Alfin of Deur, which ended his transitory command of sea power.

The next threat to Britain came from the far north, when the Easterlings gathered fresh forces, invaded the Orcades, conquering the islands, one after the other, and settling there, with shelter for their ships and abundant supplies for their men.

XVII

The turbulent years

WHEN I LEFT Britain to return to civilization, there was peace in the island, maintained by agreement between foes too exhausted to continue what had long seemed to be an inconclusive and futile struggle. British and Saxons alike were weakened in willpower and military energy. Even Artorius, though he never lost hope that he would eventually drive the barbarians back to their mountains and into the sea, knew that it was a forlorn hope. Twenty years of warfare that began with the Easterlings' invasions and Ringvald's abortive raid into the Midlands, had ended with the great battle of Badon Hill, won by Artorius, who threw away the fruits of victory when he allowed himself to be seduced by the glamour of a title that every Roman had rejected and despised. When he was hailed by the Council of Kings as Artorius Rex, he sank to the level of those tribal chiefs: he became just another British king.

That surrender of dignity and purpose marked the end of everything Roman in Britain. Artorius was no longer *dux Britan niarum*, leader of an invincible band of warriors, merely a monarch with a band of obsequious courtiers, and few people took the trouble to tell him the truth, not that he listened when they did. He had a Court, though he called it a Council, and he built what Gwinfreda called a palace, enlarging an ancient fort that stood on a low hill in the centre of the vast estate in northern Dumnonia which King Marc had given him as a thank-offering for defeating Cerdic at Badon. And in that fool's paradise he lived in contented ignorance, blind to the scandalous character of his Court.

Everybody knew what went on and everybody laughed. Messalina could have learnt a thing or two from Gwinfreda, and Artorius remained as blissfully infatuated as the Emperor Claudius had been. Messalina, a sophisticated Roman lady with the body of Venus and the heart of a whore, went too far and was found out; not so Gwinfreda, the Saxon barbarian who had acquired such superficial civilized tricks as washing and table manners; she managed her intrigues with adroit discretion. She appeared to live a respectable, well-ordered domestic life; though she was always gay, lively and an amusing companion. In that large wooden hut with its bedrooms budding off the main hall, that so-called palace, there was little privacy; but like all Saxon women Gwinfreda enjoyed far greater freedom of movement than any Roman lady. She could ride far afield over that fertile countryside, accompanied by some officer or favoured member of the Band, and she knew as much about horses as any warrior, far more in many ways, for she could talk on equal terms with stable-boys and grooms, and we never forgot that she introduced us to the estrifa, that parent of the riding iron. She had an excellent seat, and could keep up with the toughest, hard-riding sportsmen when following a stag over the hills and moors of Dumnonia, or fox-hunting in the valleys and undulating country between Corinium and Glevum. Sometimes she went for solitary rides, and picked some stalwart fellow from the Band to ride a few yards behind her: a guard was always necessary even in the civilized parts of Britain. She always selected a good-looking youth for her escort, and what happened when they were out of sight of villages and shepherds' huts was a well-kept secret between them.

During the first twelve years of her marriage, she bore five children: three sons and two daughters. I think Artorius was their father: the boys resembled him: the girls did not. Only the eldest son and the youngest daughter lived beyond childhood. But I am too far ahead: I had written about the turbulent years, of war in the Caledonian Highlands, in the Orcades, of the long battles with the Irish after they abandoned their policy of sporadic raids to avenge those made on Ireland by Maelgwyn, and invaded Demetia and Glevissig, and had to be driven out. Largely owing to British folly, and Maelgwyn's in particular, the Irish, who for two generations had become reasonably peaceful Christians, resumed their ancient habits so that no part of the far west was safe from them.

When Philonides had read through the draft account of those war years, he asked some questions. 'Not that the answers are important now,' he said; 'but I am curious. If Artorius and his followers were always victorious, why didn't he reign as King of Britain?'

'Because the latter-day Roman-British hate authority as much as their tribal ancestors did,' I reminded him. I had already written about the fierce spirit of independence that was rekindled when imperial rule ended in the province. The Council of Kings that met after Badon had acclaimed Artorius as supreme monarch, though what they said was no more than an emotional outburst of enthusiasm. Like all British proclamations and most British promises it was rich in splendid-sounding words but empty of meaning, and Artorius might not have taken it for anything but shallow flattery if he had thought about the implications; but for a long time Gwinfreda had interfered with his thinking: for her King of Britain had a sweet sound; Queen of Britain sounded even sweeter.

Reading extracts of my draft report to Philonides and answering his questions, improved my knowledge of the way his lucid, penetrating mind worked; he never asked purposeless questions, and made many reflective comments.

'Some women are born to debauch men who are or could be great,' he observed; 'this Gwinfreda is just another of Cleopatra's many imitators. Mark Antony lost the battle of Actium in bed. That's where he was defeated. So was your Artorius.' He smiled, then said: 'My own condition has great compensations: I am immune from the fluctuations of mood and blinding emotion that destroy reason and sometimes destroy empires. I owe much to my father, a skilled physician with a large practice, who decided to protect me from the major complications of life. He had no wish for descendants, for although he was of good family my mother was a dancer and an occasional whore; so before I was eight the most expert surgeon in Alexandria carried out the operation, and as I have no experience of any other condition, naturally I have no regrets.'

He picked up the sheets of my draft, and reread some of them. Then said:

'General, you were second-in-command to Artorius, and in your report you have insisted, almost too often, what a great general he was; comparing him with Julius Caesar, Tiberius and other equally famous soldiers; but surely that's an extravagant claim? I am inclined to agree with the assessment of that warrior, Wencla'—he stumbled over the pronunciation of the name—'who said that without those big horses, well-made armour and men trained to loose arrows from the saddle, Artorius was just a good, brave leader and nothing more. Compared with the campaigns of Caesar and the wars of the Empire what you have described are little more than prolonged skirmishes with half-naked savages and undisciplined barbarians.'

'Resolute barbarians,' I replied, thinking of the Easterling invasion and of Cerdic's dauntless Saxon warriors at Badon.

"What surprises me is the small size of the forces you could bring against your enemies,' he continued. 'There, I agree, Artorius displayed some military genius.'

'His strength, *our* strength, lay in the spirit of the Band,' I explained.

'I know,' he said; 'you've told me that before, and also that the members demanded no payment; at least ostensibly, but there were exceptions, it seems. This Wencla, now: he went away from the Band for some years, and after he returned from Armorica, the Band by your account was no longer animated by the same spirit. Did he challenge the leadership of Artorius? Although your draft is clear and factual, you allow your account to become vague, even obscure, when you write about the relationship of Artorius and Wencla.'

I was well aware that my pen had faltered when I tried to describe what had happened when Wencla rejoined us, and brought with him two hundred men he had recruited from his own and neighbouring estates, also the crews of three well-found ships he had acquired from Armorican owners in exchange for parcels of his lands. That young and self-reliant warrior had greatly enjoyed

being his own master; his long absence from the Band had diminished his respect for discipline and his readiness to obey orders. He
had no intention of resuming the rank of a junior officer and he told
us why. He had spent many months every year he had been away
gaining experience at sea. Since childhood he had lived near ports,
and had many friends among the fishermen along the coast, though
until he took that quick decision to come with me to Britain after
our raid on Armorica, he had never sailed on a large vessel. I
remember his long talks with Corimac, the master of that ship, his
eager questions and his unflagging interest in everything connected
with the sailing of ships and the management of seamen. I also
remembered his critical remarks when we left the Easterlings' fleet
in Maelgwyn's hands.

He was frank about his intentions. He would serve the Band
and join in campaigns but in his own way, and by using sea-power.

'At sea, you can usually pick up all that's needed to reward
your crews,' he told us; 'Seamen won't work and fight for the glory
of God. You, my lord Artorius, believe that if a man has Christ in
his heart he doesn't need more than his food and shelter: that
may suit your Holy Band of Brothers, but men who follow the sea
won't take prayers for pay.'

I began to think that Wencla had the type of mind Artorius had
once told Lunaris he would never allow in his Band: a brigand's
mind. I knew what he meant about picking up the means to reward
his crews: he fed and paid his seamen by letting them steal what
they could from trading ships. The blood of Swarf, greatest of
all Saxon sea-thieves, ran in his veins, and the riotous qualities
of his ancestors were constantly reasserted by his actions and unconcealed ambitions. Sometimes I deplored his influence on the
military discipline of the Band.

He had returned at a time when things were going badly for us in
the Orcades, where the Easterlings had established themselves, and
we were unable to land a force strong enough to dislodge them
because we lacked ships. The Orcades are treeless, naked islands,
fertile in places, but storm-swept and bitterly cold in winter, when
the sun is seen only for a short time, before and after midday. The

waters surrounding them are a terror to mariners, threaded by powerful currents, and dotted with fierce roosts that catch vessels and shake them apart; only the native islanders know the secrets of those tidal races. Wencla and his three ships changed the whole military situation. We had tried to borrow vessels from Marc, who would only consent to lend us old, small craft, useless as transports for the horses we wanted to take to the islands. Alfin of Deur lent us eight of his twelve longships, but Maelgwyn's fleet, reduced to six in number, was not seaworthy; also he had executed all his officers with sea skills.

'How like a landsman!' said Wencla, when he heard that. 'You can't trust Maelgwyn, for he's not a complete fool—only a fool part of the time. Now you know where you are with an absolute fool and can make allowances for his likely actions, but the occasional fool is always a problem, far more difficult to deal with than somebody clever or cunning.'

'You seem to have learnt a lot about people,' said Artorius, smiling.

'You learn more about men at sea than you ever learn on land,' Wencla told him; 'afloat, they are always in the presence of the enemy, the great grey cold enemy, waiting to take advantage of mistakes, and to drown the man who makes them.' He laughed, then said: 'My lord Artorius: Britain is an island, and you can't live safely on an island without ships and men who know how to use them. *I'm* one of those men, and I'm better value to you and the Band with my feet on a deck than my arse in a saddle.'

We had met in Corinium, at headquarters, and were busy making plans for resuming attacks on the Orcades. Winter was over, and Wencla had returned with his ships and his men and his vast cargo of self-confidence at the beginning of the sailing season. His fleet of three vessels had sailed into the Sabrina estuary and anchored upstream where the river begins to narrow. There he landed, took what horses he needed from local farms for mounting his escort of fifty men, and then rode to headquarters, where he reported, not as a junior officer should, but as a commander of consequence, calling as a matter of courtesy on equals. His assumption of equality with Artorius was so cool and confident, that nobody questioned it—at first. Later there was trouble and jealousy that might have been bad for discipline, but as Wencla had insisted on a separate command at sea, he was seldom with the Band. He made it known that he would welcome a few volunteers for sea service.

'Nobody over eighteen,' he said; 'younger, for choice. And you needn't think that anything you know already will be much use to you, except one thing: obeying orders.'

Only a few youngsters volunteered. Wencla was popular and was believed to be lucky, which is of immense value to any leader; but the sea does not attract young British noblemen, unless they happen to live near it, like Marc's Dumnonian subjects.

Before Wencla joined our Council of War, we had provisionally agreed on a plan for invading the Orcades, island by island, when good weather favoured our passage in small craft; but with Wencla's ships we could take all our horses and use the full mounted strength of the Band against the Easterlings; or so we thought. But Wencla would have none of it.

'My ships are weapons not floating stables,' he objected, and would have continued but Artorius interrupted.

'*Your* ships!' he said sharply; 'have you ceased to belong to the Holy Band of Brothers? Our weapons, our armour, our horses are our common property; have you forgotten that and have you also forgotten your oath?'

'Perhaps I have been too long at sea and too much in the company of plain-speaking seamen to listen with much patience to that sort of twaddle.' Wencla smiled, but his eyes were hard. 'Listen, my lord Artorius,' he went on; 'you have a fancy regarding yourself as God the Father Almighty. Cay Geladius is, I suppose the Son, and that dull old donkey Merlin, who hardly ever speaks and might just as well not be here, is the Holy Ghost—'

He got no further. Artorius was on his feet.

'This is blasphemy, rank blasphemy!' he cried.

'Better a little blasphemy than a lot of balls about common ownership as if we were field hands on an estate, being issued with tools by an overseer,' Wencla replied, rising also, while his hand crept down to the hilt of his sword.

I remained seated, but said, and I used my parade-ground voice:

'Stop this at once! Artorius, you forget your rank as senior officer present; Wencla, you forget your manners. I represent his Sacred and Imperial Majesty, the Emperor: that is why I am in Britain. That is something I never forget. We're all soldiers, and fighting on the same side.'

Wencla sat down; so did Artorius. Merlin picked up his harp, but I was in no mood for bardic performances, and said so. I had long ceased to pay serious attention to Merlin, and was inclined to agree with Wencla about him.

Wencla who had been so deliberately provocative made no amends: he was neither apologetic nor tactful, and returned to the subject of his oath to the Band.

'My lord Artorius, *dux Britanniarum*, you should remember that when I joined I qualified my oath by reserving my right to private judgement. If you don't remember, I am reminding you now that I did.' He paused, then smiled. 'Men and situations change,' he continued. 'Men grow to their responsibilities or sink under their weight and are no good to themselves or anybody else. I can carry my responsibilities, and it would be well if we now defined them and that you should understand that I am your ally, not your servant. I'll serve you well at sea, and on land too when occasion arises; but let me explain why I reject your plans for invading the Orcades. Am I to be heard, or am I just to be told what to do, whether it's right or wrong?' 'Say what's in your mind,' I invited, as Artorius remained silent and nobody else ventured to speak.

'Very well, then,' said Wencla. 'Don't land any men or horses on the Orcades. The Easterlings will be waiting for you, strong and ready: your men may be weak from sea-sickness, for the passage to the islands won't be smooth. You'll have to put a guard ashore before you try to land your horses, and, I'll say this again, the Easterlings will be waiting for you. So forget about your big horses and cavalry charges. The Easterlings took the islands with ships, and those ships must be captured or destroyed. That would be my first task, so the Easterlings couldn't leave the islands, and would lose their sea defences. That should occupy my fleet for six or seven weeks: and when we've cleared the seas of Easterling ships, we must raid the islands, every night if possible. We'll land small parties of men with plenty of fire arrows, and burn farms and barns and villages. The Easterlings must have no rest, and with command of the sea and the mobility that gives us, we can strike in a different place every night. By day, every island will see smoke rising after our raids, and if we do our work thoroughly and destroy crops and stores and cattle, a sleepless summer will be followed by a hungry winter.'

He stopped and looked at Artorius and the senior officers, seated at the long table where maps had been unrolled and spread out. Then he laughed. 'Good,' he said. 'I have your attention: nobody has yawned—not yet. Let me take you on to the spring of next year; the spring that follows a miserable winter. Winter gales will have given the Easterlings a respite from raids; but with the spring we shall return, bringing unexpected gifts for the enemy. Let's try the trick we used at Deva and give them something to drink. We can make a big daylight landing, as if we were mounting a full-scale invasion, and put our casks ashore first, then think better of it, and return to our ships and come back in a day or so—but I needn't go on. I think that trick should work again. What do you say, my lord Artorius, and brother officers of the Band?'

After a long, oppressive silence, Artorius said:

'This plan should be tried, but—,' he paused. 'I'm not belittling your judgement or capacity or skill in the managements of ships,' he explained, 'but I cannot give you the sole command of this campaign. Caius, my second-in-command, must have the overall responsibility; he is your senior, and mine too for that matter, and he is a soldier with experience of war in places other than Britain. If his expedition to Armorica some years ago hadn't been successful, you wouldn't be here, Wencla.'

This was a tactful compromise: I think that Wencla would have refused to serve under Artorius, but as he had always confided in me, and had I think real liking for my company, Artorius made it easy for him to agree. And so it was arranged, and a few days later I sailed with Wencla to Deur, to inspect the eight ships Alfin had promised to lend us.

Much against my inclination, I had to agree to Gwinfreda coming with us as a passenger. She wanted to visit her father, and as Artorius didn't object I couldn't stop her. Wencla was willing enough to have her company: certainly she gave no trouble on the voyage, and was a good sailor. Seasick men aboard ship are a curse; a seasick woman would have been intolerable; but Gwinfreda was a Saxon, born with the right stomach for seafaring. I was relieved to see that Wencla was not distracted by her presence on board and took little notice of her, being entirely absorbed in his duties as a commander.

Alfin had aged, his yellow hair and beard were now white; though his huge body was still upright, he carried himself as well as any active young man, when he happened to be sober. He agreed without arguments or reservations when I suggested that the commanders of his eight ships should take their orders from Wencla. He was, we knew, a reliable ally, and a generous-minded man. So Wencla had a fleet of eleven ships, and by midsummer we were masters of the seas, from the Pictland Strait to the waters about the far northern Orcades. The Easterlings lost all their ships, and three of ours were wrecked.

Before the days shortened, we began harassing the islands. As Wencla had hoped, we gave the Easterlings a sleepless summer; but they were tough, resolute enemies, and we lost a good many men when we landed raiding parties. The end was inevitable. By midsummer of the following year we had retaken all the islands, successfully repeating the tactics that had brought us victory at Deva.

The turbulent years were not over. After the defeat of the Easterlings when Wencla's ships had sailed south again, the Picts swarmed out of their highlands, and two long, exhausting campaigns in Caledonia kept most of the Band in the north for many months. While we were dealing with those savages, a great disaster occurred in the south-west.

We had consistently ignored King Marc's pleas for the expulsion of Cerdic: now we paid heavily for our inattention.

XVIII

Cerdic breaks out

CERDIC'S TERRITORY had over the years become thickly populated; every sailing season more hardy warriors and farmers emigrated from their German homelands, and settled down contentedly to reclaim land that had long gone to waste; and as there were thousands of empty acres awaiting them, they prospered and soon raised families and seemed peaceable and contented. Some of their more adventurous young men made quick raids now and then, across the Dumnonian border and carried off a few of King Marc's subjects, girls mostly, but that sort of thing happened all over Britain: the personal bands of big landholders in the various kingdoms often made such raids into neighbouring states, and although some royal officials blustered a little, nothing was ever done to compensate those who suffered or to restore to their owners and households the slaves and servants who had been kidnapped. Property is not respected and nobody is safe in a land that lacks central government and a properly paid standing army to back its authority.

Cerdic's subjects were not overcrowded, and under his rule, lived tax-free and were not oppressed; he and his son Cynric were strong, forceful characters, so King Marc told us, and they kept order better than most barbarians, with a small army of trained men, about three hundred he said, but of course every landlord and farmer had men who could carry a spear or wield an axe or a club, so had they been attacked by Marc or by us, they could have mustered a formidable number of defenders. Cerdic's band had fought local brigands, and also accounted for a local British chief, called Natanleod, who had, according to the usual exaggerated accounts, thousands of followers. Cerdic, after a long campaign, at last brought this elusive chief to battle, and that was the end of Natan-leod. His defeat discouraged any other attempts at organized brigandage. Meanwhile the number of Cerdic's subjects steadily increased, despite the vigilance of Marc's fleet which only managed to intercept and sink a few of the ships that ferried them across the Channel.

We never found out what impelled Cerdic to gather an army and march north: it was far more than a large-scale raid; it was a planned invasion and volunteers from the other Saxon states joined Cerdic, so that before he began his adventure he was in command of at least four thousand Saxon warriors, and perhaps as many armed field hands and runaway slaves who had taken to brigandage, but found the life too lonely and uncertain. Such an army might win new lands for its commander, that might or might not be held permanently, but the main objective was loot. Professional soldiers fight for pay; war is their trade; German barbarians fight for pleasure and with the hope of an honourable death in battle; an attitude that makes them as savage as Picts, and far more reckless and dangerous, for they are big, powerfully built men, though not as formidable as the Easterlings.

Cerdic broke out of his territory in fine spring weather. We heard nothing about it for over a year, for we were dealing with fresh Easterling invasions of the Orcades; no ships came to the far north with news, and as the Picts had swarmed again, all Caledonia, hostile and impassable, lay between us and the British kingdoms. Throughout the spring and summer of what we afterwards called Cerdic's war, the Saxons ravaged northern Dumnonia, but left the western part alone, for Marc had managed to hold his eastern border, and also used his sea power to land raiding parties in Cerdic's almost deserted countryside, where he did a lot of damage and captured many women and children for the slave market. Cerdic, though he must have had news of this trouble, was undeterred by it, and continued his march north until he reached Corinium. On his way to our military headquarters, he completed the destruction of Aquae Sulis; a senseless and wanton act, typically barbarian. As I have said, it was already ruinous through years of neglect; Cerdic's savages left the surviving great buildings, the temple of Sulis Minerva and the baths and hostels, mournful heaps of rubble, sinking into a sea of soft, warm mud. But Corinium defeated him, as Deva had defeated the Easterlings.

Staying well out of range of catapult missiles and arrows, Cerdic's army settled down for a few days, foraging in the country round about the city, devouring food stored in barns and farms, and living meanwhile in an unplanned, insanitary camp. They were neither as patient nor as competent as the Easterlings, and after nearly two weeks of inactivity abandoned the siege; Cerdic then led them north-west to Glevum, which was as well fortified and defended as Corinium, and could resist indefinitely, for supplies came to the city across the stone bridge that spanned the Sabrina. All through the summer, the Saxon army wandered at will through the rich west country, and when the great landlords regarded their ruined estates and looted villa houses they may have regretted their mean resistance to the taxation that would have given them the protection of a standing army. But I doubt whether they learnt the lesson, and if Britain is ever again part of the Empire, their resistance to taxation will be as consistent and tricky and evasive as it was when we formerly governed the land.

During the first year of his raid, Cerdic discovered that it was far easier to raise an army and invade a peaceful, settled country than to keep his men occupied and prevent them from deserting; warriors who had joined for adventure and excitement, were soon bored by inactivity, farmers and field workers who had anticipated a short summer campaign were unwilling to leave their land untended too long or their harvests ungathered. Before winter his army had begun to melt away, though it was still formidable, and occupied the fertile country between northern Dumnonia and Glevum. His men found comfortable quarters in villa houses on the great estates. They stripped the countryside bare; unable to enter towns, they burned villages and cottages and killed everybody who failed to gain the protection of strong walls.

News of these disasters reached us in the spring of the second year of Cerdic's war; just after we had finally settled matters

AR—G

with the Easterlings in the Orcades. We sailed south with Wencla and his fleet, and after a smooth, quick passage through the Irish Sea, entered the Sabrina estuary, landing in Gwent and sending messengers to the British kingdoms, calling on their rulers to attend a Council, and to bring with them as many men as they could raise and arm.

Since the last Council had met, some of the old kings had died, Lunaris of Elmet among them; a few of their young, truculent successors attemped to question the authority of Artorius as *dux Britanniarum*. Magloc, the new King of Demetia, was the most troublesome, even sillier than Honorius of Gwent, while comparatively sensible men like Marc of Dumnonia indulged the native tendency to make long, boastful and involved speeches. These men were not all fools, but on their feet, addressing an audience, they often spoke foolishly.

The Council met at Glevum, for a few mounted members of the Band had managed to clear the countryside of Cerdic's followers and that city was no longer surrounded by them. I was not present at the opening sessions, for with Marius and a strong escort, I had ridden west to the Geladii estates, to collect new mounts, for we had lost many horses in the northern wars, and the Band was sadly depleted. I had another mission, which was to reassure Artorius of the safety of his family, for when Cerdic's war began Gwinfreda and her children had fled for refuge to our well-protected and remote lands where she was well cared for by Lavinia, who disliked her greatly though prevented by good breeding from showing her aversion, so Gwinfreda never suspected how much her presence disturbed and disrupted my household.

'She would be happier in a smelly wooden hut,' Lavinia told me; 'she really detests our orderly ways and our manners and our food, and she doesn't know how to treat servants. I wish she'd brought her own. When she gives them orders, she can't always say what she means, for she hasn't a word of British speech and her Latin is so clumsy and she splutters it with such a thick guttural accent that more often than not she isn't understood; and then she loses her temper and strikes the man or the girl she's talking to, and that I won't have. I've told her, with as much restraint as I could command, that if she has any complaint about any of our servants or slaves, she must tell me, and I'll correct them if necessary.' She sighed, and added: 'I shall never get used to barbarians, but at least she's clean, though she hardly ever uses the baths; she really hates the hot steam and prefers splashing about naked in the river. She likes our children and they like her, I don't know why.'

'She likes anything male,' I said; 'if we had daughters instead of sons, she wouldn't even know that they were there.'

My sons were growing up, the eldest approaching manhood; all three desired a military life, and pestered me to allow them to join the Band, but I refused. I would never allow a member of my family to become involved in British wars, even though they were wars against barbarians. I was beginning to hope that the day was not far off when they would accompany me on my return to the civilized world. Once there, in the military heart of the Empire, they could serve if they still wished to, in the Emperor's Household Guards. The only disadvantage they would suffer would be the lilting British accent which was so unsuitable for subjects of the Emperor. I hoped that in time they might lose it, but habits of speech acquired in the nursery are apt to last a lifetime. Lavinia's speech, which was similar, never troubled me; but she had a softly modulated voice. My sons' voices were discordant. Fortunately I saw so little of them that my inclination to find fault with their manners was checked. But, as I've said before, they were always strangers.

My father-in-law, Julius Nonna, had aged greatly, and I knew why. He was not an old man, but too many energetic slave girls occupied and exhausted his abundant leisure. So the responsibility for controlling the estate and overseeing the horse breeding establishment was carried by Lavinia, for like Marius her remaining brothers had joined the Band, all four men of that generation now served with Artorius. Her younger sister had married, and lived many miles away in the Black Mountains. I mention these family matters because as Lavinia had far too much to do, she was unable to prevent that unwelcome guest, Gwinfreda, from interfering in the management of the stables, and although she loved horses and was passionately fond of riding, often with my sons for company, she was careless. Now and then wild hill ponies got at the mares, and the stock was already affected.

I stopped that, and left twenty reliable men from my escort to reinforce the stable guards. Gwinfreda unexpectedly made matters easier by announcing her intention of returning with me to join Artorius and to stay with him for the rest of the campaign. I should have refused of course; but instead I deliberately encouraged her, hoping that she would behave with her usual recklessness and get herself killed; also I wanted to relieve Lavinia of her company, and finally—and I'm not certain that this was not my chief reason —I disliked the overt attention she paid to my eldest son.

She was openly shameless. 'He's as good-looking as you are,' she told me, 'but he doesn't know it.'

She gave me a sly glance, her large blue eyes moist with desire.

'I am far from hating you,' I said, and that was a considerable lie, 'but we will leave it at that.'

She indulged her maddening habit of giggling, and then called me a stiff old Roman. 'Never mind,' she added; 'you were born one, and I'm more than halfway to admiring you.'

When we returned to Glevum, and the Band had been partly remounted by the horses we brought back, we heard about the quarrel between Artorius and Wencla over the use of the fleet. Through some defect of imagination, Artorius seemed unable to think of ships save as transports for men and horses; Wencla knew that they were mobile weapons that gave us the power of surprising our enemies anywhere along the coasts and inland waterways, and Wencla was right.

'This is an island!' he had shouted; 'and ships float on water, not on horse-dung, which is all you seem to think of!'

Wencla and King Marc had urged Artorius to use the Band to contain Cerdic's dwindling army, while our ships joined forces with Marc's and made a full-scale invasion of Cerdic's territory, so the Saxon chief would have no lands to return to, no followers either. Artorius refused. Cerdic and his army must be defeated in battle, he insisted.

'Our object is to kill the enemy,' he said.

'And is there anything in my past that suggests I'm averse to killing our enemies?' Wencla demanded. 'Fight Cerdic my way, and leave him and his people nothing but their eyes to weep with, and you'll end his power for ever. Defeat him in battle, and some of his followers are bound to escape; and they'll gather again and come back again, under another leader.'

I think that Artorius was still half-hoping that Cerdic might grow weary of the campaign, now in its second year and as far as ever from the permanent conquest the Saxon may have hoped to achieve. But he was not idle: the Band harried the Saxon forces, depleted by desertions but still large and menacing, and as the wet, chilly British spring ended, we reoccupied Corinium, which had resisted for so many months. Meanwhile, Wencla had left with his fleet, and told us that he and King Marc would fight the war in their own fashion.

'I am fighting your battles as well as mine,' he told Artorius; 'but we must go our separate ways. We have different ideas of war-making, so each to his own skill.'

'I trust you absolutely,' said Artorius; and I knew that he meant it, for although he might disagree violently with Wencla about methods he had no doubts concerning his single-minded desire to wage war successfully. But no war-plan ever made can guarantee success; especially at sea.

The Sabrina estuary broadens out into a channel with Demetia on the north and Dumnonia on the south, both coasts dangerous and rocky; and where the jaws of that channel gape wide to drink in the waves of the Atlantic that come rolling in from the sunset edge of the world, a steep-sided island stands up like a fang on which many ships are wrecked. And that is what happened to Wencla's largest warship, for his fleet was scattered by one of the early summer storms that gather so suddenly and unexpectedly in those turbulent waters. Only one vessel survived. By clinging to a spar Wencla was saved; some of the crew were washed ashore to the foot of the tall cliffs of that inhospitable island. All were injured, and Wencla had broken three ribs; but they were cared for by the half-savage farmers and fishermen who inhabited the island. No ships put in to that lonely place; the islanders had little commerce with the mainland of Dumnonia, and the only strangers they saw were shipwrecked mariners. There, perforce, Wencla stayed until his ribs were knit, and he felt strong enough to exert some authority over the fisherfolk who had sheltered him and the seven men of his crew who had survived the wreck. He borrowed a small boat, reached the coast of Dumnonia in safety, but several weeks passed before he rejoined the Band. Then he showed his quality as a man and a leader by reporting failure with the boisterous cheerfulness that a great victory would have justified.

'The waves have spewed me out, my lord Artorius,' he cried; 'so, back to the dung and the saddle.'

The Band was encamped in a valley some thirty-five miles south-west of Corinium, with the road to Calleva passing through it, and leather tents and draughty wattle huts arranged in orderly groups north and south of the road. The Band and the horse lines were separated from the areas occupied by the troops of the British kings who had brought their so-called armies with them and grudgingly placed them under the over-all command of Artorius. It was obvious to me that all the work would be done by the Band, for the royal troops were there simply to swell the numbers, so that Cerdic's Saxons might think they had to contend with a large force. Rising above the camp to the south was a high, rugged hill, crowned by the remains of an ancient British fort; something dug out, flung up, and embanked, without Roman skill or efficiency, in the old native way of fortification though affording shelter of a kind. The hill was known locally as Badon, short for Mons Badonicus, a name unlikely to be forgotten.

Merlin had returned to us after an absence of many months which he had spent travelling about Britain gathering news and sifting rumours. From him we learned that Cerdic was ravaging the Midlands; he had captured and largely destroyed what remained of Ratae, and was now making his way southwards, very slowly, for he was encumbered with masses of loot and hundreds of enslaved peasants and citizens.

Wencla had suggested that he should take Thord, Merlin's

Saxon servant, and ride north to meet Cerdic's warriors, mingle with them, volunteer to join them, and after discovering all he could about their strength and fighting quality, come back so that we should then know a lot about their strength and weakness.

I thought his plan was excellent; Merlin was willing to release Thord, but Artorius hesitated.

'How well can you speak their tongue?' he asked.

'Well enough,' Wencla answered; 'also I look like a Saxon and Thord is a Saxon, so nobody is likely to suspect what we are up to.'

Then Gwinfreda objected and I guessed that she had been trying to dissuade Artorius from granting permission for the venture.

'Every word you utter gives you away,' she said; 'you may look like one of my countrymen; indeed how could you look otherwise with Swarf and Swarfsson and a long line of Saxon ancestors; but you speak too sharply and you don't growl or splutter and splash your words about when you're excited—'

Wencla laughed. 'Perhaps I had too good a teacher,' he told her. I saw the look she gave him, and hoped that Artorius hadn't. After that she said no more.

At last Artorius agreed, and within an hour Wencla and Thord rode north towards the Saxon host.

Ten days later they were back again, cheering us all with their account of Cerdic's ill-disciplined force, which was still on the march, crawling along a few miles every day. His own small band of sworn warriors alone preserved any semblance of order; his peasant followers and the volunteers from the south and eastern Saxon states were concerned only with guarding the pack mules and hill ponies that carried great loads of gold and silver objects, broken up and bundled into sacks. Hundreds of captives on foot, representing their living loot, accompanied them; many died daily from hardship and hunger, for no proper arrangements had been made for feeding the human merchandise, and the bodies of those who succumbed were left by the roadside for wolves and foxes and birds to reduce to bones.

'Cerdic's people are animals,' Wencla concluded.

'Do not insult animals,' said Artorius: 'for God has ordained how they should behave according to nature. But men, even un-christian men, are able to rise above nature.'

He flushed with anger when Gwinfreda, giggling as usual, said: 'Nobody can rise above nature.'

'A good reply to a solemn speech,' Wencla observed; 'a speech worthy of a bishop. But Cerdic's men do behave like two-footed beasts of prey, and they're on their way here, and as our first task we should separate them from their loot. They believe in making war pay: so do I. Let's take our payment from them: your Band may be content with blessings from Heaven; *my* followers want something more tangible than God's goodwill.'

'You seem to forget that you are a sworn member of my Band,' Artorius reminded him.

Then Wencla lost his temper.

'Listen, fool!' he shouted; 'your woman there is twice the man that you are. If you think that you're leading a band of pious praying nithings, you've sunk to the level of that ass King Maël: your young men, and your seasoned troopers, have bowels and balls and loves and lusts and vices that they cover up, because they love you too much to hurt your feelings. God's teeth! I love you myself, but I think you're a fool in many ways—a fine soldier, yes, a great leader, yes, but you're trying not to be human, because you think God likes cold, wet, eunuchs. Nonsense! The God the Israelites worshipped and obeyed, was all for fruitfulness and fertility. I bet Christ wasn't a celibate; and that the apostles fucked like stoats, when they got the chance. Don't forget that some of them were sailors, well—fishermen—and I know, even if you don't, just what sailors are like, have always been like, and always will be like, so long as men are men and women are around.'

'Your blasphemies are your own concern, like your sins,' said Artorius.

The silence that followed was broken by Merlin who said:

'I foresee a great victory over the Saxon host, but Wencla must prepare the way for it.'

Wencla, who had little respect for Merlin's pronouncements, said:

'You have taken the words out of my mouth; of course there will be a great victory over the Saxons if I'm allowed to do what I suggest and break them up on the march—I believe I could do it alone leading my own people, but every king who has brought his warriors with him should let them have the chance of helping themselves to some of Cerdic's treasure. Come now, Artorius: do you agree? It is for you to say the word, so we move on the orders of the *dux Britanniarum*.'

Artorius had no choice. He knew Wencla would certainly act independently and volunteers would flock to him when they heard the master word: loot.

XIX

Badon and after

WHEN WENCLA MARCHED north to intercept Cerdic's host, three quarters of the British army went with him; only the personal bodyguards of the kings, and of course our own sworn Band, remained in the camp, though some of the new and very young members of the Band slipped away to seek adventure. Like so many youthful and inexperienced soldiers they thought that Artorius was too cautious. Unlike the kings' men they had no wish for gain; for them excitement was sufficient reward, and they knew that anyone who followed Wencla would be certain of opportunities for reckless displays of courage, which could be talked about afterwards. Talking about themselves and their deeds and their ancestors and *their* deeds is a form of recreation much enjoyed by these latter-day British, who are, I imagine, growing more and more like their tribal forbears who were so troublesome five or six generations ago.

Over twelve days passed before messengers rode into the camp with news from Wencla. Cerdic had lost his captives and his loot; his army had been roughly handled, but was still powerful and his lusty warriors were plodding on towards us, several days' march away, short of provisions but full of courage.

Meanwhile King Marc had deserted us, riding south-west to protect the borders of his kingdom, so he said, though I suspected that he was carrying out some secret plan, and my suspicion was justified, for later we knew that he had agreed with Wencla to send a fleet of his small vessels up the Sabrina to Glevum, where the captives and loot taken from Cerdic would await him. Wencla tricked the soldiers who had left the armies of the various kingdoms, eager for easy pickings from Cerdic's baggage train. He allowed them to take all the portable valuables they could carry, but they had to

176

guard the captives, as they marched westwards across country to Glevum. Wencla persuaded them to do this, appealing to their cupidity, for as he pointed out, once the loot and the captives were brought into the camp, Artorius would insist on an equal division of the spoil, though he would probably exclude his own Band, who would be amply paid by blessings tossed at them by a few bishops. A share-out to the whole assembled force would reduce the personal reward of every man, so they would be robbed of proper payment for the courage and enterprise they had shown by following him instead of staying comfortably in camp. Wencla could be very persuasive; the British soldiers were gullible fools and believed him until they reached Glevum after a weary and exasperating march, with their living wealth of captives depleted daily, for men and the especially valuable women and children died in dozens; and at the end of their journey they found King Marc and his fresh, well-fed troops and mariners in possession of the city, and a fleet of shallow-draught sailing galleys, tied up to the wharves.

I don't know what the fools had expected to find when they got to Glevum; Wencla had said vague things about a slave market where they could dispose of their possessions and then make their way back to their own homes, for they would be unwelcome at the camp; but Marc's men settled all that by herding the slave material into the holds of the waiting ships, and although many savage quarrels ended in bloodshed, Marc sailed away with the fruits of other men's labours. The leaderless soldiers, dispossessed and furious, sacked Glevum, wiped out the small garrison, and butchered many of the citizens.

Surprisingly enough, Marc and Wencla trusted each other; perhaps because Wencla had discovered that, as I have said, when Marc promised to do anything he kept his word. As he grew older and became more sure of himself, his personal vanity was modified. He became less interested in ostentation. When his two Nubian guards, Samson and Goliath died, as they did long before they became old men, he didn't replace them. Nubians seldom live long away from their African home, for the rich warmth of the sun is something no man can do without if he is born in a good climate,

and men with black or dark skins shrivel and their love of life
withers in the harsh, chilly airs of Britain. Marc knew this, and as he
was at heart a kindly man and fond of his handsome black giants, he
offered to send them back to the East, but they were too devoted to
him to leave his service.

I told Philonides about that to illustrate the quirks and inconsis-
tencies of Marc's character.

'Was he so deeply concerned with the welfare of a couple of
black slaves?' he asked. 'Really, some very odd rulers are bred in
Britain.'

'That is one of the secrets of that magic island,' I said.

He smiled, and said: 'You, too, were affected by that magic, if I
am not mistaken. I notice as you discuss your draft with me, that
you are inclined to condone the actions of the British chiefs, or kings
as they like to be called, and to accept their bad faith and deceits and
betrayals without censure. So apparently did Artorius, at least he
ignored the treacherous conduct of Wencla and Marc, though perhaps he was ignorant of their plots or too innocent to suspect
them.'

'He was innocent,' I said; 'also he trusted everybody, for he
assumed that all men were as high-minded and unselfish as he was
himself. But he was far from foolish: as a general he was a realist,
so he let Wencla have his way about attacking Cerdic, for he wanted
to keep the Band together and knew that Wencla's attack would
weaken and discourage Cerdic, and so make his own task lighter.
The Band at that time was barely seven hundred strong: and although the Saxons had not met heavy cavalry, and Cerdic had no
knowledge of our methods, his fighting strength was ten times
greater than that of our mailed horsemen. Even the superiority of
our weapons, our ability to shower arrows on the enemy as we rode
and the speed and strength of our great horses could not secure the
decisive and crushing defeat of the Saxons that Artorius intended to
inflict upon them.'

Philonides nodded, and as he had reached the point in my draft
report where I described the last and greatest battle fought and won
by Artorius, I made no more comments on those who took part.

Cerdic's army came in sight of our camp early on a hot summer's day; morning mists still floated over the little streams that threaded the valley, partly concealing the tents and huts, so the Saxons blundered into our outer defence lines. A storm of arrows drove them back, but only for a short time. They were not marching in orderly ranks or in any military formation, but in bunches and groups, and some rode on wild hill ponies and farm horses; but Wencla harrying them on the march, made their horses his chief target. Very few survived.

Two-thirds of the Band had been on morning exercises, when the trumpeters sounded the alarm; no time was lost as we were mounted and ready for instant action, so Cerdic and his Saxons quickly had their first experience of a charge of heavy cavalry. We herded those big, bewildered men like cattle; for what we had to deal with was not just a disorderly retreat, but a stampede. They were led by a stocky, elderly man, whose dirty yellow hair was mixed with grey; and that was Cerdic, not an heroic or inspiring figure, though he was obeyed and followed. In their anxiety to get away from the Band, they climbed the hill I have spoken of; tall, rugged and steep, with sides of slippery turf and those old, crumbling fortifications crowning the summit. Our big horses could not follow them, but our arrows did until they were out of range.

They stayed in the ancient fort for two days, without food or water before they attempted to challenge us. They must have known that unless they made a sortie, thirst and starvation would reduce their strength to such an extent that they would have been unable to fight an army of children, let alone mailed horsemen. But nothing deterred them once they decided to move. Cerdic was obviously a leader with courage and cunning. They tried breaking out at night, but we had dug trenches and pits that circled Badon hill and the nights were moonless so the big heavy lumbering Saxons fell into these traps and could easily be slaughtered with arrows shot at random in the dark.

The Saxons made little use of the bow. Like the Easterlings they preferred hand-to-hand fighting and that is where their height, weight and enormous muscular strength always tells. Finally they broke out of the hill fort early in the morning just after dawn, raced down to our camp and were among the tents and huts before the Band could get mounted, and while the men of the allied kings were still heavy with sleep.

These big yellow-haired men were starving and they went for the camp kitchens, emptying the cooking pots, killing the cooks, scattering the cooking fires around the tents, causing as much confusion as possible and howling like wolves the whole time. There is something chilling about the Saxon war cries. They are animal noises, inhuman and terrifying. When at last our Band was mounted they found that Cerdic's men had attacked the horse lines, hamstrung many of the horses and reduced our strength considerably.

We expected them to retreat to their hill fort again but they were too wily for that and marched away in a body. We could ride round them shooting arrows but they had a few weapons that often prevented us from closing with them. When we tried to ride them down they lashed at our horses and our legs with long-handled, double-headed axes, heavy and sharp. Wielded by a big man such an axe could do immense damage to a limb, even when protected by chain mail. We had to let them go, bringing down as many as we could with arrows shot from the saddle, but they were soon among trees where our horses could not follow and after an exhausting day battling through oak scrub and gorse and tangled undergrowth we gave up the pursuit. But that was not the end of Cerdic and his Saxons. He regained his lands and stayed there.

One thing that Saxons and other German tribes have in common with the British; they are never hopelessly downcast by defeat. Instead they tend to glorify their military failures, remembering them as magnificent and heroic occasions. So we heard later that Cerdic got far more credit and fame, and indeed congratulation, after his defeat at Badon than he had ever received before, for although he had been a consistently successful soldier, perhaps his followers could not quite forgive him for being very cautious in war, especially the young warriors who admire recklessness and dash, and are suspicious of cunning and usually get killed through sheer stupidity.

Give me old soldiers every time; the young don't know that the best soldier is a live one, and they learn that lesson too late.

The Saxons never allowed Cerdic to forget that defeat. They praised it, sang about it, and their wretched camp and court poets, who are even more of a nuisance than British bards, are likely to go on using Badon as an example of glory and a subject for songs for generations to come.

For Artorius it was a great and final victory. Philonides had reservations about that. He said:

'The battle of Badon, as you describe it, owes nothing to the generalship of Artorius; Wencla possessed the active mind that created favourable conditions for the battle; Artorius passively accepted what had been prepared for him by the far-sighted military skill of a more imaginative man, and in my view a more capable soldier. Is it possible, General, that as a good second-in-command your loyalty to Artorius clouds your judgement? In everything you have set down and read to me, you have consistently belittled your own part in the British wars, though you always give credit to Artorius where perhaps credit is not due, and, whether intentionally or not, you reveal the great capacity of Wencla as a leader. He was more than an effective leader. He was a general who had mastered the military art of surprise. Now you have said, more than once, that Artorius was a born soldier; even ranking him with outstanding generals like Julius Caesar and Tiberius, but I am better able to judge his achievements dispassionately, and would say that he was brought up and educated to create a firm belief that he was a born soldier. He was an adequate general, but no more; and you are a living proof that he could inspire devotion and retain the loyalty of those under his command. Such qualities, while useful, are insufficient to uphold a claim to greatness.'

'All the same, the Battle of Badon ended the threat of further expansion and aggression by the Saxon states,' I said.

Philonides turned back the pages of my draft, and I realized then how carefully he had followed the account.

'Correct,' he agreed. 'The only other clash with the Saxons occurred when King Marc attacked Cerdic: stupidly, for Cerdic had long recovered from his defeat at Badon and his state was repopulated and his army strong. Yes, here is the name of the battle: Cerdicsford. Now—you haven't written this—tell me what happened after Badon?'

'The usual chaotic British enthusiasm,' I said 'but I have it all in the draft that I was going to read to you. It's not in its final form.'

'Perhaps it is better so,' he said. So I read what I had put down from my reawakened memories of the crazy excitement of the British kings and their followers.

Artorius and the Band had abandoned the direct pursuit of Cerdic; the wooded nature of the country compelled them to; so they rode west and then south, intending to cut into the flank of the surviving Saxons as they tried to regain their homeland. This they did, and accounted for a few score of those tired but still formidable warriors. Cerdic, his personal guards, and a few others escaped.

'They'll live to fight another day,' said Wencla.

'That day is a long way off,' Artorius told him.

'Perhaps,' said Wencla; 'but I'm off to Dumnonia, for I think that Marc and I can make Cerdic very uncomfortable by sea raids on his coast. I presume that I have the permission of the *dux Britanniarum* to take any offensive action against the enemy that seems profitable and advisable.'

'God and my blessing go with you,' said Artorius.

So Wencla was not there when Artorius returned from chasing the last remnants of Cerdic's army, and he missed the proclamation of the British kings, assembled in Council, of Artorius as *rex Britanniarum*; had he been present I think he would have laughed and told those shouting kings that they had invented an empty title that cost nothing and meant nothing. Wencla was a realist.

'What happened to Wencla?' asked Philonides; 'I know that you have set it down, or will set it down, in your report; but when you left Britain where was he, and is he still living?'

'When I left, he ruled the Kingdom of Deur,' I told him; 'but I don't know whether he still lives and reigns. Probably he does. There was an indestructible quality about Wencla. His rise to power coincided with the decline of Artorius, who, after he became High

King of Britain, never attempted to rule.' I paused, then added: 'He made too many mistakes, because he was too trusting, and the greatest mistake he ever made was to trust Wencla. His first was to marry Gwinfreda.'

I thought of Merlin's words after Artorius accepted the title of High King.

'A woman's voice answered for him,' he had said; 'so Artorius will be remembered for all the wrong things. For deeds of bravery in battle; for a whim about a woman; for misfortunes of his own making, and as there are always fools in the world, and many of them become poets of a kind, he will be praised and glorified, not for his competence as an imperial general but for his personal prowess as a fighting king.'

There was a world of contempt in his voice as he repeated the word 'king'. Sadness as well as contempt.

Then I saw that he was an old man; without hope.

XX

The lost leader

KING MARC'S DEEDS were usually prompted by far-sighted concern for the welfare of his kingdom, and when he gave Artorius
those lands in north-eastern Dumnonia to celebrate the victory of
Badon, his high-sounding description of thank-offering artfully
disguised a well-planned piece of military policy. The presence of
Artorius and his Band would safeguard Dumnonia; such a potent
force, strategically placed a few miles from the northern border of
Cerdic's territory, would remind the defeated Saxon chieftain of
British power, should he be tempted at some future time to raise
another army and try to extend his domains. Though Cerdic's
power and the population of the lands he ruled were diminished,
and those lands had been ravaged by the seaborne raids of Marc and
Wencla, the Saxon chief could still attract men and women of
German tribal stock, always ready and eager to leave their native
country where overworked soil and poor crops could offer little
more than equal shares of poverty. Britain was still a place of promise
to hungry and adventurous German tribesmen, and Cerdic could
give land and protection without taxation to anyone prepared to
risk the Channel crossing. Though greatly weakened after his famous
defeat, he was still a ruler to be reckoned with, commanding a
small personal bodyguard of veterans and a few devoted and lucky
youngsters who had survived after Badon.

The site Artorius chose for building what he intended to be his
southern headquarters overlooked the countryside; I have already
said that the ancient fort on that small hill was enlarged, and though
Gwinfreda called the place her palace, it was essentially a stronghold:
uncomfortable, impregnable and intimidating. The encircling walls
were high, and the towers of the gatehouse reminded me of the

gateway at Onnum on Hadrian's Wall; the design was similar but instead of masonry, wood had been used, for King Marc, who supplied the labour, had plenty of carpenters, but no masons. There was no proper drainage; the latrines, although separated from the great hall—the royal hall as Gwinfreda named it—were far too close to the living quarters, and they stank, for the water supply, insufficient and intermittent, came from two deep wells that dried up in the summer months, so the sewers, never properly washed out, became clogged with filth. I had now lived for many years in Britain, but could never ignore squalor with the cheerful indifference of the native-born.

Fortunately my military duties demanded prolonged absences from headquarters, when, with a strong escort I made tours of inspection, to satisfy myself that officers responsible for defence were properly alert. They seldom were, and had forgotten all about external dangers: Badon, they would tell me, had settled the Saxon threat, once and for all. Inspecting the state of British defences was the ostensible reason for my visits to the various kingdoms: actually Artorius wanted to be certain that the little kings were not preparing to fight each other. Quarrelsome, proud, sensitive and always ready to take offence for some trifling reason, the rulers of the smaller states, particularly those of the west, had, like their officials, forgotten about the strength and potential power of the Saxon kingdoms and the frequent reinforcements those states had from overseas. Alfin's realm of Deur was slowly spreading southwards, by peaceful settlement, never violently, for Alfin honoured his pact of friendship with Artorius.

The Anglian kingdom, still ruled by Haldred and Cuthvald, caused us no anxiety; as the Angles were quiet, sullen, independent and intent on minding their own affairs. Their fertile realm was a tempting invitation to kindred tribesmen who were still living in their impoverished and overcrowded homelands; and year after year shiploads of fresh settlers crossed the North Sea in the summer sailing season. There was ample space for them. Artorius, untroubled by the steadily increasing population of that east coast kingdom, thought that it might become a client kingdom, like Deur. The only potentially aggressive states were the south-eastern and southern Saxons: Cerdic, he said, was a spent force.

Wencla disagreed with him; so did Merlin. Both were influenced by the opinions of Marc. The King of Dumnonia, while admitting that Badon had been a great victory, never ceased to worry about Cerdic's presence on his eastern border. I have related how, long after Badon, Marc attacked Cerdic and lost his army at the battle of Cerdicsford. But by then Artorius was no longer High King of Britain: nor was he the commander-in-chief, the inspired and inspiring military leader; his authority had dwindled, the Holy Band of Brothers, long demoralized, had dispersed, and once again the British kingdoms were rearranged, and power had passed into the hands of two kings who knew what they wanted and were strong enough to extend and protect their new borders.

I should have killed that woman.

I did not write that in my draft report; I said it aloud when Philonides reached the point in my account where Artorius discovered Gwinfreda in bed with Wencla in a farmhouse a few miles from the royal palace.

'It is often expedient to kill women,' Philonides agreed.

'I think I could have done so if I hadn't detested her and everything she stood for,' I told him. 'I've always avoided being governed by emotional impulses.'

'Surely it was a matter of politics not personal feelings,' he said, 'and you could easily have arranged a fatal accident.'

Although I approved of such cold realism, I was well aware that when the moment for action came I should not have been able to cut down such a radiant, vital animal, or even connive at her removal by others.

I was perplexed by my own reluctance, but Lavinia knew me better than I knew myself. I had few relations with women; the occasional playmate never counted with me; such casual affairs were wholly physical, as lacking in significance as opening my bowels; after I married they ended, nor were they ever resumed after Lavinia's death. Women have wasted only a very small part of my life.

'I think that you loathe Gwinfreda as much as I do,' Lavinia had told me, after we agreed not to move into quarters in the royal palace; 'but you could never harm her. No man could. She is everyman's secret appetite.' She smiled, and added: 'Oh, I know that *you* would never yield to her, like Marius and Wencla and every personable member of the Band and God alone knows how many others, but to destroy her would be like self-immolation.'

I hardly expected Philonides to understand that point of view, but he did, and observed that my wife must have been a wise and exceptional woman.

Marius, who had risen to high rank, for he was not only a brilliant soldier but a fortunate one, acted as my deputy when I was absent from headquarters; and nobody was small-minded about it or stupidly jealous about his advancement or attributed it to our tenuous family relationship, for he was as popular as Wencla. So it happened that on an autumn day two years after Badon he had accompanied Artorius who had ridden south with a bodyguard of ten mounted archers, almost as far as the border of Cerdic's domain, and on their return journey they were blinded by one of those heavy mists that suddenly rise, billowing up like smoke from the undulating moorland. They lost their way, and as the moor they were crossing had many dangerous bogs that could gulp down men and horses without warning, for the bog surfaces looked like good firm turf, they rode very slowly and cautiously. Night fell before the mist thinned, and they found a track that led them to a big, lime-washed farmhouse, that gleamed in the light of a waning moon.

'We'll shelter here for the night, and stable the horses,' Artorius had said; while Marius dismounted and hammered at the stout wooden door with the hilt of his sword. Although he heard some muttered exclamations from within, no bolts were drawn, so he banged at the door again and shouted,

'Open in the King's name!'

At last the door was opened by a frightened old woman, who babbled about thieves and robbers prowling and how nobody dared unbolt a door after dark. Marius asked for shelter for the night and stabling for the horses; and then from an inner room a sleepy voice had said:

'Woman, I told you that we were not to be disturbed.'

Marius had recognized the voice at once; so had Artorius. They pushed past the old woman into a large, dimly-lit kitchen, with logs flickering on an open stone hearth, and a rush-light standing on a rough wooden table; beyond the kitchen was another door, which was exceptional in a farmhouse, for usually one big room occupied the whole area with shut-beds against one wall; but this was an ancient house, well-built, with the inside walls smoothly plastered and whitewashed. Artorius strode across to the inner door and flung it open. The room beyond was almost as large as the kitchen, and luxuriously furnished, so far as luxury was understood in Britain; a brazier of glowing charcoal gave out some warmth, three rush-lights showed a huge bed piled with fur rugs where Wencla and Gwinfreda lay side by side.

Marius told me that he was ready to stop, if he could, a fight to the death between husband and lover; but when Wencla leapt out of the bed, and reached for his sword, Artorius raised his hand and said:

'No—there are too many wounds already without bloodshed. Inflicted by a wanton wife and a false companion. Enough.' He crossed himself, and then added: 'The Lord gave; the Lord taketh away; blessed be the Name of the Lord.' Then he wept, and, to his surprise, Marius found that he too was weeping.

The mist had cleared, and together they rode back, with their escorts following. For some miles Artorius was silent, then at last he said:

'She must go. Yes, Marius, she must return to her father's kingdom, though even the thought of parting drains the blood from my heart.'

Although the affair had happened years ago, Marius told me that he felt crushed by an overwhelming weight of guilt, because he had once been one of Gwinfreda's many lovers. She had, of course, been common to the Band—at least to the more virile and personable members; but that knowledge gave Marius no comfort, and on the ride back to the royal palace, he resolved to leave the Band, and with his brothers, to form one of his own, to reside on the Geladii estates, and rule their own secluded valley and the countryside around the Black Seat. Never again, he said, could he be at ease in the presence of Artorius. Marius and his brothers were the first to leave, and during the year that followed many others deserted.

King Honorius of Gwent died, and his little kingdom was promptly invaded by Magloc, King of Demetia, who marched through Glevissig, after announcing his intention of conquering and ruling all the lands north of the Sabrina and south of the Black Mountains. This roused Artorius, who ordered Magloc back to Demetia, mustered what remained of the Band, crossed the Sabrina estuary, and established his court at Isca Caerleon, the fortified city that had once been the British headquarters of the IInd Legion.

Had Artorius given those orders to Magloc as the British commander-in-chief, as *dux Britanniarum*, Magloc would almost certainly have defied him; but as Artorius Rex, the proclaimed High King of Britain, he was instantly obeyed. Magloc and his army returned to Demetia, and no more was heard of extending his kingdom. Artorius decided to stay permanently at Isca Caerleon, and never returned to the palace, which a few years later was raided and burnt by Irish pirates.

Gwinfreda returned to Deur by sea, in one of King Marc's largest warships, and Wencla and his own followers went with her. Her two surviving children remained with Artorius: she had always been a careless and casual mother, perhaps because she could never be sure who had fathered them. Alfin, now a very old man, welcomed Wencla, and openly proclaimed him as his successor to the kingdom, for years earlier his own sons had been killed in the sporadic border warfare with Pictish raiders.

Merlin announced that he was leaving us. He was going to Armorica and did not intend to return.

'I can no longer be your councillor,' he told Artorius.

He said this at the end of a Council meeting, after we had settled a border dispute (or thought we had settled it) between Demetia and Glevissig. Artorius merely nodded: ever since he had parted from Gwinfreda he seemed to have lost all interest in life, and spent much of his time praying.

'You weren't much of a councillor,' I said; 'your prophetic song about Artorius was hopelessly wrong, wasn't it?'

He replied, calmly and complacently:

'Not altogether. But when those who are empowered to, look along the road to the future, they sometimes follow a byway that leads to a time and place that will never be.'

What was left of the Band was useless. The spiritual fire had flickered out. The survivors, no longer made strong by inspired leadership, were rotted by self-indulgence. All the men of noble British blood had left and returned to their own estates in different parts of the still almost civilized West: the very purpose of the Band had gone.

Soon I began to feel that I had completed the task entrusted to me by the Emperor so many years ago. I had stayed with Artorius as long as he was a power in the land: so long as any hope remained of achieving his original plan of uniting Britain; but tired, old and empty, he accepted compromise. So Britain was permanently divided into a group of virile Saxon states, ruled by barbaric kings, extending from Cerdic's territory, all along the south and east coasts, beyond the Anglian kingdoms, up through Lindissi to Eburacum.

When Alfin died, and Wencla who had married Gwinfreda, ruled in Deur, he abandoned Christianity—which I don't think he ever took very seriously—and turned his kingdom into a strong aggressive state. His first action as an independent ruler was to invade Maelgwyn's conquered kingdom of Reged. He defeated Maelgwyn in three battles, transporting troops in his own fleet, round the north of Britain, down into the Irish Sea, and harrying the coasts of Reged and Gwynedd.

When I left Britain with my wife and three sons and personal servants, Wencla reigned over a kingdom that extended from the North Sea to the Irish Sea, south of Hadrian's Wall. He invaded the little city state of Eburacum, captured it and moved against Elmet and I don't know what happened to him after that. He may still rule in northern Britain, and have come to some border agreement with Maelgwyn.

Artorius is dead; but how or where he met his death is a mystery. Maelgwyn tried to extend his kingdom southwards beyond the Black Mountains, after Wencla had occupied Reged; but Marius and his brothers raised an army, defended their lands, and an inconclusive war dragged on for many years in those far western hills and valleys, until Maelgwyn wearied of losing men; but whether Artorius was involved I never knew. All this happened after I returned to Constantinople, and at odd times I heard vague, unreliable rumours.

One thing only was certain: Britain had lost the leader who could have brought unity of purpose to the quarrelsome barbarians whose forefathers had been citizens of a prosperous Roman province. Artorius failed, not splendidly but foolishly; but he may live on as a legend, for the British are addicted to legends and are not cast down by defeat and disaster. That we must always remember, if we try to reconquer the lost province.

XXI

The Imperial decision

I FINISHED writing my draft report, and found myself thinking of what Merlin had said to me the last time I saw him. He rode away from Caerleon with his two servants, now elderly men, one pack mule bearing all his possessions corded in nets slung over its back. Slumped in the saddle and wrapped in a thick, long grey cloak, he looked frail and feeble.

'I am without hope for this land,' he said. 'The Britons have gone back to what they were before Rome rescued them, but are unguided by the ancient faith that came from our wisdom, the wisdom and rule of my Order. And now they have lost five centuries of Roman civilization, and can look forward to nothing but blood and darkness for a thousand years; then they may rise again.' He shivered, drew his cloak closer about him and pulled up the peaked hood to cover his head.

'The people of Britain, however mixed their blood becomes, will always be mostly fools,' he added, talking more to himself than to me. 'The Christian Church may save them for a few generations,' he went on; 'not the ancient wisdom. That dies with me, for I am the last of the Order. As for the Church, that too will be destroyed, not violently, but through decay.'

I decided to add those words of ill omen to my report, but Philonides told me to strike them out, so they remain only in the draft. He had edited and controlled the form of the final document so that it would tempt his Sacred and Imperial Majesty to read and not appear too formidable.

On my last visit to the palace I found that Philonides had forsaken his normal calm. I did not expect him to explain his changed demeanour, but he did so.

'I am afraid,' he said, 'that much of the excellent work you have put into your report may be of no avail. His Sacred and Imperial Majesty had become afflicted by doubts and although her Resplendency, the Empress, favours the project of completely reconquering the West, her advice may not prevail.'

After a very long pause, he said:

'You have never been presented to the Empress. It is a great privilege and I shall try to arrange an audience.'

He seemed to be choosing his words very carefully before he continued. 'I think that you should read your draft to her and be ready to answer questions. Her questions will be penetrating, always to the point, and she likes short answers.'

As weeks went by without any further summons from Philonides, I resumed my secluded, agreeable routine of life. The delays and fumbling obstruction of the administration had amused me many years ago, when I was a junior officer in the Household Guards; we all made jokes about it then; exasperation with officials only came as I rose in rank and urgently awaited some decision. Now I realized that nothing had changed. I doubted whether my report would ever be read by anybody other than Philonides. Not that I regretted the time I had given to its preparation. Then, when half a year had passed, I was ordered to report to him, abruptly and with less than an hour's warning.

When I reported, he said that the Empress had graciously granted an audience and we must attend immediately; and together we went to a wing of the Palace that few were privileged to visit. (I had heard that some of those who did, never returned.) We passed through long, high corridors, their walls hung with purple silk; innumerable doors were opened by armed guards, and after climbing a broad stairway we entered a large sparsely furnished room, with one vast window that overlooked the port and shipping.

After we had made our ceremonial obeisance, I was conscious of astonishment. I had heard many descriptions of Theodora's beauty; on a few rare occasions, in the great Church of Sancta Sophia, I had seen her in the distance; a rigid, stately figure, like a jewelled image; but I had never seen her close to or heard her voice, and my astonishment was caused because she reminded me of Gwinfreda, though certainly not in appearance. But she had the same stark feminine power that can hurl men down to the level of obedient and docile animals. I could well understand how such a woman could dominate an Emperor, or indeed, any man. She was small, lithe and very graceful. Her large luminous eyes, full of dark fire, held you. Her voice was deep, rather harsh, and she spoke rapidly. Her questions about Britain, about Artorius, about the places I had known, the character of the people and the power of the Saxon states, were shrewd. Somebody had read my report to her carefully, and she had remembered it. The audience was short; but she ordered Philonides to bring me again into her presence.

My second visit was my last.

'She will make the decisions,' Philonides had warned me. 'She has for many years now, but how long that will continue I cannot predict. His Sacred and Imperial Majesty is a changeable man and he is too closely preoccupied in his relationship with God to pay much heed to earthly missions and I think already his vision of the restored and united Empire is becoming as insubstantial and colourless as a tiresome dream. Once, not so long ago, it was a bright and vivid hope and he could think of nothing else and there were victories to begin with but . . .'

Philonides stopped. He smiled at me and said:

'General, you are one of the few people who ever tempt me to indiscretions of speech and I think I know why. You are totally uninterested in personal advancement; in the Emperor's plans; or the restoration of Britain to the Empire. Why?'

'The answer is simple,' I told him. 'I spent too many years in that hopeless island and I am thankful to be back once more in the civilized world. The suggestion you made to me some time ago, that I might be a suitable commander of the expeditionary force to recover Britain, filled me with dismay. I should, of course, have obeyed orders, but I don't think I should have been a good commander or a successful one, and anyway I am too old. I hope that you have forgotten that suggestion.'

'No,' said Philonides. 'I still think you would be the best commander for the expedition, but it will never be sanctioned. From what you have told me about the new savage world the barbarians are making for themselves in the West, I realize that Rome can never go back.' He reflected awhile, then said: 'Perhaps Artorius was the saddest of all Rome's failures.'

I have discharged the Imperial Commission, and am much relieved by the imperial decision. My Official Report on the state of Britain will repose in the imperial archives, and probably never be seen again. My draft with my own reflections and comments, I shall leave to my eldest son, who, if it is safe to do so, may pass it on to his sons, so at some future time, far distant, unknown and unknowable, men may read the truth about Artorius.

Historical note

THE REPORT by Caius Geladius on the state of Britain, written for submission to the Emperor Justinian, would have had some practical value for the imperial military staff, had the Emperor ever attempted the complete reconquest of the West. But such an undertaking was beyond his resources. After North Africa, south-eastern Spain, Italy and Sicily were restored to the Empire, no further campaigns were mounted. When Justinian died in 565, his gimcrack reconstruction of the Western Empire collapsed, and the barbarian successors resumed their control.

Britain in the late fifth and early sixth centuries may have preserved some features of the administration and amenities of a Roman province, probably confined to the west and south-western parts of the Island. A desolate No-Man's-Land separated the Romano-British kingdoms from the Saxons, who consolidated their conquered territory, establishing a semi-rural civilization, far inferior to the sophisticated, efficient civilization of a well-run Roman province; isolated rustic settlements, for the Saxons were farmers, countrymen who rejected towns and town life. The British kingdoms, ruled by quarrelsome and temperamental monarchs, occasionally pooled their military resources under a commander-in-chief. Ambrosius Aurelianus was apparently such a war leader, Artorius another; both were successful generals. Artorius, that remote Romano-British commander, has lived on as a fairy-tale figure, the legendary King Arthur, whose deeds were magnified and glorified and fabulously embellished by mediaeval writers. As such he inspired Sir Thomas Malory's *Le Morte d'Arthur*, also *Idylls of the King*, once described by Arnold Bennett as 'Tennyson's nearly worst work', and in a wholly different vein, Mark Twain's hilarious burlesque, *A Connecticut Yankee at the Court of King Arthur*, and T. H. White's fantasy, *The Sword in the Stone*.

The report by Caius Geladius is, of course, a purely imaginary document; but some such person as Caius may have been the original of Cay or Chei.

The period has been studied and the documentary and archaeological evidence assembled and assessed by Dr John Morris in *The Age of Arthur* (London: 1973), and by Dr Leslie Alcock in *Arthur's Britain* (London: 1971), both works of outstanding scholarship.